HELEN DICKSON

A Vow for an Heiress

5451

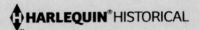

HARLEQUIN® HISTORICAL

Recycling programs for this product may not exist in your area.

ISBN-13: 978-1-335-63490-0

A Vow for an Heiress

Copyright © 2018 by Helen Dickson

Printed in U.S.A.

HARLEQUIN®
www.Harlequin.com

Kissed and caressed into almost unconscious sensibility, Rosa's slumberous dark green eyes fluttered open.

William smiled down at the incredibly desirable young woman who had the power to set his body on fire. He had only wanted to kiss her then walk away. Instead he'd ended up wanting to make love to her. Her magnificent eyes were naked and defenseless. His tanned features were hard with desire. "Well, Miss Ingram," he murmured, his voice a purr of pleasure. "You have hidden talents I knew nothing about."

Rosa trembled in the aftermath of his kiss, unable to believe what had happened and that she desperately wanted him to repeat the kiss that had stunned her with its wild sweetness. William was still holding her gaze, and she looked with longing at his lips.

Helen Dickson was born in and still lives in South Yorkshire, with her retired farm manager husband. Having moved out of the busy farmhouse where she raised their two sons, she has more time to indulge in her favorite pastimes. She enjoys being outdoors, traveling, reading and music. An incurable romantic, she writes for pleasure. It was a love of history that drove her to writing historical fiction.

Books by Helen Dickson

Harlequin Historical

When Marrying a Duke...
The Devil Claims a Wife
The Master of Stonegrave Hall
Mishap Marriage
A Traitor's Touch
Caught in Scandal's Storm
Lucy Lane and the Lieutenant
Lord Lansbury's Christmas Wedding
Royalist on the Run
The Foundling Bride
Carrying the Gentleman's Secret
A Vow for an Heiress

Castonbury Park

The Housemaid's Scandalous Secret

Visit the Author Profile page at Harlequin.com for more titles.

Prologue

1816

The Indian sunset was magnificent, illuminating the towers and domes of the Rajinda Palace in a princely state in the north of India. They caught the light—bright gold in the flaming glory of the setting sun. On the wide horizon the gold gradually turned to rose and purple. It was a vision of fantastic splendour—one William had marvelled at since he was a boy. A deep, aching sadness touched his heart. He was soon to leave this beautiful country, the land of his birth—his home, never to return.

Having served as an officer with distinction in the honourable East India Company, William's ambition and ability elevating him to the position of Colonel, on receiving a letter informing him of the demise of his cousin, bound by the ties of family, he had resigned his post. He was to go to England to take up the position of the sixth Earl of Ashurst, an event he looked on with little joy. India held his heart and his imagination, and it would be hard adapting to life as a member of the English aristocracy.

Throughout the years with his regiment he had been motivated by a sense of adventure and driven by the excitement of battle, but the sights of the battlefields and the loss of his friends had left their scars.

He passed through an enormous gated entrance, large enough for elephants two abreast and an army to pass through. Being a familiar figure at the palace, allowed to come and go at will, he was not apprehended. The vast, marble magnificence of the ornately decorated royal residence with its orchards and groves inside the massive, crenellated Mogul walls never failed to impress him. He walked beneath tall archways and through scented courtyards full of statuary and on through marble pavilions to a place where a cool breeze drifted through detailed latticework from the flower-scented gardens. Colourful ring-necked parrots graced the branches of mango trees, loud with quarrelling monkeys and squabbling mynah birds.

As a surgeon in the British East India Company, William's father had come to the palace on the request of the Rajah—the present Rajah's father—to treat his youngest son, Tipu, who had been thrown from his horse and almost trampled to death. His medical skill had saved the boy's life, although the accident had left him crippled. His father had been highly thought of by the Rajah and he had brought William with him on many occasions to spend time with the Rajah's youngest son.

William watched as a figure materialised from the shadows. This was his friend Tipu Chandra, dressed in silks and winking jewels. He was small and slight, his eyes brilliant and watchful. Tipu was intelligent and imaginative, a man of brains and breeding whose enthusiasm for life had been broken by the crippling riding accident. He was twenty-six years old, yet he shuffled towards him like a frail old man, dragging his injured leg behind him. There was close friendship and brotherhood between them, and a great measure of mutual respect. The two men embraced, then Tipu stepped back.

'William, my friend. I am so glad you have come. I understand you are to go to England.'

'I am. I have had word that my cousin has died. I am his heir and must return to take over the running of the estate—such as it is at this present time. According to his solicitor it is practically bankrupt, so you understand my haste to leave India.'

'Knowing you, my friend, you are most reluctant to leave. I know you look upon India as your home.'

'You are right, I do, and I would not have left without seeing you, Tipu.'

'And you will not forget me when you are no longer in India?'

'I could never do that.'

'That is good. You are much changed from the boy who came to the palace with your father all those years ago and took pity on the crippled child.'

'I never pitied you, Tipu. You know that.'

'I do and thank you for it. I always looked forward to your visits and valued the time you spent with me. Few people wanted to spend time with a cripple, but you were different.'

'I'd like to think I saw beneath your disability. You

are my lifelong friend and I shall miss you. I got your message saying you wanted to see me. What about?'

'My nephew—Dhanu. I have an important and rather delicate task for you to do for me. In fact...' he paused, studying William's face '...it is a task I am taking a tremendous risk in entrusting to you. But I know that you can do it. If anybody can, it is you. I want you to take Dhanu with you when you go to England.'

William's eyes opened wide. 'What? Why would you want me to? Tipu—has something happened?'

'I am afraid for his safety. Here anything might happen to him. It is not only wild beasts that prowl beyond the walls that are a danger to him. It is here, within the palace. My brother's wife, the Rani, and her brother Kamal hate him. Kamal is ambitious. All he wants is power, lots of it. He is greedy and cruel and if he could get rid of my brother so much the better, once he has dealt with Dhanu. He will use his sister's children like counters in the games he likes to play and once he has achieved his aim, he will sit upon his achievements like a large spider and weave his plots. The boys will be like pawns in his games, to be put forward as bait, to draw rich prizes into his web. I do all I can, but I cannot watch Dhanu all of the time.'

William knew Kamal Kapoor and how throughout the years he had taunted Tipu mercilessly about his crippled state. He also knew how much Tipu loved the boy, the five-year-old son of his brother, Rohan, the Rajah. He also knew how deeply he had loved Zoya, Dhanu's mother, how devoted to her he had been. But her ambitious family had overlooked the crippled Tipu in favour of the more able-bodied, more powerful Rajah. Something in Tipu's eyes caught his attention. Ever since Zoya had died, he had seen a deep sadness in his friend's eyes. But now it was worse. It was more than sadness—it was fear. Fear for Dhanu.

When Zoya had died, the Rajah had taken another wife, Anisha. She was very beautiful. Her position was strengthened by the birth of their twin sons. Courtiers flattered and fawned on her and hastened to ingratiate themselves with the new power behind the throne—not so Tipu. Intrigue and ambition haunted the new wife's quarters. Anisha was a devious woman, a woman whose heart would never rule her head. She would not rest until she had put her firstborn son in Dhanu's place, such was her jealousy of the boy.

Unfortunately, the Rajah was besotted with his new wife and he did not see what was happening. On the birth of their sons, suddenly his firstborn was of less importance. He would do anything to please her. She held him in the palm of her hand. Her hatred of Dhanu knew no bounds. She would not be secure in her position until the Rajah's eldest son was removed. Accidents had begun to happen and Tipu now employed an official taster for the child lest she try to poison him.

'Steps have to be taken to protect Dhanu,' Tipu said. 'He is still grieving deeply the death of his mother—he misses her every day. Take him with you—in secret—until it is safe for him to return.'

'And his father—the Rajah?'

'My brother is weak. He would do anything to please his wife. Despite my own aversion to the woman and other differences, as brothers we have always been close. He has agreed to let me remove him from the palace.'

'But not to have him go to England.'

'He is so blinded by his love and susceptible to his wife's influence, I doubt he will notice he is gone. I will deal with him when he finds out what I have done.'

The Rajah's deep affection and his protection of his younger brother could not be denied, but how he would react when he discovered Dhanu had been spirited out of India William could not imagine. 'You have been more of a father to Dhanu than his own, Tipu. Zoya should have married you.'

A sad smile touched Tipu's lips. 'No. She was very beautiful—such beauty would have been wasted on a cripple. It was enough for me that I could be near her. You are my good friend, William. I beg you, do this for me and you will be suitably rewarded.'

'You and I are friends, Tipu. I look for no reward.'

'Nevertheless I will not forget what you have done for me, my friend—or your father. Had he not treated me when I was thrown from my horse when I was a boy and everyone almost gave me up for dead, I would not be here now. Better to live the life of a cripple than to have no life at all. So—you will do it, you will take Dhanu with you?'

'Yes—I will take him.'

'You will protect him, I know.'

'I will protect him with my life. You know that.'

'Do not underestimate Kamal Kapoor, William. You know the depth of his cruelty, his deviousness and his mastery of poisons and debilitating drugs. Keep what you are to do to yourself. If he hears of it, he will strike before you have a chance to board ship.'

William's expression was grave. 'I will not utter a word, although I would not put it past him to follow me to England to do the deed—or hire someone to do it for him.'

'That is my concern. Take care, William—of yourself and Dhanu. You are precious to me, both of you. Because of our friendship Kamal hates you enough to tear your life to shreds. Be warned.'

Chapter One

Having left the ship that had brought them from India, William Barrington, the Earl of Ashurst, escorted the child and his Indian nurse, Mishka, along the busy wharf of the East India Dock. The air heavy with the odour of hemp and pitch, it was a seething mass of noisy humanity. A number of heavily armed Company-owned vessels were at anchor in the deep water. Tall masts and webs of rigging swayed with the motion of the River Thames, the charcoal-grey water lapping at the great hulls. Workshops and warehouses all within a mile of India House stored all kinds of exotic commodities from the east that stirred the imagination. Ropes and barrels were piled high and stevedores carried trunks and crates from the ship.

Dhanu, the five-year-old child, had difficulty keeping up with William's long strides so he hoisted him up into his arms. Tall, lean and as olive skinned as a native Indian, his hair dark, thick and curling, William was a man who inspired awe in all those he met.

His mind was very much on what he had to do now he was in London. After much deliberation and letters passing to and fro between him and his solicitor, there was only one solution that he could see to satisfy the creditors. He must marry a rich wife, a prospect he little relished after his ill-fated betrothal to Lydia Mannering. Lydia was the only daughter of an Englishman who had made his money in India as countless others had done and continued to do. Lydia was beautiful, witty and fun to be with, he had adored her, believing she would fulfil all his yearnings and dreams and light up his life with love and laughter and children. She was impressed to learn he was the cousin of the Earl of Ashurst and enthralled with the idea of going to London and mixing with the cream of society. Despite his aristocratic connections, William came from the poorer branches of his parents' respective families. He did not have a private fortune and did not give a damn for titles, when all Lydia's mercenary heart cared about was wealth and rank.

How utterly stupid and gullible he had been to let himself believe she cared for him. On returning from a long tour of duty he was devastated to discover Lydia had married someone else, an officer whose credentials and wealth far outshone his own.

William was the last in a long line of Barringtons. If he didn't produce a legitimate heir, the title would become extinct. It troubled him more than anyone realised, and he knew he could not ignore the issue. He would marry with great reluctance, unless he could find a wife who would bear his children and make no demands on him. Hurt and angry by Lydia's betrayal, with grim determination he had forced himself to come to grips with what she had done, managing to keep his emotions well hidden. Never again would he let his emotions get the better of him, and he vowed that he would not allow himself to be so weakened by a woman's body and a pair of seductive eyes. His heart was closed to all women.

Apparently his solicitor had a wealthy client, the mother of a man—Jeremiah Ingram—who had made his fortune as a sugar cane planter in the West Indies, and she was looking to marry her two granddaughters to titled gentlemen. He was to be introduced to the eldest of the two before he left the city for Berkshire. William was single-minded and completely unreadable, and at that particular moment he had an uneasy feeling of being watched. His stride was unhurried and, apart from a muscle that ticked in his clenched jaw, there was nothing about him to betray the fact that every nerve and faculty was tense and alert. His sharp, bright blue eyes observed everything that was going on around him, looking closely at individuals and probing the shadows for the dark faces of the two men who had followed him from India on another Company vessel, two men who posed a direct threat to the child.

As he left the docks he was unaware of the two figures that emerged from the shadows. One of the men was Kamal Kapoor. His dark eyes held a steadiness of sinister intent as they followed in William's wake.

Glancing out of the window of her grandmother's well-sprung travelling chaise, Rosa Ingram wished the weather wasn't so depressingly dull and cold, with rain falling heavily. Clouds darkened the sky, obliterating the sun as if it was probably too afraid to show its face.

Rosa felt no attachment to England. With its depressing weather and capital city a confusion of people and noise, it was a world away from the vibrancy and gently waving palms against the splendid vivid blue sky of her plantation home on her beloved island of Antigua, where she and her sister, Clarissa, older than her by two years, had been raised. A lump appeared in her throat when she thought of the circumstances that had brought them to this day, of the anguish that had engulfed them, almost drowning them in a sea of despair when their beloved parents had been laid to rest.

Abiding by their father's wishes, they had come to England on his demise to live with their paternal grandmother at Fountains Lodge in Berkshire. With just her maid, Dilys, for company, Rosa was travelling to Berkshire after staying with Aunt Clara and Uncle Michael in London.

Their grandmother was resolved to find suitable husbands for both her granddaughters before her death, which, since she suffered ill health, could happen at any time. She was afraid that should it come to pass before she had seen them both settled, as immensely wealthy young women they would be besieged by fortune hunters. It could prove disastrous with no one to guide them. She was assured their beauty and wealth would secure some penniless nobleman.

But how Rosa wished she could put her share of their father's wealth to better use. Shoring up some penniless nobleman's estate seemed a dreadful waste of money when so many people were in want. Deeply concerned with the sorry plight of London's destitute children, Aunt Clara was involved in charity work. It was the kind of work that appealed to Rosa, something she could apply herself to that would be both worthwhile and rewarding. When she had broached

the subject with her aunt, much as she would welcome
the funds that would benefit her charities, she had refused, telling Rosa that she was far too young to become involved with such things. Besides, Rosa's father
had made his mother, Amelia Ingram, her guardian. It
was up to her to decide what she should do.

And so Rosa had set off for Berkshire. Clarissa
had protested tearfully against marrying the Earl of
Ashurst, openly declaring her love for Andrew Nicholson, a young man she had met on Antigua. He had
been visiting friends on the island and had travelled to
England to visit relatives on the same ship. His family
home was on the island of Barbados, where his father,
like their own, also had a sugar cane plantation. The
Nicholson family were wealthy and well connected and
held considerable influence on the island. Clarissa had
appealed to her grandmother to let them wed before
he had to return to Barbados, but she had dismissed
Clarissa's entreaties, stubbornly refusing to discuss
the matter further.

She believed she had found the perfect match for her
elder granddaughter in William Barrington, the Earl
of Ashurst. Having distinguished himself as a soldier
in the East India Company, he had recently returned to
England to fill the role of the next Earl of Ashurst, heir
to the vast Barrington estate in the county of Berkshire.
Unfortunately it was almost bankrupt. To avoid closing the house and selling land and the Barrington town
house in Grosvenor Square, an enormous amount of
money must be acquired—and quickly. With no means
of his own, William Barrington had agreed to his lawyers' suggestion that he found himself a wealthy wife.

The Ingram family's small land portion bordered the

Ashurst estate. Miss Clarissa and Miss Rosa Ingram's widowed grandmother had been in London for the sole purpose of calling on the Earl's lawyers to propose a match between the Earl and her eldest granddaughter. Matters had been approved but nothing signed, and following a brief meeting between the Earl and Clarissa, their grandmother had returned to Berkshire with Clarissa. Unfortunately, Aunt Clara had taken to her bed with a severe cold. Concerned for her aunt, Rosa had remained behind until she was well enough for her to leave.

The travelling chaise pulled into the yard of a busy inn, where coaches going to and from London stopped for their passengers to partake of refreshment. Rosa uttered a sigh of relief. The journey was proving to be long and tedious, made worse by her maid's sniffles and coughing. The poor girl did look most unwell. The sooner they reached their destination and the girl was in bed the better.

'Come along inside, Dilys,' Rosa urged as they climbed down from the coach, pulling the hood of her cloak over her head to protect herself from the relentless rain while stepping round the deep puddles that had formed in the yard. 'Something to eat and a hot drink will probably make you feel better.'

The inn was thronged with a rumpled assortment of noisy travellers, trying to get close to the warmth of the crackling fire as they waited to resume their journeys. Seeing her dismay on finding the inn so crowded, the driver sought out the landlord. After speaking to him they were shown into a less crowded room.

Rosa found a quiet corner for herself and Dilys while the driver left them to take care of the horses.

After removing her fur-trimmed cloak and bonnet and ordering their meal, she glanced at the other occupants. Her gaze came to rest on a foreign woman and child seated across the room. She was conspicuous in the silk tunic of an Indian lady and she was trying to coax the child of the same race to eat. She was perhaps nearing thirty. A purple silk scarf was wrapped around her head, framing and half-covering her face. She appeared to be ill at ease, her eyes darting around the room and constantly looking towards the door.

Rosa's observations were interrupted when food was brought to them, but she did notice the gentleman who came into the room and went to sit at the same table as the foreign woman. His eyes flicked around the room. They met Rosa's briefly and without undue interest, then moved on.

Distracted, Rosa found herself staring at him. She judged him to be about thirty years of age, and he was tall and impressive—over six foot and lean of body—in the athletic sense. His skin was a golden olive shade—almost as dark as those people of mixed race on her island home. His hair was near black and thick, but it was his eyes that held her attention. They were piercing and ice blue, darkly fringed with lashes beneath fiercely swooping brows.

Unlike her sister and most of her friends Rosa was not a romantic at heart, but she thought him to be the most handsome man she had ever seen. He had an unmistakable aura of authority about him, of forcefulness and power. He also had an air of unease and the deep frown that furrowed his brow told her he didn't appear to be in the best of moods. Her attention was diverted when Dilys was suddenly overcome with a fit of sneezing. The man shot a glance of irritation in their direction before concentrating his attention on the boy.

Having eaten and eager to be on her way, Rosa left the inn. Dilys excused herself and disappeared into the ladies' retiring room. The yard was busy with carriages and people alighting and some setting off. Holding her skirts free of the puddles, she pushed her way through the people mingling about. The woman and child she had seen inside the inn were among them. Rosa heard the sound of hoofbeats and could feel them pounding the ground. She saw the crowd break up and part and then she saw a coach and four careering madly towards them.

Out of the corner of her eye she caught a movement next to her and two hands seemed to leap out of the crowd beside her. The next thing she saw was the little boy suddenly propelled into the path of the horses. Without conscious thought she leapt forward and grasped the child, pulling him back before the horses galloped past and came to a halt. The child began to cry and the woman, who had been distracted and was looking the other way, turned back and took his hand.

'What are you doing? You must be more careful.'

The woman spoke crossly in a voice whose faintly sing-song intonation alone betrayed the fact that it was not an Englishwoman who spoke.

The dark, frightened eyes of the child overflowed with tears. 'I—I was pushed,' he cried. 'Someone pushed me.'

The woman focused her attention on Rosa. On seeing the flush on her face and her closeness to the child, she immediately assumed Rosa to be the guilty party, having no idea that she had just saved the child from being trampled to death. She was unable to truly comprehend what had just happened but the look she cast Rosa was cold and accusing.

The small, silent boy, who now had tears streaming down his cheeks, stared up at her, clasping the Indian woman's hand. He was a strikingly attractive child, his Indian ancestry evident in his features and his jet-black hair. What entrapped Rosa more than anything was the compelling blackness of his eyes. They were large and widely spaced and fringed by glossy lashes. The woman began to drag him away, but not before Rosa had heard the child say in a small, quivering voice, 'I was so frightened.'

Then the man she had seen inside the inn stepped between them and gently brushed away the child's tears while bending his head to hear what the woman had to say. They spoke together in a language Rosa did not understand. After a moment he stood up straight and looked at Rosa, anger blazing in his eyes.

Some deep-rooted feminine instinct made Rosa's breath catch in her throat at being confronted by a man of such powerful physical presence. He had an expression of strength and marked intelligence. His eyes drew another's like a magnet to a pin. They were so full of life, so charged with the expression of their owner's awareness. Unexpectedly, she found herself the victim of an acute attack of awkwardness and momentarily at a loss for words, for in such close proximity, his overwhelming masculinity seemed more pronounced. When her eyes locked on his she was quite unprepared for the effect he had on her—her pulse seemed to leap. With his piercing blue eyes and his rich dark hair, he was an extremely attractive man.

'The child is unhurt—'

She was brusquely interrupted. 'No thanks to you.'

His words had an aggressive ring to them. Bright colour flamed in her face and her slender figure stiffened and drew itself erect. She stared at him. 'I beg your pardon?'

He looked at her full in the eyes, fixing her with a gaze of angry accusation. 'I realise that your carelessness may have been accidental and if that is the case then I advise you to be more careful in the future.'

His condemnation was unnecessarily severe. She thought his anger had been brought about out of concern for the child, but she would not excuse his rudeness. 'I would be obliged, sir, if you would voice your unjust accusation in a more temperate manner and apologise.'

The young woman's anger and animosity might at any other time have amused William and, looking into a pair of eyes the colour of green moss in which gold and brown flecks shone and seemed to dance about, he might have taken time to admire her slender form and the flawless beauty of her face beneath the high-brimmed silk bonnet, but now, his major concern being for the child, he did not smile. His temper was not improved by her bold attack, which caused his lean features to darken and his lip to curl scornfully across even white teeth.

'And I would be obliged if you would see fit to mind your own business.'

'That is exactly what I was doing and from what I have witnessed, sir, I would advise you to mind yours. It may have escaped your notice, but the inn yard with horses and carriages coming and going is a dangerous place to be for a young child.'

William's jaw hardened and his eyes snapped fiercely as he fixed her with a savage look. There was a murderous expression on his face and it was with a great deal of effort that he restrained himself. 'You are an extremely outspoken young lady—too outspoken for your own good.'

For a long moment he stared at her hard, then turned away, but Rosa could feel his contained anger as he stepped aside. The look he had given, cold and dismissive, had sent chills up her spine.

'Not usually,' she replied, refusing to be so rudely dismissed. When he turned and looked at her once more she met his eyes with a cool hauteur that belied the anger mounting inside her to match his own. 'Only when I find myself in the presence of someone as insufferable as yourself. Your accusation that I pushed the child—accidental or otherwise—into the path of the horses was harsh indeed. I did neither.'

'Her nurse tells me otherwise.'

'Then she was mistaken. She had taken her eyes off the child and someone from the crowd pushed him. I witnessed what happened with my own eyes and reached out just in time to save him from being trampled to death. So you see, sir, you might have made certain of the facts before accusing me. Your time would be best spent seeking out the real culprit.'

For a moment he appeared to freeze as he absorbed her words. 'Someone else pushed him? You saw who it was?'

'No, I did not. My whole attention was on the child. I do not know you, sir, but someone must have a very deep grievance against you to want to hurt the child.'

'That may be so, but *I* will decide that. You are a

stranger. Do not take it upon yourself to assume. Is that understood?'

Rosa stared at him. How dare this man speak to her in this condescending manner? She was so taken aback by his rudeness she could hardly speak, but when she did so it was with a fine, cultured accent like frosted glass. 'You, sir, are the most insufferable, rudest man I have ever had the misfortune to meet. Is it your habit to attack those who have done you a kindness?'

William's face paled significantly beneath his dark countenance, although he was furious with himself more than with her for he seldom betrayed his feelings in this manner. He had misjudged her, he could see that now, but before he could reply to her cutting remark she had turned on her heel. He caught her arm, halting her, his eyes doing a quick search of those around him.

'Not usually. I urge you to think back. It is most important that you do. Did you by any chance manage to see who it was?'

'No, I did not. I cannot help you.' Her chin lifted haughtily. 'Now please let go of my arm.'

Immediately he dropped his hand. 'In that case there is nothing more to be said.'

Realising that she was being dismissed, Rosa stepped back. 'You are right. There isn't. I expect it is beneath you to offer an apology.'

William gave her an uneasy glance, well aware that she, too, might have been hurt had she not stepped in to pull the child out of the way of the horses and that she was probably scared out of her wits by her show of bravado. 'If I have offended you, then I beg your pardon. Are you harmed at all?'

'I am perfectly all right—not that it is any of your

affair,' she remarked, still too angry to be mollified by his apology. 'Good day, sir.'

Turning on her heel, she hurried towards the waiting coach, relieved to see Dilys already inside. She had no idea who the man was and handsome though he was, that was the only thing to his credit. He was exceedingly rude. She did not suppose she would see him again and she thanked God for it. But, rude though he might be, one thing was certain—she was hardly likely to forget him in a hurry.

Before climbing inside Rosa looked back at the foreign woman, feeling that her show of ill temper might be a refuge from fear. But fear of what? she wondered curiously. Turning away, she saw a man backing away into the crowd. He, too, was foreign, of Indian origin, she thought as she noted his brown face and long tunic-like coat and European trousers, both in black. She felt his stare. There was a stillness about him, a silence, that was entirely menacing. She felt the hairs stand up at the back of her neck. She was taken aback by the ugliness of his expression—a scowl of such concentrated venom that made her draw back.

William's unease about what had just happened failed to lose its grip. His face betrayed very little of the emotions swirling through his body and his eyes remained impassive as he made a silent observation of the scene around him. But rage flooded through his veins as he thought of the danger that had presented itself to the child. His jaw hardened. The complexity of his emotions exasperated him. At a time when he should be focusing on his new role in life and trying to keep the Ashurst estate from being sold off, he was finding his time taken up protecting Dhanu. He was seeing danger in every shadow. That he had been followed from India he was certain, but he had thought he'd thrown them off the trail in London. However, if what the young lady had told him was true, then it would appear he was mistaken.

Suddenly he felt as if everything was spinning out of control. He had promised he would keep Dhanu safe, yet he felt as if he had just stepped into his worst nightmare. Slowly, carefully, he took a deep breath. He must not allow this to prevent him from thinking straight. His intelligence, his clever mind, which he had developed during all his years as a soldier, was his greatest asset. If he was to outwit this threat and keep Dhanu safe, then he must use his mind to do it. But, he thought, glancing around at the jostling crowd, how did one arm oneself against a foe that had no face?

Guilt overwhelmed him when he considered his ill-mannered treatment of the young woman. Her skin was golden. That surprised him, for most of the female population in England prided themselves on their milky-white complexion and took precautions to protect it from the sun. He had failed to do the decent thing and apologise properly to her. Beginning to feel a sense of shame for his unforgivable conduct and wanting to right the wrong he had done her, he turned to walk to her carriage, only to find it disappearing out of the inn yard.

Tense and irritable, Rosa suffered what remained of the journey in silence. The encounter with the stranger and the intended harm to the child had affected her more than she realised. Who was he, she wondered, and what was his association to the Indian woman? He spoke her language, which suggested that he had spent some time in India. She told herself that it did not concern her and tried putting it from her mind, instead concentrating on her arrival at Fountains Lodge. She managed to put it to the back of her mind, but she could not disassociate her personal feelings altogether.

Her thoughts turned to Clarissa and her distress at being forced to wed the Earl of Ashurst. Rosa knew what she was going through. She could empathise with her, for had she not lost her own love, Simon Garfield? His death had been final. It need not be like that for Clarissa. Andrew was not dead. Rosa closed her eyes, close to tears. Angry and emotional, everything inside her wanted to reach out to her dear sister, knowing how traumatised she would be if she was forced to go through with this marriage. Rosa felt she needed to help her defenceless sister, but to do that she would have to stand up to their grandmother. Amelia Ingram was a formidable lady, but she also suffered ill health and Rosa had been deeply concerned about her when she had seen her in London. She was worried that her grandmother wouldn't be strong enough to take on the task of arranging marriages for Clarissa and herself.

On a sigh she leaned her head against the cushioned upholstery and closed her eyes, letting her mind drift back to Antigua and Simon. What they'd had had been sweet and gentle, their relationship happy and fun loving. His sunny smile and dark brown eyes were imprinted on her soul. His death on a fishing trip had been a blow she had believed she would never recover from. She had successfully repressed her feelings for him, but at times like this, they rose to the surface. It was impossible to stop loving someone just because they had died. The pain of her lost love was still there and she knew it would be a long time before she was truly able to say it didn't hurt so much.

The coach made good speed, the horses moving briskly through winding, narrow roads overhung with branches as they neared Fountains Lodge. With Clarissa, she had been to England only once in her life, when she had come to Berkshire for an extended visit. The surprising thing when they neared the house was how familiar everything seemed, from the unfolding landscape and the villages they passed through, to the impressive Ashurst Park in the dip of a valley, the sprawling ancestral home of the Earl of Ashurst. They passed the gilded, tall wrought-iron gates which carried the Earl's crest. The house could not be seen from the road, but on her rides she had looked down on it from the surrounding wooded hills.

Soon Fountains Lodge, a fine seventeenth-century manor house, came into view. Set back from the village of Ashurst, it was a spacious house, east of which were outbuildings and stables arranged around a sizeable courtyard. The Ingram family had built it and remained in possession since. Apart from Amelia Ingram's maid and housekeeper, who had their own rooms, the staff needed to run the house lived in the village.

On reaching Fountains Lodge, Rosa strode into the hall with a winning smile for the hovering servants while removing her bonnet and shaking out her bright chestnut mop of curls, which rioted in a wild explosion about her head.

'Hello, Grandmother,' she said when the elderly lady entered the hall, her cane tapping the tiles as she walked stiffly forward to welcome her granddaughter. Elegant with a regal bearing, at seventy-five she was a small fragile woman. Arthritis and the years had worn away the muscles of her youth, leaving behind a shell of a woman. Her aloof, unshakeable confidence and bearing came from living a thoroughly privileged life. Being a small frail lady, it was difficult to believe she could be so formidably assertive.

'You're here at last and about time, too.'

'It's good to be here. How are you, Grandmother?'

'Better now I am home.'

Amelia cast her eye over her younger granddaughter, knowing she would have her work cut out if she was to see her married in the near future. Rosa's manners were unrefined and, unlike Clarissa, she knew nothing about genteel behaviour. She was a wild child, as wild as could be. She was intelligent and sharp-witted. She remembered her as being a problematical child—a constant headache. She was also proud and wilful and followed her own rules, but Amelia would not concede defeat.

'We expected you some three days ago. I trust Clara was feeling better when you left London?'

'She was much improved and sends her love to you both. But I'm here now and it's lovely to see you again.'

Sweetly Rosa kissed her grandmother's cheek before going to Clarissa, who followed in her grandmother's wake. There was an almost translucent quality about Clarissa. As sisters they were not unalike, apart from the colour of Clarissa's eyes, which were blue, and her hair, which was a light shade of brown. But where Clarissa was of a gentle, placid nature, Rosa was more spirited and inclined towards downright rebellion when crossed, with a wilful determination to have her own way. She was two years younger than Clarissa, but she always felt the eldest. As a result, without any parental control, Rosa had a strong sense of responsibility towards her sister. The sisters hugged one another, uttering little cries of welcome and pleasure. At last they drew apart.

'I've looked forward to your coming, Rosa. I imagine Aunt Clara was reluctant to let you leave.'

'She was, but she hopes to see us soon when she comes here for your wedding.' Clarissa's smile faded, making Rosa wish she had never mentioned it.

Amelia tapped her cane on the floor. 'We have much to do if Clarissa is to marry our neighbour, the Earl of Ashurst.'

'I shall do all I can to help with the arrangements. I like to be kept busy.'

'I intend to see that you are—with matters concerning your future role in life. I haven't forgotten that a husband must be found for you when Clarissa is settled—although I realise how difficult and unyielding is your nature.'

'Father would doubtless have agreed with you. He ever despaired of me—but the same could not be said of Clarissa,' she said, reaching out and squeezing her sister's hand affectionately. She was worried about her sister, who seemed to have lost all her usual vitality. 'In his eyes you could do no wrong. But where I am concerned, Grandmother, I am in no hurry to wed. I am not like my father. I am a realist. I can see things for what they are and I know I will never be accepted into the upper echelons of the aristocratic society my father aspired to. He could never see that.'

Their father had been known on the island of Antigua as a hard, authoritative man who worked long hours on his plantation and fully expected everyone else to do the same. Unfortunately, the authority he showed in his working life did not produce the same results in his younger daughter, who was known for her lack of discipline and her inclination to defy his direction, which did not apply to his elder daughter, who was a credit to him.

'You are right, Rosa,' her grandmother remarked, 'but nevertheless he was your father and you must respect what he wanted for you and Clarissa.' There was a hoarseness in her voice that told Rosa of her grandmother's inner grief over the death of her only son. 'He may be dead, but you have a duty to abide by his wishes,' she reminded Rosa, as she did every time Rosa broached the matter. 'It was his wish that you come to England, where you will be taught the finer points of being a lady—and I shall see that you do if I expire in the attempt. And despite what you have just said, a title will open many doors that will otherwise remain closed while ever you remain plain Miss Ingram. God willing, I will see you both suitably settled before I die.'

Rosa swallowed down the lump in her throat. How difficult life had suddenly become and how difficult the transition had been for her to leave her beloved Antigua and come to England. 'I will try not to be a disappointment to you, Grandmother. I will try not to let you down.'

She spoke truthfully, for she really didn't want to disappoint her grandmother or upset her in any way, but she was determined to have some say over her future.

* * *

Rosa, always intuitive to her sister's moods, looked at her, her brow creased with concern. Not until they were in Rosa's bedchamber and Clarissa had closed the door did they have the chance to talk.

'What is to be done, Rosa?' Clarissa said, thankful that she had her sister to confide in at last.

'I think you speak of this marriage to the Earl of Ashurst. What can be done, Clarissa? Grandmother is adamant that the two of you will wed.'

'But I don't want to marry him,' Clarissa cried tearfully. 'He is a stranger to me.'

'You will soon get to know him.'

'But I don't want to get to know him—not now. Not ever. I cannot go through with it. I love Andrew. I love him so much it hurts. I have never known such love—such sweetness…'

Rosa listened as her sister seemed to shine, her eyes brightly lit with adoration as she continued to speak of her love, her passion for Andrew. 'Then, feeling as you do, you must speak to Grandmother.'

'I've tried, but she refuses to listen. I cannot think of a life without Andrew. I cannot live without him,' she murmured despairingly.

Rosa sighed. Never had she seen Clarissa in such a state. Alarmed by this, she sat on the bed. Feeling a great need to protect her, she took her hand and drew her down beside her. 'Listen to me, Clarissa. She cannot force you to marry the Earl. You are twenty-one. You have a perfect right to decide who you will and will not marry. You must make her understand that you are your own mistress now. How does Andrew feel about all this?'

'He loves me as I love him. B-but he will not marry me without Grandmother's blessing.'

Rosa did not need convincing. Andrew's adoration and the gallantry he showed towards Clarissa when they were together were plain for all to see, but because his family were planters in a small way, Grandmother had refused to encourage the relationship and had departed London as soon as a meeting had taken place between the Earl of Ashurst and Clarissa.

'What is he like—the Earl?'

'To be quite honest we were together no more than a few minutes. He had another engagement and his mind seemed to be elsewhere. Oh, he is handsome and quite charming—in fact, I am certain there is not a woman in the whole of England who would not welcome a rendezvous with him. His lineage is impeccable and he has distinguished himself in India...'

'But?'

'He is not for me.' Clarissa looked at her sister imploringly. 'In truth, he is so—so excessively male and formidable. He radiates a force and vitality that scares me to death. I cannot possibly marry such a man.' Sighing deeply, she looked down at her hands in her lap. 'How foolish you must think me. You, who have never been afraid of anything or anyone in your entire life.'

Rosa sighed, for Clarissa spoke the truth. Clarissa was quiet and self-effacing, while she was too outspoken and never afraid to voice her own opinions, of which she had many—from any subject that was topical at the time to slavery, which had been a constant irritant to her father since the smooth running of the plantation depended on slave labour. He was forever chastising her, telling her to stop going on about matters which did not concern her and of which she knew nothing.

Should Clarissa marry the Earl of Ashurst, not only would he have sweet and gentle Clarissa to run his home, grace his table and warm his bed, but he would be in possession of a large portion of her father's considerable assets to repair his fractured estate. Their grandmother was right in one respect. With such an inheritance they would become prey to every fortune hunter in London. Better they were settled in good marriages.

'I wish I could think of something comforting to say that would alleviate your fears, Clarissa, but do not be too downhearted,' she said gently. 'Who knows what the future holds? Why, if the love between yourself and Andrew is as deeply committed as you say it is, then when Grandmother realises this and sees that you will be happy with no other, then maybe she will relent. When Father gave Grandmother control over us he was only doing what he considered best. I'm sure he wouldn't want you to be unhappy. She wants to make quite sure we are settled and everything taken care of before—before she...'

Something in Rosa's faltering tone caused Clarissa to look at her sharply. 'Do you think she is very ill, Rosa?'

Rosa nodded. 'There is no denying that there is a frailty about her and I noted when we were in London that there are times when she appears to suffer breathlessness and a great deal of discomfort.'

'She does tire easily.'

'But you must not let that stop you from telling

her how you feel—that you cannot marry the Earl of Ashurst.'

'I know I should feel honoured—and I am—but I would give all my prospects to anyone who would take them from me…simply to marry Andrew without the kind of wealth we have.'

'The Earl does not have our wealth, but marriage to you would change all that,' Rosa retorted coldly, feeling some resentment towards the Earl of Ashurst. What manner of man was it that would take a wife merely to pay off debts incurred by his cousin and to repair the neglect to his estate? She could feel nothing but contempt for a man who would marry a woman for the size of her dowry rather than for the woman herself. And who was to know that he wouldn't do the same as his erstwhile cousin and squander his new-found fortune?

Lying in her bed and thinking about Clarissa, Rosa was deeply unsettled by her concern for her sister. What was to be done? If only she could find a way to circumvent her grandmother. There must be some way to stop Clarissa marrying a man not of her choosing. The more she thought about it a plan began forming in her mind, a plan so shocking she feared to enlarge on it. It caused her heart to pound so hard she could scarcely breathe, for it was a plan no gently bred young woman would dare think of, let alone consider.

Yet the more she thought about it the more she fixed her mind on the plan and, with a cold logic, let it grow until she could think of nothing else. At one stroke she had presented herself with an answer to Clarissa's problem.

She would marry the Earl of Ashurst instead of Clarissa.

To contemplate marrying a man she had never even met surprised her—indeed, it sent a chill down her spine, but it did not shock her. If there was a way of helping Clarissa, then she would do everything in her power to do so. Clarissa said the Earl was handsome—at least he wasn't in his dotage so she would have that to be thankful for. However, the biggest obstacle was her grandmother, but she need know nothing about what she was planning until she had been to Ashurst Park. She would take a closer look at the Earl of Ashurst's noble pile to give her an insight into the house and its owner, to see what awaited her if she went ahead with her plan.

After breakfast two days later, relieved that her grandmother was still in bed—she never left her bed before mid-morning—without a word to Clarissa of what she was to do, she left the house. She was dressed in her best riding habit. The colour was dark blue, the jacket cut tight in at the waist, to slope away at the sides, the ensemble set off by a jaunty feather-trimmed hat. There was no sign that she had spent a sleepless night wrestling with the wild plan she had conceived. But her delicate jaw was set with determination.

Feeling deeply sad for Clarissa, she was prepared to sacrifice herself. So what did it matter that the Earl of Ashurst was a stranger to her? Whoever she married would not possess the qualities Simon had. She would never forget what had happened to Simon, but she must put it behind her if she was to forge a new life for herself here in England. It was important to her that she rediscover something within herself, something she had lost the day he had drowned. She would love to fulfil her desire to do something more worthwhile with her life, for she would dearly like to become involved with Aunt Clara's charities and help underprivileged children, but since that was to be denied her then she was pretty confident that she would be able to persuade the Earl of Ashurst to marry her and he would be well rewarded for it.

The Berkshire countryside was lush and green, with the sleepiness of late summer. Pausing on a rise, she looked down into a gently sweeping basin, where the gracious Ashurst Park was situated in what she thought was a pastoral paradise. It took her breath away, for it was the most beautiful house her eyes had ever beheld. Facing due south, it sat like a gracious queen in the centre of her domain. It had been built in the sixteenth century in the classical style of Brittany in France, which had been a fashionable form of architecture at the time. It stood among tall beech trees and oaks, guarding the brooding house like sentinels. Lawns adorned with flowerbeds and statues added to its beauty and further afield a rolling deer park stretched to the horizon.

A shiver crept along her spine. It was the same as she remembered, every detail. It was hard to believe that if Clarissa did marry the Earl of Ashurst, this beautiful house would be her home. Rosa's heart warmed to it. She would not mind being mistress of such a beautiful, noble house and, as the Countess of Ashurst, whether she was accepted or not, she would be in the forefront of society.

Since Simon's death, followed so soon by her father's, and coming to England, she had existed in some kind of daze. Halting her horse and looking at Ashurst Park, she felt all that was about to change. Determined not to think of the impropriety of an unaccompanied lady visiting a bachelor's residence, urging her horse on, she had not felt this energised for a long time. In some way she was back to being the old Rosa, head-strong and tempestuous and accustomed to having her own way.

But suppose the Earl wouldn't marry her? Suppose, despite all the money that would come his way, he still insisted on marrying Clarissa? Then what would she do? As she clenched her jaw, her eyes took on a deter-mined gleam. She wasn't fool enough to think it would be easy, but she would make him want to marry her, she vowed.

Chapter Two

It seemed to Rosa that she was entering a new world as she rode through the wrought-iron gates. When the gatekeeper closed them behind her she continued along the winding drive. Riding slowly past the lake, she took a moment to pause beneath the leafy canopy of a great sycamore tree. A cascade of water tumbled down a hill into a deep pool on the other side of a gracious three-arched bridge which spanned the narrow head of the lake. The still surface of the water was broken by the occasional swallow diving for midges on the surface. A boathouse could be seen in a recess among the trees on the other side.

She breathed deeply, the summer smells wafting about her. A sudden glow warmed her heart. She decided there and then that whatever drawbacks the Earl of Ashurst might possess, she would be well compensated by the beauty of Ashurst Park.

Coming to a halt at the foot of a low flight of stone steps, she dismounted. As she looked about her, a young man she assumed must be a groom hurried towards her.

'Is Lord Ashurst at home?'

'Yes, miss. Would you like me to take your horse?'

'Yes—thank you.' She watched him walk away leading her horse before climbing the steps. When she stood facing the door, she experienced her first signs of genuine apprehension. As if on cue the door was opened by a middle-aged male servant attired in black jacket and knee breeches.

'I am here to see Lord Ashurst.'

He nodded. 'Who shall I say, Miss…?'

'Ingram,' Rosa provided.

Waiting for the servant to return and removing her bonnet, Rosa looked about the large panelled hall. It was sun filled, polished and scented. She stood in awe of her surroundings. Beautiful artefacts reposed on a gleaming table in the centre, and on the walls were paintings of long-dead family members in gilded frames. The house exuded an indefinable quality—a sense of order, centuries of happiness and disappointments, memories of men and women who had lived and breathed within these walls—all folded into the fabric. The house was living, breathing, but empty of life.

Her eyes shone and she felt a peculiar excitement. It was unlike anything she had felt before and she found herself ensnared, as if this wonderful house was trying to wrap itself around her. She wanted to claim it for herself—she felt it was part of her destiny.

An elaborately carved oak staircase rose on one side of the hall to the upper floors, forming a gallery. She was conscious of a small contingent of curious maids lurking there. Open to their searching scrutiny, she was aware they stole lingering looks down at her. She managed to direct a self-conscious smile at them, but her mind was braced on the meeting with the Earl of Ashurst.

The servant reappeared.

'Lord Ashurst will see you now. Please come this way.'

Keeping her eyes straight ahead of her, Rosa followed in his wake along an assortment of corridors, taking note of everything she saw. The house was awe-inspiring and, despite the crippling debts that the Earl was desperately trying to meet, the atmosphere was of comfort and luxury, of elegance and a style of living she could never have imagined in her island home. The servant swept open a pair of carved oaken doors and stepped aside to admit her into the study, a comfortable, tastefully furnished room lined with books and discerningly furnished. Large French windows were open, the scent of freshly mown grass drifting in.

The servant closed the door behind him as the man she assumed to be the Earl got up from his desk with a welcoming smile on his face, clearly expecting to see Miss Clarissa Ingram. He halted in surprise, staring instead at a vaguely familiar, beautiful young woman wearing a stylish riding habit.

Rosa was equally surprised when she recognised him. In that moment she noticed the startling intensity of his light blue eyes and again she thought how extraordinarily attractive he was. His tall frame was clad in impeccably tailored dark blue trousers and coat and white shirt and neckcloth at the throat. He stood, his shadow stretching across the room. Then he was striding towards her. The room jumped to life about him as his presence filled it, infusing it with his own energy and vigour.

Her heart seemed to suddenly leap in her chest in a ridiculous way. 'Oh! It's you! You are the man I met at the inn the other day. Are you the Earl of Ashurst?'

Momentarily stunned, William continued to stare at her. His blood stirred as she came into the light thrown by the sun through the leaded windows. The young woman was a beauty, her hat dangling by its ribbons from her fingers, a riding crop in her other hand. The rich vibrancy of her chestnut curls framed a heart-shaped face and the green eyes beneath long dark lashes that had caught his attention previously held his gaze now. She had a healthy and unblemished beauty that radiated a striking personal confidence. There was about her a kind of warm sensuality, something instantly suggestive to him of pleasurable fulfilment. It was something she could not help, something that was an inherent part of her.

'I am Lord Ashurst, the Earl of Ashurst.'

On discovering the identity of her hoped-to-be husband and recalling their contentious previous encounter, she remembered that as she had walked away from him he had made a strong impression on her. And now here he was and the irony of it was that if her grandmother had her way then he was about to become betrothed to her sister.

Her momentary shock gave way to a cold anger. 'Had I known who you are I would not have come here. You were very rude to me.'

His mouth curled into a thin smile. 'After spending my entire adult life as a soldier, Miss Ingram, I'm afraid I shall have to relearn the art of gallantry. But as a matter of fact, I agree with you. My behaviour towards you was unmannerly. Believe me when I tell you that my conscience smote me and I wanted to do the right thing and apologise to you properly, but when I looked for you, you had left. Can I offer you refreshment?'

'No, thank you. I have not come here to make polite conversation, but on a matter of the utmost importance. I realise you are a busy man so I will be brief and take up as little of your time as possible.'

He lifted an eyebrow. Tilting his head to one side, he gave her his whole attention. 'What brings you here with such urgency?'

There was something in the depths of his eyes that Rosa could not fathom. Blue and narrowed by a knowing, intrusive smile, they seemed to look right past her face and into herself. For that split second she felt completely exposed and vulnerable—traits unfamiliar to her, traits she did not like. His direct, masculine assurance disconcerted her. She was vividly conscious that they were alone. She felt the mad, unfamiliar rush of blood singing through her veins, which she had never experienced before—not even with Simon. Instantly she felt resentful towards the Earl of Ashurst. He had made too much of an impact on her.

'I am Rosalind Ingram—everyone calls me Rosa. I have come to speak to you about my sister, Clarissa. I don't quite know how to begin. I have never done this sort of thing before, you see, and…my grandmother knows nothing of this visit. When she does I will feel the full force of her displeasure, but it will be worth it if you agree to what I propose. I have come to ask your help. I realise it is very presumptuous of me, and of course you are quite free to refuse, but the matter is urgent.'

'Is there no one else who can help you?'

'No—I'm afraid not. If I had…'

'Because of what transpired between us on our first encounter you certainly would not have come to me.'

'No, that's not right. I'm afraid you are the *only* person I can ask to help.'

A muscle twitched in his cheek and his light blue eyes rested on her ironically. 'My curiosity is aroused as to why you have come here without your grandmother's knowledge to visit a man you don't even know.'

Crossing to the fireplace, he draped his arm across the mantel and turned, regarding his visitor with a cool and speculative gaze. He could not help but admire the way she looked. Her overall appearance was flawless and he was quickly coming to the conclusion that she would set the standard by which all other women have to be judged, at least in his mind.

Her hair had been arranged artfully about her head and several feathery curls brushed her cheeks, lending a charming softness to her skin. The appeal in her large, silkily lashed green eyes was so strong that he had to mentally shake himself free of their spell. Something stirred within him that he was at a loss to identify.

'I am intrigued. Please—sit down,' he said, indicating a chair placed at an angle in front of the fireplace. 'Now, tell me, what can I do for you?'

Now she knew the identity of the Earl of Ashurst, Rosa's regret at coming to Ashurst Park increased a thousandfold as she perched stiffly on the edge of the comfortably upholstered chair. Never had she felt so unsure of herself.

'So, Clarissa is your sister. I thought there must be some connection. She is well, I hope?'

'She is perfectly well—only...'

He waited a moment, studying her with those strongly arched eyebrows slightly raised. When she wasn't forthcoming he prompted, 'Only? Only what?'

'She—she does not want to marry you and I recognise that I must lend her all my support.'

'I see. Do you mind telling me why?'

'Because she's in love with someone else.' Apart from a tightening to his jaw, his expression remained unchanged.

'Then that is as good a reason as any. Why was I not told this earlier—and why has your grandmother not thought to inform me?'

'I'm sorry. She was following my father's wishes in arranging Clarissa to marry a man with a title. Clarissa has never defied our father, sir. She loved him dearly and understands perfectly why it was so important to him that we both make suitable marriages.'

'And you have ridden all this way to tell me this?'

'Yes. I—I thought you should know.'

'Thank you. I appreciate your thoughtfulness. However, nothing has been signed so there is nothing to bind us.'

'You—will not pursue her?'

'No, Miss Ingram, I would not do that. To force the issue when she is in love with another man would make her loathe me.'

'If you discerned anything in her manner when you met in London—which, she has told me, was brief— you would know that she does not loathe you. Clarissa is the most gentle person you could wish to meet.'

'That is the impression she gave me,' he said, remembering that when he had met Clarissa Ingram how he had admired her refinement of character, her charm and sensibility—in fact, there was nothing about her with which he could find fault and he could not deny that he had been tempted by her grandmother's proposition that she become his wife. But that had been in London.

As a soldier, he listened to his head and not his heart in all things. Nothing in his life was accidental or unplanned and everything was carefully thought out.

He'd agreed to consider his lawyer's suggestion that he marry a wealthy woman, which would enable him to retain Ashurst Park, but his abhorrence to doing such a thing was as strong as ever. Miss Rosa Ingram's revelation had come as something of a surprise to him and also a relief that he would not have to do battle with his conscience.

'However, it is clear to me that your grandmother made the proposal without a thought to her finer feelings. It changes things considerably and has helped me with my decision. I will go and see your grandmother and tell her that I have changed my mind about marrying Clarissa—which is the truth. I would not contemplate marrying a woman whose heart is elsewhere.'

'Not even to save your estate?'

'No. Not even to save Ashurst Park,' he answered with icy calm. 'Since I agreed to consider marriage to your sister I, too, have had a change of heart. So you see, Miss Ingram, I am not as mercenary as you think.'

Taken by surprise, Rosa stared at him. 'I see. What did you intend doing about it?'

'I was going to see your grandmother to explain.'

'But—I have come here to offer a solution to your problems.'

'And how did you intend doing that?'

'I—have come to offer myself in Clarissa's place. I wondered if you would consider marrying me instead.'

His eyes flashed unexpectedly. 'Good Lord!' The words were exhaled slowly, but otherwise, he simply stared at her. 'Have you taken leave of your senses?'

She tossed her head, causing her hair to shimmer. 'I assure you I am quite sane.'

'Are you serious?' he asked, raising an eyebrow.

'I am perfectly serious,' she replied, thinking everything about him bespoke power and control. He was much too in command of himself to toy with.

'Yes, you are,' he replied coldly, 'and the answer is no.' It was an instant response. Unconsidered. Automatic. Already William could feel his pride and self-respect being stripped away bit by agonising bit. Her proposal unsettled him. The feeling was something complex and disturbing. Instinct told him he'd be best served not to prolong Miss Ingram's visit, for he was quite bewildered by his own interest in this young woman. Her manner was forthright, but there was a vulnerability about her. She had no flirtatious wiles and her candour threw him somewhat, so what was it about her that disturbed him—and how was it possible for her to have made such a strong impact on him on so short an acquaintance? Her eyes seemed to search his face as if she were looking into his soul.

Suddenly he found himself wondering what it would be like to have her as his wife. Would she light up his life with warmth and laughter? Would she banish the dark emptiness within him? He caught himself up short, dispelling any youthful dreams and unfulfilled yearnings he had consigned to the past. He had experienced them once before and realised his mistake in the most brutal manner. He scowled darkly as he realised Miss Ingram was suddenly bringing all those old foolish yearnings back to torment him. He would have none of that. After his turbulent relationship with Lydia he had reconciled himself to a life of transient affairs, which satisfied and relieved his body and left his emotions intact, but he suspected that if he were to take Rosa Ingram as his wife she would be a threat to everything he had determined never to feel again. His hurt went too deep. However difficult his life had been since Lydia's betrayal, he had not deviated from his determination never to fall into the same trap again.

What might this woman do to him if he let her?

Disappointed by his response, forcing herself to ignore the fluttering in her stomach, Rosa ploughed on before her courage and confidence deserted her. 'Please—hear me out. I have given the matter a great deal of thought and I have decided that it is a solution that would suit us both. I should mention that my father left both Clarissa and me a substantial inheritance.'

'My lawyer has made me aware of that. Whatever you have heard about me and expected to find when you came here, I am not a charity case, nor am I a beggar who is so impoverished that I will grab the offer of a proposal of marriage from a woman I do not know and sink to my knees with gratitude.'

'Not for one moment would I expect you to do that. It would be ridiculous.' Seeing how one well-defined dark eyebrow shot up in annoyance, she plunged bravely on. 'I would like to point out that marrying me instead of Clarissa would make no difference to the money. A large dowry I am sure would make marriage to me palatable...' She fell silent when he held up a hand and halted her.

'Miss Ingram, let me assure myself that I understand you,' he said, recovering from the shock her proposal had caused. 'You are asking me to throw over your sister for you? Is that right?'

'Yes.'

'You must excuse me,' he said, controlling his ire with difficulty. 'I have never before been engaged in such a conversation, and to be frank I do not know the rules of the game.'

'Neither do I,' she admitted. 'But let me assure you that it is not a game, Lord Ashurst.' Rosa flushed violently and stiffened with indignation. She refused to retreat now she had come so far. 'I know it may sound mad to you, but it is not like that at all. You are not the first Englishman who finds himself down on his luck and required to marry a wealthy woman as an answer to his financial difficulties. I am not ignorant of the fact that in the upper classes large sums of money and extensive estates are involved in such marriages.'

With surprise, she was conscious that he was studying her with a different interest. She sat and returned his look. His expression did not alter, yet she felt the air between them charged with emotion. He cocked an eyebrow at her and for a moment it seemed as if he would agree, then he looked away.

'You are very sure of yourself, Miss Ingram.'

'I have always been sure of myself, Lord Ashurst. It is other people that often puzzle me.' When he looked at her once more, his eyes hard and direct, she sighed. 'You don't want to marry me, is that it?'

'Miss Ingram, I don't *want* to marry anyone,' he said, going to sit in a large winged chair opposite her, propping his right ankle on his left knee and steepling his fingers in front of him. 'I find the manner of your offer a cold-blooded business arrangement—in fact, some might call it vulgar for a lady to discuss money matters and propose marriage to a complete stranger.'

Mentally chiding herself for lacking the poise and behaviour of the lady she had been brought up to be, Rosa lifted her chin, undaunted. 'Yes, I suppose they would, but I have no time for such niceties. I came here to make you an offer since I have no one else to speak for me.'

'You do have your grandmother.'

'She does not always see things my way and I know she was hoping you would marry Clarissa.'

He was silent for a full ten seconds and then he gave her a smile that didn't quite reach his eyes. 'How old are you, Miss Ingram?'

'I shall soon be twenty.'

'I see. Why are you so intent on marrying me?'

Uncomfortable with both his question and the penetrating look in his eyes, Rosa tried to smile and make light of his question.

'One of the reasons is that I have fallen in love with your house. One cannot fail to be impressed by it. Ashurst Park is beautiful.'

'I cannot disagree with that. The fabric of the house is as it was when I was here as a youth. My inheritance is both ancient and beautiful, and I consider it a privilege to call it my home. Although,' he said, his mood somewhat despondent and thoughtful, 'in this present financial climate one cannot fail to observe unavoidable signs of wear and tear here and there. Countless tasks await me to be done in order to restore the estate to its former glory. I have not yet had time to discover the full extent of the neglect. The lawyer has kept on a skeleton staff even though there was no family member living here. According to my lawyer, a great deal of money is needed to put things right.'

'Have you considered selling the estate and returning to India?'

'I confess that it did cross my mind—but I considered it no further. I am bound by the ties of present and future relationships to the house of Barrington. I had a vision of my grandfather and his proud and noble bearing and of the long line of my forebears who suffered to preserve intact the honour and noble name of Barrington, who subdued their own lives and fought their own individual battles for that same sense of honour— some making the ultimate sacrifice in one battle or another. I owe it to them to see that Ashurst Park is made secure for future generations.'

'Finding yourself in such dire straits, I am sure they would understand if you were to sell.'

He shook his head. 'If I were to do that, then the Barrington ghosts would be justified in rising up in anger at my dishonourable deed.'

'That is where I come in. You want a rich wife. I am available.'

Not a muscle flickered on William's face. He was silent, looking at her hard, incredulously, as though she had suddenly changed before his eyes. His face instantly became shuttered and aloof. He looked her over carefully, as if to judge her for her worth, and appeared dubious as his brows snapped together and a feral gleam appeared in his narrowed eyes with angry disgust.

'Contrary to what you might think, Miss Ingram, I cannot be bought. I am a man of honour and honour cannot be bought or measured in wealth. No matter how much money you may bring with you to shore up the walls of Ashurst Park, what makes you think you are worth it?'

Rosa stiffened her spine. 'Now you insult me,' she declared, a surge of anger rising up inside her like flames licking around a dry log, furious with herself to think she had been so stupid as to think he would accept her offer.

'It is not my intention to give offence. Forgive me if I appear surprised, but I fail to understand why you would wish to marry a complete stranger. And why would you think I would agree to marry you? Since your sister is no longer available to me, there is nothing to stop me looking elsewhere for another heiress to marry if I so wished.'

'Surely one wife is much like another if she comes to you with a fortune.'

'I disagree,' he replied, thinking that Miss Rosa Ingram would prove to be more trouble to his carefully held sensibilities than she was worth. 'Although there must be hundreds of ambitious parents who would be only too ready to offer their daughters for an increase in position—a generous dowry in exchange for the grand title of Countess of Ashurst.'

Rosa looked at him directly. 'I am sure you are right—which is exactly what my father was thinking. The choice is yours, of course. But, unlike Clarissa, I am not in love with another—so it is not as difficult for me to accept.'

'Accept?' His face might have been carved out of stone when he fastened his hard gaze on hers and there was a saturnine twist to his mouth. 'I do not recall proposing marriage to you, Miss Ingram—or your sister, come to that.'

Lord Ashurst's taunting remark flicked over Rosa like a whiplash. The hot colour in her cheeks deepened and her soft lips tightened as she exerted every ounce of her control to keep her temper and her emotions in check. 'No, of course you haven't. How could you? Where Clarissa is concerned I thought there was an understanding.'

'No. Our meeting was brief. Nothing was decided.'

'You must bear with me, sir. I have only recently come to England myself and I have much to learn. I frown upon marriages arranged without reference to the feelings of the bride—with sole regard to titles and the increase of family fortunes. When Grandmother has seen Clarissa settled in a marriage of her choosing, it will be my turn. An arranged marriage is what she intends for me.'

'And your father, by all accounts. It is not my intention to be disrespectful towards your family, Miss Ingram, but from the little I know of him he set more importance to his daughters marrying a title than he did their happiness. Finding yourself in the same situation as your sister, how will you react if you do not approve of your grandmother's choice of husband?'

Rosa's face had taken on a youthful dignity as she looked at his directly. Her age and inexperience were evident, yet she was prepared to stand her ground to defend her father's good name if required. 'My father was a private man, Lord Ashurst, and benevolent, with a rational and cultivated mind. There was no one better.'

'Yes—I am sure you are right and your loyalty towards him is to be commended.'

'I have never defied either him or my grandmother. I loved my father and I love my grandmother dearly and understand perfectly why it is so important to them both that Clarissa and I make suitable marriages. But I will find it difficult to meekly submit to my grandmother's rules as a matter of course, which is why I have decided to be my own advocate and make my own case. If I fail in this I will be completely helpless and defenceless before my grandmother's determination to find me a husband of the nobility.'

'No helpless female would dare to come all the way here—alone, I might add—and propose marriage to a complete stranger. A woman who can do what you are doing, Miss Ingram, is not helpless—or defenceless. Reckless, yes, but certainly not helpless.'

Rosa looked into his eyes, trying to read his expression. There was a moment's silence and William watched her face with a slightly cynical lift to his eyebrows.

'I salute your courage and your boldness. I feel this is your style—setting out on some impulsive adventure, with little thought of the consequences. I cannot for one moment believe you have thought it out properly. You are being a little selfish in throwing yourself at me, a stranger, daring me to take advantage of your offer. But have you not for one moment thought that you might be playing with fire? I will not satisfy your scheme.'

Rosa's heart fell at his unexpected cynicism. She had agonised over the steps she had taken. Did he understand nothing of what she had said at all? 'Whatever you think of me, my offer was well meant. If you think my coming here is nothing but a silly, reckless adventure on my part, then there is nothing more I can say to convince you that it is otherwise.'

William studied her gravely for a moment. 'Perhaps you do have it all worked out. You are undeniably brave—and beautiful—and impetuous, with very little thought of the consequences of your actions. What you are doing for your sister is highly unusual, Miss Ingram—and commendable, though it leads me to question your motives.'

Rosa's green eyes snapped with disdain and for a brief instant William glimpsed the proud, spirited young woman behind the carefully controlled façade. 'I told you. Clarissa is in love with someone else. It would break her heart if she didn't marry him.'

'Then why put yourself forward? You didn't have to. Your sister is twenty-one, old enough to make her own decisions. She could just walk away.'

'Not Clarissa. Our father wanted the very best for her: marriage, title, everything he aspired to be himself—he always did have aspirations of grandeur—which was why, ill as he was and knowing he would not be around to see his wishes for both of us come to fruition, he placed us in Grandmother's hands with the stipulation that she finds us noble husbands. Clarissa loved and respected him too much to go against his wishes.'

'Your grandmother is a formidable lady.'

'Yes, she is.'

'So why me? If it is a husband you require, then surely London is full of gentlemen who would prove to be far less trouble than me—although in exchange for your wealth you would obtain a title if I agree to the marriage.'

'Titles are meaningless to me. Besides, I know it is my father's money that attracts them to me and nothing else. It would act like a beacon to every impoverished nobleman in England.'

'Then I am no different from them—an impoverished lord who would be marrying you for your money.'

'There is a difference. I chose you, Lord Ashurst. I see marriage to you and being able to reside at Ashurst Park a good way of investing in my own future.'

'I see,' William replied caustically, getting to his feet and turning from her. In silence he took a thoughtful turn about the room. He was feeling more humiliated and degraded than he cared to admit.

His immense fears as his lawyer had told him the extent of the estate's insurmountable debts was deep-rooted, and the shadow of Lydia continued to haunt him, making it impossible for him to get on with his life with ease. She had been a bright and beautiful beacon in his world and he had found an untold happiness when he was with her. She had used all her witchery to captivate him, making him her willing, pliant slave. He had later come to deplore the fact that he had kept such a large streak of naivete in his make-up and had found it hard to grasp the guile behind the soft smiles and fond words. He had believed she loved him. How soft and persuasive her voice could be. He could not have guessed for a moment what weight of treachery it concealed.

It was strange that Miss Ingram's presence and her proposal had brought what had happened with Lydia—

that ultimate betrayal when she had thrown him over for someone else—back to him with each sordid detail. He stopped in front of her, knowing he was right to turn her down. 'I am sorry, Miss Ingram. I cannot help you. I cannot make rash promises I may not keep.'

Rosa stared at his rigid stance. 'I do understand how difficult this is for you, Lord Ashurst.'

Struggling to keep the irritation out of his voice, he said, 'Believe me, Miss Ingram, no part of this dilemma is remotely easy for me. You have so much money that what you do should not be a problem. You've had life handed to you on a silver platter. Wealth gives you an advantage over me I don't like.'

Rosa stared at him. A great wave of crushing disappointment filled her heart, banishing everything but her regret that she had been foolish to come to Ashurst Park and humiliate herself before this stranger. She averted her eyes. She had at least done what she could. But it was small comfort. She knew with rising dread that no one could push the Earl of Ashurst into any decision not of his own making. She realised how misguided she had been. For the first time since she had devised this wild scheme, she knew the real meaning of failure.

Her small chin lifted primly and her spine stiffened, and before his eyes William saw her valiant struggle for control—a struggle she won.

'Then I suppose there is nothing more to be said,' she murmured in a colourless voice.

William hadn't missed the flare of temper in her eyes. 'I'm afraid not.'

'And you will visit my grandmother to explain about Clarissa?'

'Of course. Thankfully nothing was signed so your grandmother can hardly sue me for breach of promise.'

Rosa cocked her head to one side, trying to see beyond his cool façade. 'Is there something you do not like about my family—something you object to?' Frowning thoughtfully, she said, 'I wonder... You must know how my father became rich—the source of his wealth.'

'My lawyer did make me aware of the facts.'

'And that his plantation was worked with slave labour?'

He nodded. 'I don't imagine there is a plantation in the Caribbean worked any other way.'

'And that concerns you?'

'Yes, as a matter of fact it does but it has nothing to do with my decision. Slavery is not something people in England are accustomed to. It is a shocking practice. To take a man by force from his native country, to be chained and taken across the Atlantic to be sold in the markets that deal in human flesh, to work the plantations without the right to call themselves men, is unacceptable.'

'It may surprise you when I tell you that I agree with you completely. I have despised the practice ever since I was old enough to understand it. It is as much an abomination to me as it clearly is to you. I make no excuses for my father but I ask you not to judge him too harshly. It is a subject I argued constantly with him about. Had I the power and the means, I would have changed everything. However, that is clearly not an issue since you rejected my proposal.'

'I am glad to know you share my views, Miss Ingram, but that was not the reason why I refused to marry you.'

Rosa's sense of defeat was augmented by the knowledge, which had grown on her since their first encounter, that she had made a fool of herself in attempting to appeal to such a man as Lord Ashurst. He was hard and unfeeling, and all that was left for her was to retreat with what dignity she could muster. She was too proud to let him see that she was confused and disappointed by his rejection.

'Then I will keep you no longer. Thank you for taking the time to see me.'

'It was my pleasure.'

To know that she shared his views on the abomination of trade in human beings touched him deeply, almost weakening his resolve not to become involved with her in the way he had been with Lydia. But he would not allow it. Rosa Ingram posed a threat, a danger to his peace of mind, and he could so easily become enamoured of her—and become completely undone into the bargain. He had been there once and had no mind to travel down the same road twice. However, he could not fail to notice the pain and discomfort she was feeling and admired the dignity with which she had received his pronouncement.

'One moment, Miss Ingram,' he said. She had turned from him but paused at his request and turned and looked at him. He looked down at her with gravity in his eyes, but a half-smile on his lips. 'I have my own reasons for refusing you which you can know nothing about. As yet I have not become fully acquainted with the estate and the tenant farmers. I still have much to consider and discuss with my bailiff and lawyer—but no matter. I have enjoyed meeting you and I wish you well. You are a woman of spirit, even if a little too impetuous.'

'I feel that I must agree with you.'

'You should not have come here today,' he went on. 'Not that I do not appreciate your visit—quite the contrary. But this is a bachelor establishment, something which perhaps did not cross your mind—perhaps you also did not realise that since I live here and I am a newcomer to the area and few people know anything about me, it is a very dubious bachelor establishment.'

'Please do not concern yourself,' she replied stiffly. 'My action was entirely innocent and I am persuaded than my reputation cannot suffer, as a consequence, in the eyes of those people who know me, and those who don't will never know.'

'A woman of spirit indeed! I would not like to see you cowed by gossip.'

'Lord Ashurst, I know well enough what my impetuosity and my meddling has cost me today and I would thank you not to rub it in.'

Her words brought a broad smile to his lips and, in spite of her anger Rosa caught herself wondering why a man with such an unpleasant character should be gifted with such a lovely smile.

'Excuse me. I will leave you now,' she said, making for the door.

'I will call on your grandmother shortly.'

Neither of them spoke as they left the room and crossed the hall. Rosa looked squarely at the Earl as he held the door open for her to pass through, and as she met his gaze her small chin lifted and her spine stiffened. William saw her put up a valiant fight for control, a fight she won. She looked as regally erect as a proud young queen as she went down the short flight of steps and took possession of her horse the stable boy was holding. The boy held his hands for her booted foot, hoisting her atop her horse. Riding astride as he had seen no lady do since coming to England—normally they rode side-saddle—that was the moment William saw she was wearing skintight buff-coloured breeches beneath her skirt.

Rosa sat on her horse unmoving, as if she were some stone goddess, insensate but powerful. She gripped the reins in her slender fingers and stared back to where he stood in the open doorway.

'I realise how concerned you must be about the state of the finances. My offer was sincere. I would like to help—if you would let me,' she offered.

'Thank you. That is extremely generous of you. I appreciate your offer but I cannot accept it.'

'Not now, perhaps, but think about it.' About to ride off, she paused when she remembered something. 'Oh—there is something I forgot to mention which you may like to know.'

'Which is?'

'At the inn—when I was leaving—I saw the man who I am certain pushed the boy. He was mingling with the other passengers and looked extremely angry.'

William froze and then he was striding down the steps to where she was trying to settle her restless mount. 'Are you certain?'

'As certain as I can be.'

'What did he look like? Can you describe him?'

'He was of medium height, gaunt looking, with short, straight black hair and dark skin. The look he gave me made me thankful I was not his enemy.'

'Was he alone? Was anyone else with him?'

'I don't know. I didn't see anyone else—but then,

there were so many people.' She jerked her horse round. 'I must go. Good day, sir.'

Leaving the Earl staring after her as she rode away, she couldn't help thinking that she had made things a whole lot worse. As she put a distance between her and Ashurst Park, something inside her, some hopeful light that had shone bright on her journey to meet with Lord Ashurst, faded and winked out of existence. But out of sheer pride she held herself tightly together against the disappointment and humiliation. She was sorry he had turned her down, but having such strong principles concerning slavery, she really could not blame him.

As soon as her grandmother had married Clarissa off she would be thrown onto the marriage market and she would be expected to go trustingly and placidly into the unknown. The man chosen for her might be old or ugly or both. The thought was intolerable. At least Lord Ashurst was a young man and handsome.

As it was there was nothing for it but to tell her grandmother everything. Her heart was filled with dread in anticipation of the condemnation she would ultimately receive. There would be no redemption, she knew that.

As Rosa rode away from the house, William let his eyes sweep over the wide parkland, narrowing them against the glare of the sun. Filled with deep concern for the boy, he prayed God that soon Tipu would have this matter with Dhanu resolved and he could return to India. He was inclined to believe what Miss Ingram had told him and he would ensure that every precaution to safeguard his well-being would be taken. The idea that someone was stalking him with every intent of permanently removing Dhanu awakened in him a dangerous, quiet anger.

He continued to watch Miss Ingram ride away, her hat tied loosely round her neck and bouncing madly against her back, only the ragged pulse that had leapt to life in his throat attesting to his own disquiet as he stared after her with mingled feelings of regret and concern.

As he turned and went back into the house he refused to be moved by her offer. Until his cousin's death, he had been a man who had made his own choices and, as much as he would like to appease his manly appetites with the lovely Rosa Ingram, he would not be so easily manipulated. How could he like some lapdog blindly accept what she was offering without yielding his mind and his principles?

But she was far too beautiful for any man to turn his back on. It would be no easy matter banishing her from his mind. She was physically appealing, with a face and body he found attractive, but she was also appealing in other ways, with an intelligent sharpness of mind. He suspected on knowing her better she would possess a clever wit that he would admire, making her pleasant company and interesting to be with. However distasteful the prospect was, perhaps he should consider her proposal. After all, heiresses were few and far between.

As an only child, the times he had spent with Charles had been precious to him and his untimely death had upset him profoundly. He had loved his cousin like a brother and deeply regretted that he had been unable to help him when he had fallen into financial difficulties, which had driven him to take his own life. William felt honour-bound to make the estate prosper as it had in the past. It would be a massive undertaking but he would do it—not only for himself but for Charles. Perhaps if he agreed to marry Miss Rosa Ingram he wouldn't come out of it too badly. It could be the answer to a problem he could see no other way of solving at this present time.

The noble certainty that she had been doing the right thing when she had set out for Ashurst Park had disappeared as Rosa rode back to Fountains Lodge. She felt abased in her own eyes. What she had done had been foolish in the extreme. She had acted impetuously, rashly and unthinkingly and most importantly without common sense in Lord Ashurst's eyes, earning his derision and her profound dislike. He had been hard, cold and cynical and had done nothing to put her at her ease.

Thinking of all the things she didn't like about Lord Ashurst was a barrier against recalling her own shortcomings, so by the time she reached Fountains Lodge she had worked herself up into a temper and a very thorough dislike of the man. She hoped she would not have the misfortune to meet him again in the future, but somehow she felt that she would.

Chapter Three

Rosa watched her grandmother's sharp eyes narrow with disapproval, for perching on a chair in front of her she presented a wild, untidy vision. Her laced leather boots were smeared with mud and her skirts were creased, and Rosa knew her grandmother was not fooled, that she was painfully aware that underneath she was wearing the outrageous breeches she insisted on putting on when she went riding. But above it all there was a passion in Rosa that was so potent it changed the atmosphere of the room.

'Did you enjoy your ride, Rosa?' Amelia enquired, pressing a perfumed handkerchief to her nose as the smell of horses wafted in her direction.

'Yes, very much,' Rosa answered, shoving her untidy mop of chestnut hair back from her face, putting off the moment to tell her of her visit to Ashurst Park. 'I always enjoy riding and the horse the groom selected for me excelled itself.'

Her grandmother's gaze became pointed. 'Are you feeling well, Rosa? You are very flushed.'

'Yes—I am quite well. If my face is red, then it

must have something to do with the exhilaration of the ride. But I—I didn't sleep very well,' she said, looking down at her hands folded in her lap. 'I—I am concerned about Clarissa and your insistence that she marry Lord Ashurst.'

'You have no reason to be. It is my duty to stop her becoming involved with any man who cannot support her in a respectable lifestyle. Clarissa is no longer under age, I realise that, but it changes nothing. She must abide by your father's wishes.'

'Father would not want her to be unhappy. He would not force her into a marriage she did not want.'

'Who is to say she will be unhappy? The Earl is an honourable man and Ashurst Park is a beautiful, noble house.' She sat back in her chair with a determined expression on her aged face. 'I am resolved that the decision I have made is the right one and will benefit Clarissa.'

With a worried, haunted look, as though carrying a burden too heavy to bear on her young shoulders, raising her head she looked at her grandmother, meeting her questioning eyes. She would have to tell her everything. It could not be avoided.

Rosa thought her grandmother was going to have a fit as she hesitantly told her what she had done. Her eyes never moved from her granddaughter's face. She seemed unable to speak, to form any words, from between her rigidly clamped lips. When Rosa had finished speaking Amelia remained for a while in contemplation of her clasped hands. Her ashen face was set in lines of concern. Rosa respected her silence, stifling her painful anxiety.

Unable to contain herself any longer Amelia raised

her eyelids and looked at her. Rosa shivered at the anger and disappointment in her eyes.

'I am shocked, Rosa—deeply so. You had a plan, you say, one that would suit everyone concerned. It was a very stupid, thoughtless action to take. You had no right to take it upon yourself to do that. Lord Ashurst will never agree to such an outrageous idea.'

'I know that now. He made it quite plain what he thought of it. Grandmother, I am so sorry.'

'Being sorry is not enough. What you have done is outrageous. Among other things, to call on a gentleman uninvited and unaccompanied was disgraceful. Why on earth didn't you take your maid?'

'Dilys is still unwell. Besides, she does not ride. I told her to stay in bed until she's feeling better.'

'Then you should have taken a groom. The expensive education your father provided for you should have taught you about behaviour and comportment. You may not have been born into Lord Ashurst's league, but you are still quality born with good breeding. And to offer yourself in marriage to a man who to all intents and purposes is about to become affianced to Clarissa is not to be borne.'

'But he isn't—at least he won't be when he has told you that he has had a change of heart and will withdraw his suit.'

'But why would he do that? Did Clarissa displease him in some way?'

'No, not at all. He—he will not marry Clarissa knowing she is in love with someone else—and he has no wish to marry me, either.'

Amelia became quiet. She looked deflated. 'I cannot blame him. He must think you're too forward by far. At least he is honest. But until I have seen him and spoken to him myself, nothing is changed. You should not have gone to see him, Rosa, you should not.'

Having expected to be severely chastised, Rosa squared her shoulders. 'I am truly sorry, Grandmother. I should not have gone to Ashurst Park without talking to you first.'

'You should not have gone there at all. What were you thinking? To go there in the first place without prior invitation was an act of rudeness. Now what is to be done? What must Lord Ashurst think?'

'He—he is going to call on you shortly. But—when I explained about Clarissa—he understands.'

Amelia looked at her hard, knowing just how single-minded she could be, how stubborn. God help her if ever she experienced the sheer driving force of passionate love—and the man it was focused on. Amelia knew how determined she could be, that when she had something on her mind she would have her own way at any cost, and if that kind of love touched her, she would not deny herself having it. Amelia also knew about the young man she had formed a deep friendship with on Antigua, that he had drowned and Rosa had been grief-stricken by his death. But that had been an adolescent love, the kind most young people experienced at one time or another, but not enduring.

'I did not get the impression that Lord Ashurst was the kind of man to comply to the whim of a young woman he has never met.'

'I know that now—and understand his reasons—but I had to try. All this is a quandary for you, I know, but it needn't be.'

Amelia looked at her granddaughter with a keen eye.

'Oh? You have the answer, do you, Rosa? I know you are sympathetic to your sister's plight, but how can I let her wed that young man in London? It's quite out of the question.'

'But they love each other. Forgive me, Grandmother, but I must speak out,' Rosa said softly, unable to remain silent any longer on the subject. 'I know you have Clarissa's best interests at heart—but she should not be forced into a marriage she does not want. She is feeling quite wretched about it all, knowing how much Father wanted her to make a splendid marriage—and you, too. If you insist on this she will not disobey you, but I know the last thing you want is to see her unhappy. Let her have her way and marry Andrew.'

'I can't, Rosa. What would your father say?'

Rosa studied her grandmother's stern face for a moment and then affection came and softened her features. Rosa found herself bursting with affection for her. Slipping to her knees beside her grandmother's chair, she took her crooked fingers in her own. 'I think Father would not object to Andrew. His father is an influential man on Barbados—a sugar cane planter, too. Sadly, Father died before Andrew came to Antigua, but I know he would have liked him. Clarissa loves the Caribbean, Grandmother. She considers it her home. Let her go back.'

'And what of you? It must have been a wrench for you when the plantation was sold and you were forced to leave Antigua. It was your home also.'

'Taking my leave of our home and the island was not easy—and after Simon drowned...' She faltered, biting her lip as the memories drifted into her mind. She remembered everything of that last summer on the island with Simon—the laughter, the foolishness, the lazy summer days, the intensity of a time which had meant everything to her. 'Everywhere I looked held reminders, precious memories of the years too quickly gone by. But I am not like Clarissa. I will adapt to whatever life has to offer.' She would like to have pressed her own case, that she be allowed to go to London to help Aunt Clara with her charities and to forget all about marrying anyone, but her aunt had already said no to her on that matter and her grandmother looked so crestfallen that she hadn't the heart to add to her worries. Amelia remained silent, thoughtful. To Rosa, watching her with concern, she seemed so very frail and appeared to shrink into herself. Sighing deeply, Amelia shook her head slowly.

'What a business this is.' Her eyes looked bleak, her voice hollow with emotion. 'What is to be done? If only your dear father were still here to guide you. It was my dearest wish that he would not go before me, but…' Her voice faltered and she bit her lip to keep it from trembling. 'I have buried all my children. No mother should have to do that.'

Rosa gazed at her, at her misshapen hands. Her face bore lines of grief. Deep inside the awesome, formidable lady was a profound loneliness, the loss of her three children who had died in infancy, her husband and only child who had lived to manhood its wellspring.

'What can I do to help?' she whispered.

'Nothing, my dear, nothing at all. If you don't mind, Rosa, I'll return to my room. Ring for Margaret, will you? She will take me up.'

'Are you feeling unwell?' Rosa asked anxiously, getting to her feet. 'Should I send for Dr Parish?'

'No, there is no need for that. I'm just tired—nothing that a little sleep won't cure.'

Rosa wasn't convinced. According to Clarissa, their grandmother was spending more and more of her time in bed and hardly ate anything. Rosa hated to see her fading like this. Margaret had been her grandmother's personal maid for twenty years. She watched the maid accompany her grandmother out of the room. Her movements were weary, her small body stiff. Rosa felt a constriction in her throat which she swallowed down and went in search of Clarissa.

Rosa and Clarissa were at breakfast the following morning when Margaret burst in on them, her distress so acute that Rosa felt her heart leap to her throat. She stood in the doorway, so out of breath she could hardly speak.

Rosa sprang to her feet. 'What is it, Margaret? Is Grandmother…?' Her blood seemed to chill in her veins.

'Oh—it's terrible, Miss Ingram. She—she's had some kind of attack. She is asking for you.'

Instructing Margaret to go to the village to fetch Dr Parish, Rosa and Clarissa went immediately to their grandmother's room. She was propped against the pillows in the big, canopied bed she had shared for forty-five years with her husband. Her eyes were closed, her cheeks sunken, her lank, lacklustre hair spread over the pillows. Her thin, deeply veined hands plucked at the bedcovers in a distracted fashion.

Rosa was shocked. She had not expected to find her so reduced, so ill in such a short space of time. She was filled with self-recrimination, feeling her foolishness in going to Ashurst Park had brought her grandmother to this, tears stinging her eyes. She would never do anything intentionally to hurt her.

Amelia opened her eyes and looked at her granddaughters, trying to draw breath.

'What is it, Grandmother?' Rosa said, gently taking her hand, terrified that something might happen to her grandmother. 'Margaret has gone for Dr Parish—he won't be long.'

'I—I've had some kind of turn…' Her voice was a thread, but her blue-tinged lips turned up in a small smile. 'I—I'll be all right soon…'

The doctor came, old Dr Parish who had attended Amelia on a regular basis. He took her wrist and put his ear to her chest, and told Rosa when they had left the room that he didn't like the sound of it, but they were to take care of her and give her a few drops of laudanum to settle her and to help her sleep. He would call the following morning.

She became worse in the night, worrying about what would become of her granddaughters should she be taken. She died a few moments later, her hand in that of younger granddaughter.

Rosa and Clarissa were bereft. Their grandmother had been very dear to both of them. What did the future hold for them now?

Dealing with their grandmother's affairs kept both sisters occupied during the ensuing days. Funeral arrangements had to be made and her lawyer paid them a visit to deal with her financial matters. Her death had affected everyone. Rosa missed her terribly, but it wasn't like when Simon had died, when she had wanted to drown in her sorrow.

Two days before the funeral, on a lovely sunny day, escaping the confines of the house, the sisters took the carriage into Ashurst to purchase some black ribbon to trim their bonnets from the haberdasher's in the High Street.

They had just stepped out of the shop into the street and were returning to their carriage when a prickling sensation at the nape of Rosa's neck told her she was being watched. Curious, she turned her head to find herself looking into the black, impertinent eyes of the Indian gentleman she had seen at the inn, the same man she believed had pushed the boy into the path of the horses. She could see the unconcealed hostility in his eyes. Although never of a nervous disposition, she felt the chilling hand of fear clutch at her. Her heart began to race, urging her to turn and walk on, but she held her ground.

Another Indian gentleman came to stand a little behind him. He was not quite as tall, but like his companion his face was long and thin, his nose hooked. Shifting her gaze back to the taller of the two, when she looked into his eyes she saw nothing. No emotion, nothing. If, as it was said, the eyes were the windows to the soul, then this man's windows were firmly closed and shuttered. Both men had an air of menace and cold ruthlessness about them that inspired fear. Rosa stiffened, finding the encounter curiously distasteful. With their faces as inscrutable as a rock, they looked like the harbingers of woe.

Unaware of what was happening, Clarissa carried on walking. Averting her eyes, Rosa was about to walk on, but paused once more. A feeling of unreality crept over her and she shuddered.

Overcoming her initial surprise, she automatically found herself speaking to them. 'Who are you? What do you want?'

The taller man took a step towards her, the pupils of his eyes narrowed like a cat's in the light. When he spoke, his voice was heavily accented with his native tongue. From between his parted lips a gold tooth gleamed as it caught the sun. 'I know who you are— and that you are acquainted with William Barrington. I know what you did that day. We want nothing from you. Our presence here does not concern you. Do not interfere in what we do.'

Thinking it a strange thing for him to say, Rosa forced herself to back away, her heart beating faster than normal. She shared another glance of hostility with the Indian man before he turned and walked away, closely followed by his companion. Gradually her pulse steadied, but she wore an air of acute unease.

Clarissa came to her side, a curious frown creasing her brow.

'Who were those men, Rosa? Do you know them?'

'No, not at all. I saw one of them at the inn where we took refreshment on our journey from London. I think he is connected to Lord Ashurst in some way.'

'Quite possibly,' Clarissa said. 'Those gentlemen are clearly Asian and Lord Ashurst has just returned from India so it would not be unusual.'

'I don't think they are nice men, Clarissa.'

Clarissa looked at her curiously. 'How do you know that?'

'Because Lord Ashurst was also at the inn that

day—not that I knew who he was then—but I have an uneasy feeling that the men you have just seen are dangerous individuals—men Lord Ashurst has reason to fear.'

They attended their grandmother's funeral as did many others who had known her. It was a warm sunny day, marred only by the sorrow. It was then that Rosa realised just how well known and respected her grandmother had been. The funeral service was held in Ashurst village church, the service simple and moving. Afterwards Amelia Ingram was laid to rest with her beloved husband in the churchyard.

At the back of the church on the opposite side to where the Ingram sisters sat, enclosed in a boxed pew, William rested his gaze on the two young women at the front. Their heads were bent over their prayer books as the priest in his ornate robes intoned the solemn, centuries-old words of the funeral service. His gaze passed over Clarissa to her sister, where he let it rest, looking at Rosa with interest. Remote and slender, she had a purity of profile which arrested and compelled his eyes. Her devotions as she knelt and prayed seemed absolute. Her black-bonneted head was haloed in the light penetrating the windows and he saw, when she lifted her head and let her gaze fall on the cross on the altar, that her expression was sorrowful and tense. There was a shadowed hollowness to her cheekbones and she was pale, which told William how affected she was by her grandmother's death.

Along with the rest of the mourners he followed the service, automatically saying the familiar words of the prayer, but his gaze kept straying to Rosa Ingram, to

the gracefulness of her head, now bent in utter sub-
mission, her lips moving in silent prayer.

As if aware of his gaze, suddenly she turned her
head and looked directly at him, her eyes a brilliant
green and intensely secretive in the atmosphere of rev-
erence, a recognition stirring in their depths. The sheer
intensity of that glance, the nakedness of it, and the intimacy, made William feel that they were the only two
people inside the church.

Then the service was over and he stood, momentarily distracted by the people moving all around him,
following the funeral procession outside into the blazing sunlight. Outside the church he stood back, watching the proceedings as the coffin was lowered into the
ground, but all he could think about was Rosa Ingram
and the imprint of her secretive glance. He had been
made uneasy by it. There was something about her that
reached out to him and touched him in half-forgotten,
obscure places.

Rosa and a tearful Clarissa greeted the steady
stream of guests as they arrived at the house. Rosa
had noted Lord Ashurst's presence in the church. He
had become the focus of everyone's scrutiny. Everyone
knew the new Earl of Ashurst had taken up residence
at Ashurst Park, but few people in the surrounding dis-
trict had seen him. It was well known that he had spent
almost his entire life in India, which made him a somewhat mysterious, curious figure, but there were those
who remembered him as a youth when he had come to
England for his education and resided at Ashurst Park.

Rosa saw him arrive and studied him for a moment
in silence before moving forward to greet him. He was

clad in jet black with the exception of his snowy-white shirt and cravat, which gleamed in stark contrast to his black suit and silk waistcoat. As she had noted on their first meeting there was a strong, arrogant set to his jaw. Everything about him exuded brute strength and arrogant handsomeness. He was the kind of man who was capable of silencing a room full of people by just appearing in the doorway, whose attitude was that of a man who knew his own worth.

His appearance in the church had pulled her from the strange melancholy that had seemed to enclose her since her grandmother's death. She had experienced a feeling of alarm on seeing him again. He had appeared too suddenly for her to prepare herself, so she had been unable to suppress the heady surge of pleasure she experienced.

As Rosa faced him, it was difficult to set aside their last meeting and what had transpired. 'Lord Ashurst, thank you for coming.'

'I won't stay, but I wanted to speak to you both personally to convey my condolences. I must apologise for not coming sooner, but pressing matters of business have taken up my time.'

'Yes, I can understand that, but no apology is necessary, I assure you,' Rosa said. 'We are grateful to you for coming. Grandmother did not have the best of health, but we did not expect her to leave us so soon. Her death has come as a crippling blow to both of us.'

William shifted his gaze to Clarissa, who hovered shyly a step behind her sister. 'I intended riding over to see you, Miss Ingram.' He saw her moist eyes light with hope and an underlying uncertainty. 'Worry not. Your sister has explained everything to me so we need not discuss the matter further.' Seeing Clarissa's happy response, he smiled. 'We will speak of it no more and I wish you well in your future happiness.'

'Thank you,' Clarissa murmured, clearly relieved that she had escaped marriage to this formidable man. 'I appreciate your understanding.' Her eyes filled up with tears. 'Please—excuse me.'

Rosa watched her go before turning back to Lord Ashurst. 'Clarissa's taken Grandmother's death badly. She is quite overwhelmed by all this and will probably go to her room to lie down.'

William noted a change in Rosa Ingram from their previous two encounters. This was not the face of the young woman who had boldly come to his home and proposed marriage to him. Then, her haughty manner had marked her as strong of character whereas now, with her eyes full of grief and a gentle smile on her lips, there was a softness about her, an elusive gentleness that declared her to be as vulnerable as the roses that clambered over the garden walls. Clearly she was a woman of ever-changing moods and subtle contradictions, and while her physical beauty first arrested the attention, it was this spectrum, this bewildering, indefinable quality that held him captive.

'And you, Miss Ingram? Your grandmother's death must have come as a shock to you, too.'

'Yes, it has. I am going to miss her terribly. To have only recently arrived in England and then to lose her so soon is heartbreaking.'

A strange, sweet melting feeling softened William's innermost core without warning, the place in him that he usually kept as hard as steel. 'And it will affect your future, no doubt.'

'Of course,' she replied stiffly.

'What will you do? Have you decided?'

'I'm not sure. I don't have to do anything at present.'

'And the house?'

'My grandfather's nephew has inherited Fountains Lodge—Antony Ingram. He is a businessman and married with a young family so this house will be perfect for them.'

'He was not at the funeral?'

'No. He lives in Scotland. He is held in the highest regard. His reputation as a gentleman and a businessman is unequalled and, I regret to say, as yet I have not had the pleasure of making his acquaintance. He has many things to take care of before he can leave. Ingrams have lived at Fountains Lodge since the day it was built over two hundred years ago. I'm glad it's to remain in the family.'

'Will you stay until he arrives?'

'No, I don't think so. It could be several weeks before he manages to get here. I might go with Clarissa to London, where we will stay with my mother's sister, Aunt Clara.'

'And Clarissa?'

'Will marry Andrew and return to the West Indies. His family lives on Barbados. His father is also a planter of sugar cane. She will be happy there.'

'I sincerely hope so.' He looked beyond her to the knot of people looking curiously his way. He stepped back. 'If you will forgive me, I will bid you good day, Miss Ingram. I have pressing matters to attend to.'

'Yes—of course. Thank you for coming.' She watched him leave the house before remembering there was something of importance she wanted to say to him.

Quickly she went after him, halting him in his stride as he strode towards his carriage. 'Please, Lord Ashurst, wait. There is something I have to tell you. It may be important, it may not, but I think you should know.'

Pausing, he turned and looked at her, waiting for her to speak.

'It's about the Indian gentleman I saw at the inn on our journey here. He was in Ashurst two days ago.'

William froze. He felt nausea strike within him and a sudden grinding pain behind his eyes. 'How do you know this?'

'I saw him. I was with Clarissa. He was tall and thin with a hook nose. I also noticed that one of his teeth at the front was gold. There was another Indian gentleman with him, very similar in looks, but not quite as tall.' As he listened she observed his reaction, saw his jaw clenched so tightly that a muscle began to throb in his cheek.

'I see,' he retorted tightly.

'You—know who they are?' she queried tentatively, curious as to their identity and their connection to Lord Ashurst and the woman and boy she had seen at the inn.

He nodded. 'I do.' He felt as if he had stepped into his worst nightmare. Kamal Kapoor had a gold tooth.

'Who are these men?' she ventured to ask.

His eyes narrowed to dark blue shards. Unable to quell the cauldron of emotions that were seething inside him, his fury escaped him. It vibrated around her. 'Believe me, Miss Ingram, you don't want to know.'

His reply was brusque, warning Rosa to pry no further, but she was curious as to the bitterness her question had evoked. 'Of course not. I understand. It is none of my business—which is what one of the men said to me.'

There was a steely strength to him as he gave her a slow, studied glance. 'They spoke to you?'

'Yes. One of them recognised me.' She looked at him directly. 'He told me not to interfere in what they do. Tell me, Lord Ashurst—am I in danger?'

'No. You have no need to feel threatened by them. It's me they are interested in—and the child,' he said in a controlled voice, while inside he was seething with rage, knowing Anisha's assassins—her brother Kamal Kapoor and his cohort—had followed him to Ashurst. 'Don't let it concern you, but should you see them again I would appreciate being told.'

On that note William left her, knowing there was nothing he could do about the two men unless he was prepared to commit murder. His temper, a true Barrington temper, was never a wise thing to stir. Right now, he was prowling, a hungry wolf seeking blood. If anyone harmed Dhanu, that equated to an act of aggression against him and the experienced soldier beneath the veneer of an elegant gentleman reacted and responded appropriately.

He asked himself why a man could kill his fellow man in battle and why a man could be shot or hanged for a crime he has committed, yet he was not permitted to kill a man who was intent on murdering Dhanu.

The early-morning mist had lifted and the day was crystal clear as William rode up the valley, his mount's hooves striking sharp against the rocks.

Although the estate employed a very efficient bailiff, William considered running the estate a full-time occupation, and the concerns of his tenant farmers were his own concerns. He rode out to make himself known to his tenants and their families and inspected properties and land. He talked to them in depth and made mental notes of their needs—which were many. No doubt some of his fellow landed aristocrats considered his work habits most eccentric, but he didn't care a jot. The welfare of his farmers was most important to him and he hadn't realised what dire straits they were in. Unable to make a decent living from the land and their livestock, some of them were considering coming out of their farms. In all conscience he could not let that happen. Something must be done and it was up to him entirely.

But on this particular morning he felt at ease and at peace among the gently rolling hills and valleys that lay all about him. Why this should be so was a mystery to him since his situation was more serious than he had realised when he had come to Berkshire. The last few months had been full of anxiety, tension and infuriating frustration for him and finding out the extent of the debts had driven him almost to breaking point. His lawyer had informed him that time was running out. Only yesterday he had sat at his desk looking with despair at the list of debts that far exceeded what he had imagined. It had sent a chill through his heart.

In the past, under the diligent care of previous earls, Ashurst Park and all its land and properties had prospered. With the death of his cousin and the troubles, it was as if the life and soul had gone out of the place. Everyone connected to it knew there were dark days ahead. He could not rest until the money that was owed was paid back. It was not right that his family's bad luck should impact on the livelihood of others. If he couldn't find his way out of the financial mess within the next two weeks, with creditors coming at him from all directions, there would be nothing for it but to sell the estate.

Knowing there was no time to go heiress hunting and loath to leave Dhanu at Ashurst Park too long because of the dangers the two men posed to his safety, William's thoughts turned to Rosa Ingram and the proposal she had made to him. Women had been drawn to him since he was a youth, but he had never left himself vulnerable, as he was now. The thought that he would marry her to secure his estate was acutely distasteful to him.

In truth he didn't want to dwell on the threat she posed to his carefully held feelings and emotions. But she had offered him a solution to his situation that could prove useful to him. And though furious at not having the upper hand, he was considering trading his aristocratic lineage for the sake of his future security and Miss Ingram's money—a commonly accepted practice, but it made him feel less of a man.

Halting his horse on the wooded hill overlooking Ashurst Park and the lake, he gazed about him. Crushed by all the unsupportable issues he was involved with, he had taken to coming to the tranquil and everlasting peaceful countryside to gain relief from the empty stillness, which was quite profound. The durability all around him gave him hope for the future.

Rosa loved to ride in the early morning. As soon as breakfast was over, eager to get out of the house and away from the sombre funereal atmosphere that clung to it, she made her way to the stables. Clarissa didn't join her, preferring to stay and help Margaret and Dilys sort through their grandmother's possessions and put them into storage, but she stressed that Rosa should be accompanied by one of the stable hands. To placate her, Rosa agreed.

In no time a horse was saddled and she was cantering out of the yard, Thomas, the stable boy, hard pressed to keep up. The air was warm and heavy with a fragrance of the trees and undergrowth. She halted her horse on a rise, beneath some giant elms that cast a web of shadows around her. Below her the lake was bathed in bright sunlight, a shimmering, radiant expanse of water. She sighed. It was perfect. She felt dazed with the colours and the sunlight and the beauty of it all. The water beckoned. What a pity she was unable to bathe.

To the left of her a ribbon of water cascaded over stone steps carved out of the hillside. A splendid baroque temple stood at the top. The water tumbled into a deep pool spanned by the three-arched stone bridge before flowing into the wider body of the lake. To the right the house was perfect in its setting. With its surrounding gardens and fronted by the lake, it seemed to be slumbering in a golden peacefulness.

Breathing deeply, she closed her eyes. Ashurst Park had a timeless quality. Nothing mattered. Nothing existed but the moment.

It left her totally unprepared for what was about to unfold. Seeing a flash of bright blue on the bridge, she watched as it took form. It was the Indian child, out walking with his Indian nurse and a maid. Unconcerned, she continued to watch, the boy's happy laughter reaching her. She saw him point to the temple above, and before the nurse could take his hand he scampered off, the nurse, hampered by her skirts, shouting for him to come back as she ran after him. Fear began to unfurl in the pit of Rosa's stomach. She saw the child leave the bridge and run round the pool at the bottom of the cascade to begin to climb the slope beside the tumbling water and move closer to danger.

Alarm shot through her and, calling to Thomas to follow her, she urged her horse on. On reaching the bridge she flung herself off her mount and looked up the slope, hoping to see the boy. There was no sight of him, only the nurse and maid scrambling up the grassy slope. Then she saw a flash of bright blue in the fast-flowing cascade, carrying the boy down and into the pool. Without thought she hurriedly unfastened her boots and kicked them off her feet before throwing off her hat and removing her jacket and the skirt she wore over her breeches, knowing the heaviness of the thick fabric would drag her down. Over the parapet she saw the boy gasping for breath and flailing and floundering about wildly, before disappearing beneath the water.

Scrambling down the steep bank, filling her lungs with air, Rosa dived into the water, trying not to think of the unimaginable depths beneath her. After bobbing up to the surface once more, terror and panic on his little face, the child was dragged down once more.

Upon seeing a horse and rider emerge from the trees further along the hill from where he was and go tearing down towards the lake, another rider following in her wake, William also saw Dhanu climbing up beside the cascade of fiercely tumbling water. Fully alert to the fact that he was liable to fall in, William touched his heels to the stallion's flanks, sending him forward.

He now knew that the rider who had reached the bridge before him was Rosa Ingram. A strange mixture of fear and relief swept over him. Reaching the bridge, he threw himself out of the saddle at the same moment she disappeared from his sight beneath the dark swirling, frothing water.

As he watched, his expression turned rock hard as a suspended memory broke free and he recalled his lawyer informing him of his cousin's suicide and the manner of it—of how Charles had ended his life in this place.

'Oh, my God!' he whispered. 'You little fool! You brave, courageous little fool!'

His breath left his body and immediately he vaulted over the end of the bridge and slithered down the bank, more frightened than he'd ever been in his life. In the space of a split second, fear consumed him, fear that both Rosa Ingram and Dhanu would perish in the same pool of water.

Rosa went down into the endless darkness. The seconds seemed limitless as she felt around for the boy, but she couldn't see a thing. She came up for more air before disappearing beneath the water once more, hampered by the water swirling around her from the tumbling cascade pushing her down. From somewhere a long way off she could hear her name being called above the roaring in her ears. Unable to breathe, she felt as though her lungs would burst. And then her hands touched an arm and then a small body. Holding on to him, she kicked strongly and they were rising once more, the bright light coming closer, larger, until she burst through its centre and felt the warm sun on her

face once more, before being thrust back by the raft
of water and hitting her head on the rocks at the bottom of the cascade.

Momentarily stunned, a red haze began to cloud her
vision and for a moment she almost lost her hold on
the boy. Somehow she managed to hold on to him and
when he coughed and spluttered and wriggled against
her, her heart swelled and she offered up a prayer of
thankfulness. Despite the dizziness inside her head,
clutching the small body tightly to her with one arm,
she swam desperately towards the bank. Someone was
kneeling and holding out a hand and shouting for her
to take it.

'Take the boy first,' she gasped, having recognised
the voice as belonging to Lord Ashurst.

William reached out and took the boy from her,
passing him to his nurse before turning his attention
to Rosa.

Knowing that the boy was safe, with an ache in her
head and the red haze increasing before her eyes, Rosa
felt her consciousness begin to recede and a calmness
begin to descend on her. Just when she thought she
was lost and about to sink beneath the surface of the
water once more, strong hands grasped her arms in a
paralysing grip.

'Hold on to me,' William ordered. 'We'll soon have
you out.'

Instinctively Rosa obeyed, unable to do anything
else as with much slipping and sliding he hoisted her
out of the water with what seemed to be superhuman
strength. She collapsed, gasping and helpless, onto the
grass at his feet, where she lay with her eyes closed,
her chest heaving for breath.

'You're safe now,' she heard Lord Ashurst say, but she couldn't move. Everything seemed so far away and her body felt like lead. The pain in her head, which had momentarily disappeared, returned to torment her with a savage vengeance. When she was able to breathe more easily, her eyes fluttered open to see Lord Ashurst's darkly handsome face. He was kneeling beside her. His light blue eyes were clear and shone as bright as jewels. Black brows were puckered together in frowning concern.

'My—my head,' she managed to whisper. 'I seem to have bumped my head.'

'I can see that,' he murmured, wiping back the veil of wet hair from her pale face and looking down at her in silent contemplation, 'but you'll be all right. You're out of danger. You little fool—jumping in like that. You could have drowned.'

'No, I wouldn't. I can swim. Living on an island surrounded by sea, I had every opportunity to learn.' She wondered what he would say if he knew she often swam naked in the clear blue Caribbean Sea, her hair floating free. 'I'm sorry if I frightened you. I only went in to retrieve the boy. I wasn't in any danger until I hit my head on a rock.'

William believed her. He had watched her swim beneath the surface of the water, her figure moving swiftly as if she had been born there. Taking her face gently between his lean fingers, William turned it to one side, brushing back tangles of her hair to reveal a small gash just above her ear, from which a thin trickle of blood oozed. He smiled down at her, making an instant appraisal of the rest of her. Sheathed in her clothes clinging to her body, her blouse moulding the curve of her soft breasts and her legs encased in tight cream-coloured breeches, she was as slender as a wand.

'The wound is superficial and I don't think any permanent damage has been done—but no doubt your head will ache for a while.'

'The boy? Is he conscious?'

'Yes. Thank the Lord you got here in time—and that you can swim. I, too, was out riding. I saw Dhanu on the bridge and rode hell for leather to get to him. You beat me to it.'

'I really thought he was going to drown. With the amount of water pouring into the pool from above, I knew the current would drag him down. I was up on the hill overlooking the lake when I saw him.'

Rosa struggled up from her dazed trauma to prop herself up on her elbows, glancing towards the boy, who was weeping and trembling in his nurse's arms. Deeply affected by the boy's ordeal and her own distraction which had allowed him to wander off, the woman sobbed over him, clutching so desperately at him that she was in danger of smothering him.

'Poor woman. She tried so hard to reach him when he ran from her.'

'I saw,' William said, glancing at the nurse who was visibly distressed.

Her voice was becoming very high pitched as she said over and over, 'You are safe, little one, you are safe now. Never run away from me again.' The ragged note of relief was apparent as she pressed her cheek against his hair, offering strength and comfort to the trembling child.

'We have got him back to the house. Mishka is

very good with him but he is a boisterous child. He is watched all the time.'

'Why? Why does he have to be watched?'

'It's no matter,' he said quickly. 'Do you feel that you can stand? We'll get you back to the house where you can be tended to.'

'No—I mean, no, thank you. I'll be all right to ride home.'

'I won't hear of it. I see you have a groom with you. I'll send him to your house for a change of clothes. He can take your horse with him. When you are ready I'll have you sent home in the carriage. Now, let's get you onto your feet.'

Knowing it was useless to argue, taking his hand she allowed him to pull her to her feet.

In silence, William looked down into her upturned face. 'You did well just now. Dhanu owes you his life and I owe you my unending gratitude. The lake can be hazardous. Even when the water looks calm there are eddies there. It's treacherous where the water enters the pool.' His eyes narrowed on hers and his expression softened. 'You're not afraid of anything, are you?'

'I'm not afraid of water,' she told him blithely. She was deeply touched by how alarmed he'd seemed. His voice had been hoarse with concern when he'd pulled her from the water, his face ravaged with worry as he had called her a little fool.

'I'm glad,' he said. 'I wouldn't want you to be.' He looked down at her dripping clothes, trying to ignore how delectable she looked at that moment. 'Come. You must get out of those clothes and into dry ones before you catch a chill.'

After instructing Thomas to return to Fountains

Lodge with her horse and inform Clarissa of what had happened and to have a change of clothes sent to Ashurst Park, it was a sorry, bedraggled little group who made their way at a steady pace to the house, the child, now quiet, walking slowly beside Mishka.

Chapter Four

Carrying her jacket over her arm and holding her hat, Rosa walked beside Mishka, noting how her full cotton skirts swung rhythmically to her straight-backed graceful stride. Her glistening black hair hung down her back in a long braid tied at the end with colourful cotton tassels. She was clearly upset by what had occurred and to some extent blamed herself for failing to keep hold of Dhanu's hand on the bridge. Rosa spoke to her, trying to comfort her with soft words of encouragement. She was rewarded with a little smile as Mishka thanked her and told her that she recognised her as being the lady at the inn who had saved Dhanu before. She was most grateful.

'Saving him from those galloping horses was a great act of bravery done with extreme promptness. I am usually so protective of Dhanu and I only took my eyes off him for a second. It was wrong of me to accuse you. I hope you will forgive me, but I panicked and it was how it seemed to me at the time. I have no words sufficient for my gratitude.'

'I was glad I was able to help. I hope he suffers no ill effects from falling into the water.'

'He is a strong boy. He looks unharmed.'

Rosa looked down at Dhanu, feeling most relieved that she had managed to reach him before his fall into the pond had ended in tragedy. 'Tell me your name?' she asked the boy. Even though she knew it, she wanted to hear him say it. He was a lovely child, sturdy and big for his age. It was easy to forget he was only five years old. His hair was a lustrous dark brown, his complexion smooth and the eyes that regarded her so seriously were soft and dark. He looked at her for a long moment, as if weighing her up, then said softly, 'Dhanu. I wanted to go outside to the little building on the hill but I fell into the water.'

'You must not run from Mishka, Dhanu,' William remarked softly. 'We are going back to the house and there you must stay. Do you understand?'

'Yes,' Dhanu whispered. This was the limit of their conversation, but he took Rosa's proffered hand and walked beside her contentedly.

As they walked William turned his thoughts to what had happened. It proved that Miss Ingram's courage in the face of danger both to herself and others set her apart from her contemporaries. He was filled with admiration for what she had done. Without doubt, her prompt actions had saved Dhanu's life. How many of the women of his acquaintance would have had the nerve to kick off their shoes and dive into a terrifyingly deep pool to save the life of a child?

He cast a glance at her walking a few steps ahead of him and in fascination watched the swing of her long wet hair which hung down her spine and the sway of her hips as she walked along the road with a lithe, liquid movement—like a dancer to music only she could hear, he thought as his gaze lingered with appreciation on her slim ankles and slender legs enhanced by the clinging breeches.

On reaching the house they were greeted by the tense, waiting faces of the servants, all worried over the fate of the young boy who had captured their hearts. Lord Ashurst reassured them all that Dhanu seemed to be unhurt, but he would like him to be examined by a doctor. One of the servants immediately left the house to fetch the resident doctor from the village and the child and his nurse were hustled off to the nursery, where he would be given a hot bath. Lord Ashurst cast a disapproving glance at the two footmen to remind them of their duties as their eyes became fixed with frank approval on the young woman who stood beside him. Mrs Hope, the housekeeper, stepped forward to take charge.

'And you, my dear? Are you all right? That's a nasty bump you have to your head.'

In appreciation of her thoughtfulness, Rosa gave her a smile that was slightly forced. 'My head aches a little, but otherwise I am suffering no ill effects from my dip in the lake. Although I would appreciate getting out of my wet things.'

'Of course you would. Come with me now and we will see to it right away.'

'I think the doctor should take a look at you all the same,' Lord Ashurst said. 'Just to make sure.'

'I'll take him to her as soon as he's checked the boy over.'

'Thank you, Mrs Hope. I am sure you will look after Miss Ingram.' William turned to Rosa. 'For the time you are here please make yourself comfortable. Mrs Hope will see that you have a hot bath and refreshment.'

The housekeeper walked a little ahead of Rosa up the stairs. They reached a landing which opened out on to a long gallery. Huge portrait paintings of stern-faced Barringtons dressed in outdated costumes lined the walls. If she hadn't felt so uncomfortable, Rosa would have taken time to study them, but her body was cold beneath the wet garments clinging to her and she couldn't wait to discard them. Halfway along the gallery they entered another landing, walking past closed doors until Mrs Hope stopped in front of one and pushed it open.

'Here we are. I am sure you will be comfortable in here while you wait for your sister to send your clothes. I'll have some water sent up for your bath right away. You will feel better for it after your ordeal and a maid will come and attend you. If you would like to make a start there's a dressing robe on the bed.'

'Thank you, Mrs Hope,' Rosa said, her eyes doing a quick sweep of the comfortable sunny room with its large four-poster bed hung with rich green and gold brocade curtains. 'You are most kind, but I don't want to put you to any trouble.'

'You're no trouble at all, Miss Ingram. It's the least we can do after you jumped into the lake to save that young boy—poor little mite. Ever since he arrived he's been fascinated by the water. No matter how vigilant we all are to make sure he doesn't leave the house, it was only a matter of time before he slipped the net. He's a mischievous little boy. After what happened to his lordship's cousin, we can only thank the Lord that he didn't suffer the same fate.'

Rosa glanced at her sharply. 'Why, Mrs Hope? What did happen to him?'

'Goodness me! Didn't your grandmother tell you? He drowned—in the pool where the water from above flows into the lake.' She shook her head, her expression becoming solemn. 'Terrible business it was, just terrible. Such a nice man, too.'

Rosa stared at her. The words branded themselves into her memory and she felt a lump of constricting sorrow in her chest, knowing the deceased Earl had drowned in the same pool that she had dived into to save the child earlier.

Rosa quickly stripped away her clothes and wrapped herself in the warm robe. Going to the window, she stared out, feeling suddenly weary. Her head ached and she longed to rest, yet she would wait until she was home. Thinking of Lord Ashurst, she was disquieted. Her situation had become confusing—she should not be feeling anything towards him, but he was causing her usual calm to disappear. She remembered the moment when he had pulled her from the water and the concerned expression on his face when she had opened her eyes and found him leaning over her. Despite her sorry state, she had been almost smothered by his nearness, by the heady smell of him, a clean masculine scent of sandalwood that had shot like tiny darts through her senses. In all truthfulness, of stature and face and features she had seen no match and he could be the stuff of any girl's dreams.

Rosa mentally shook herself as she realised where her mind was wandering. In some embarrassment she moved away from the window, relieved when at that moment the door opened and a maid came in carrying the first jug of hot water for her bath.

By the time she had bathed and taken some light refreshment her clothes had arrived along with the doctor. After examining her face and declaring her fit enough to go home, she went in search of Lord Ashurst.

She found him in his study—a solitary brooding man standing with his shoulder propped against the window, staring out over the gardens, but seeing nothing. Compassion swelled in her heart as she realised that although he appeared cold and unemotional in front of her, he had come in here to worry in lonely privacy.

Suppressing the urge to go to him, she quietly said, 'Lord Ashurst?' He turned and looked at her, his face impassive. He looked tired and Rosa could just make out the fine lines beginning to form at the corners of his eyes. 'How is Dhanu?'

'He is settled and has the whole household fussing over him.' Sighing deeply he pushed himself away from the window, running his fingers through his hair. 'He's had an awful time of it—losing his mother and being removed from his home—from India and all that was familiar. God knows what harm the upheaval and now this latest trauma has done him.'

'Possibly not much. I have had little to do with children but from what I do know they are very resilient. All they need at Dhanu's age is nourishment, warmth—and love.'

'I hope you are right. Dhanu has been placed in my care and I feel a profound need to protect him. Unfortunately I have to be away from the house for long periods—I am trying to familiarise myself with my tenants and assess their needs. Mishka finds the house daunting and having to keep a constant eye on Dhanu difficult. Like Dhanu she is easily distracted and my mischievous charge takes advantage of that.'

Rosa watched him, her throat tight with emotion. She could see that Dhanu's escapade that had almost resulted in his death had affected William deeply. She had not given a thought to his relationship with the child, but now, struck by the various emotions playing over his features, the love he felt for his young charge reflected in his eyes could not be concealed.

'Tell me about Dhanu. Why is he here with you— and the woman Mishka?'

He became thoughtful, his expression unreadable. 'Dhanu is the nephew of a dear friend of mine in India. His name is Tipu. The boy's father is a very important man—a rajah. Dhanu is his heir.'

'I don't understand. What is he doing here—in England with you?'

'It's a long and complicated story. When his mother died his father took another wife, who bore him twin sons. Anisha is beautiful and ambitious and courtiers try to ingratiate themselves with her. The Rajah is blinded by his love for her and he will do anything to please her. He is so besotted with her he can see nothing else—suddenly Dhanu is of less importance. She has great influence over him and is referred to as the new power behind the throne. Her jealousy and hatred of Dhanu knows no bounds and she will not rest until her firstborn son is put in his place.'

Rosa was horrified by what he was telling her. 'But—he is just a child.'

'Anisha will not be secure in her position until Dhanu is removed—permanently.'

'You mean she would do him harm?'

'Accidents happen. I often went to the court in the Rajah's palace on Tipu's invitation—although I was away for long periods on military matters. When I returned after one long spell I was sensitive to the atmosphere. At first I dismissed Tipu's accusation against his brother's new wife. It did not take long for me to change my mind. Beneath the surface ran hidden undercurrents of plots and counterplots to get rid of the boy. Bribery, intrigue and ambition haunted the new wife's quarters. Tipu was so concerned he employed an official taster for Dhanu lest Anisha try to poison him.'

'But—that is evil.'

'Tipu was insistent that steps had to be taken to protect Dhanu, which was why he asked me to bring him to England with me—along with his nurse, Mishka. She is devoted to the boy and is beside herself with remorse and more than a little guilt that she let go of his hand.'

'I can imagine how she must feel. And the two men? Who are they?'

'One of them is Anisha's brother. His name is Kamal Kapoor. From your description of the man you saw in the village I am certain of it. He enjoys the kudos of being Anisha's brother and he is as evil as she is. Hooked by ambition and greed, through her sons he would be all powerful. He is like a predatory animal and he will not stop until he has achieved his aim to remove Dhanu for good—and his father, the Rajah, when he gets back to India.'

Rosa stared at him in disbelief. 'You—you mean they will harm the boy?'

He nodded. 'Anisha and Kamal will not be content until he is dead. While ever he is alive he stands as an obstacle to her own sons. You have first-hand knowledge of the lengths they will go to, to harm him.'

'Yes—yes, I have. But—you can't keep him here for ever. There will come a time when he has to return to India. Will his father not miss him?'

'Tipu will deal with him. Because his presence upset the Rajah's wife so much, he had already decided to remove him from the palace. When it is the right time for Dhanu to return to India Tipu will send for him.'

'But that could be a long way in the future.'

'In which case I will keep him here with me. I have him watched all the time, but it is not always easy. He is an active boy and quietly determined. Whenever Mishka turns her back for a moment he is away on some mischief or other. She says she is tempted to tie a rope to him so she can reel him in from wherever he is hiding. Ever since he saw the lake he has been drawn to it. Perhaps it's because he has nothing like it where he lives in India. It will not happen again.'

'Your friend must love the child a great deal.'

'He does. Tipu was in love with his mother. It broke his heart when she died. He would do anything for Dhanu. He's been more of a father to him than his own.'

'It's a pity she didn't marry Tipu instead of the Rajah.'

'Her family would not hear of it. As the result of a riding accident when he was a boy, Tipu is crippled.'

'I am sorry to hear that. You are fond of him, I can see that.'

'We have been friends since childhood.'

William fell silent, staring into the distance, thinking of his past and his insecurities.

His silence prompted Rosa to turn and look at him. 'What is it?' she asked.

William started and glanced at her. 'I'm sorry. I was miles away. Another time. Another life.' He gave her a wan smile. 'Sometimes memories return unbidden.'

'But not unwanted, I suspect.'

'Some are,' he confessed quietly, his gaze fixed unseeing on something in the distance that Rosa could not imagine and made her wonder what he could be thinking. 'But thoughts of India return to me all the time.' He sighed. 'India was my home. Home,' he mused. 'How empty the word sounds. I suppose I shall have to get used to calling Ashurst Park my home from now on. But how can it be home when I am a virtual stranger here? There was a time not so very long go when I believed I could make my own destiny—when I would have married the woman...' He fell silent, reluctant to say more, making Rose curious as to what he might have divulged. 'That was not to be. Suddenly I feel that I am at the mercy of fate.'

'Maybe it's a bit of both,' Rosa said softly, wondering if a woman he had loved—might still love, was at the heart of why he had been reluctant to accept her proposal of marriage. If this was so, where was she? Who was she? Had he loved her so much that he was blinded to all other women? 'We are born with things that define us—character, humour, resilience—but we can make our own future, too.'

William turned and looked at her. Their eyes linked and held, hers open, frank, with understanding in their depths, his a blend of seriousness and sadness and frustration.

'I want so much to believe that. Is that what you told yourself—when you left Antigua?'

She nodded, fixing her gaze ahead. 'Yes. I, too, want to believe that. I came to England only once before—Grandmother spent some time with us on Antigua. I really should have got to know more about England—so that I would not have been so entirely at a disadvantage.'

William saw that sudden, questioning vulnerability. It required an answer. 'I, more than anyone, can understand that. We both have to acclimatise to new situations—a new life, no tears, no regrets, just memories.'

Rosa gave a wistful, almost shy smile. His handsome face was sombre. She was acutely aware of his powerful male body seated next to her, strong and sure. The combination of all that was becoming dangerously, sweetly appealing. 'Thank you for saying that.'

'My pleasure.' He meant what he said. Beneath the heavy fringe of dark lashes, her eyes were amazing, mesmerising in their lack of guile, and her smooth cheeks were flushed a becoming pink. Strands of her hastily arranged shining hair brushed her face. She was, he decided, refreshingly open and honest, with a gentle pride he admired. He smiled. 'Thank you for saving Dhanu's life, by the way.'

His words were sincere and heartfelt. Rosa was deeply moved.

'You have already thanked me. I only did what anyone else would have done when seeing a child in danger.'

'Not everyone can swim.'

'I was taught at an early age.' She glanced at the cascade in the distance, trying not to think of what had happened earlier. 'That's a rather splendid temple up on the hill. Where does the water that feeds the lake come from?'

'Fortunately Ashurst Park has been blessed with a ready supply of water. One of my ancestors was responsible for collecting water from streams and rainwater and storing it in an elaborate system of ponds, watercourses and pipes on the high ground above the lake. The view of the lake and the house from up there is quite something. But come, I expect you'll be wanting to get home. The carriage is waiting. I'll drive you myself,' he said.

'Thank you.'

Leaving the house and crossing to the waiting carriage, an inexplicable, lazy smile swept over his face as he looked at her and held out his hand. Automatically she placed her hand in his and he helped her step up into the carriage, before climbing in and taking the reins and turning the horses towards the drive. His eyes were warm with admiration as they looked straight into hers.

'I trust you are feeling no ill effects from your ordeal?'

'No, I am perfectly all right. I'm just glad I got to Dhanu in time.'

'So am I. You did well.'

For the rest of the journey they either sat in companionable silence or talked of inconsequential things. When William halted the carriage at Fountains Lodge he assisted Rosa down.

Walking towards the house and aware that he

seemed in no hurry to drive away, having the stirrings of an idea she turned to look back at him. The idea was perhaps ridiculous, and if she had any sense at all she would abandon the notion without giving it a moment's consideration, but all her feelings and her concern for Lord Ashurst's charge were heightened.

'Lord Ashurst, may I make a suggestion?'

He regarded her intently. 'Please do.'

'Would you consider letting Dhanu and Mishka come here for a while. You have told me you have serious concerns about his safety. The more I think about it, the more it seems a plausible solution.'

'What?' His amazement was genuine and he looked at her incredulously. 'Are you serious?'

'Yes—yes I am. I realise that this is a difficult time for you and that you have a problem making sure he is safe. Fountains Lodge is nowhere near as big as Ashurst Park and there are enough of us in the house to watch him. There is a reasonable sized garden at the back of the house with a containing high wall so he would not be deprived of fresh air. The men who wish to do him harm will not know he is here. I imagine they will be watching your home. From what I have seen of Dhanu he is a friendly boy. He will have no problem settling in here.'

Without taking his eyes off her, William began reviewing her proposition seriously, making two lists in his mind—one for accepting her offer and one against. The former won. Because he had to spend so much time away from the house at present, it would be an answer to his problem. Folding his arms casually across his chest he leaned against the carriage. Miss Ingram was surveying him with a steady gaze and he considered the danger of encouraging a deepening of their relationship. Hers was a dangerous kind of beauty, for she had the power to touch upon a man's vulnerability with a flash of her lovely green eyes.

Holding his gaze with her challenging stare and quietly determined manner, she closed the distance between them with a smooth fluid grace and he felt suddenly exposed. He knew he was staring at her, but he couldn't help himself. Perhaps unlike so many other women—excluding Lydia—she refused to be intimidated or impressed by him. Maybe she even disliked him a little, and he wouldn't blame her one bit after his harsh treatment of her when she had come to offer herself in marriage. But if she did, then why was she offering her help—and why did the thought hurt?

'And you are certain Dhanu will be safe here with you?'

'As safe as he can be. Are you willing to consider seriously my proposition?'

He nodded. 'I am a cautious man and there are many aspects to consider.'

'But you will?'

He nodded. 'What you propose does make sense—but it will be a temporary arrangement.'

'Of course.'

'Then I will make arrangements to bring them over.' Climbing up into the carriage and taking the reins, he looked down at her. 'Thank you for your concern and your kindness. It means a great deal to me.' On that note he flicked the reins and drove away.

William brought Dhanu and Mishka to Fountains Lodge in a closed carriage. Rosa, closely followed by Clarissa, hurried out to meet them. Lord Ashurst stepped down, sweeping Dhanu into his arms before setting him on his feet. His pride and affection as he looked down at the boy could not have been more evident.

Stepping forward, Rosa smiled softly. On impulse she reached out and took his small hand in her own, and bending down, so that her face was on a level with his, she smiled warmly into his eyes, hoping to put him at ease. 'Hello, Dhanu. I'm so pleased to see you again and happy you have come to stay with us for a while.'

Dhanu made no attempt to pull away and a little smile began to tug at the corners of his mouth. He seemed to be assessing her, and when his eyes ceased to regard her so seriously his smile broadened, which was a delight to see.

'I remember you. You jumped into the water to save me.'

'I did. We both got a soaking. I hope you are recovered now, Dhanu.'

'Yes—thank you.'

Everyone began to relax and look at one another, certain that he had no objections to living at Fountains Lodge and that a good start had been made. It also brought a relieved smile to William's features and he seemed to relax, which told Rosa how apprehensive he had been about removing him from Ashurst Park.

Rosa watched Clarissa take Mishka and Dhanu into the house before looking at Lord Ashurst. 'He'll be all right. Try not to worry about him. Rooms have been prepared for them. He need not be afraid.'

'If he is then it is not you he's afraid of. It's the upheaval. Ever since he lost his mother he's been confused about everything that's happened to him and doesn't understand it.'

'I know. He'll settle down here, I'm sure of it. You must visit him as often as you wish. Will you come in?'

He shook his head. 'No—thank you. I have appointments to keep.' He looked down at her. His gaze became intent on her upturned face, her free-flowing chestnut hair gilded by the sun's rays. He was impressed and intrigued, and would never cease to be amazed at some new character of this woman he was considering making his wife. 'Thank you for all you have done. I do appreciate it.'

Rosa watched him go, a delightful flush on her cheeks.

Dhanu loved being at Fountains Lodge. Having so much attention was a new experience for him, and after his initial shyness had worn off, he had surprised everyone by responding to all the fuss and attention with a startling vitality, which poured from him like heat from the sun. He was such a happy, bright child, and charged with energy, the playful devilment in his nature a joy.

William had left the house for his early-morning ride before returning to pore over the ledgers in his study. Knowing Miss Ingram often rode early he was not surprised when she rode into view. Concealed from view beneath the cover of trees, perched atop his large brown stallion, William paused to drink in the sight of her. He had watched her as she had galloped over the terrain, her companion way behind as he struggled to keep up. With a thin scarf tied around her riding hat, rippling behind her like a pennant in the wind, she rode with the blind bravado of a rider who has never fallen off. There was jubilant simplicity as she soared over each hedge and ditch, at one with her mount—confident, trusting and elated—its tail floating behind like a bright defiant banner.

Now she sat her horse supple and trim, her black mourning skirt spread over the horse's flanks, her long legs encased in breeches. Her hair beneath her hat had come loose and the breeze played with and gave colour to her cheeks, but she wore a determined expression and exuded an air of openness and extreme capability William found attractive. The clash of his emotions as he watched her left him irritated and he broke his cover and rode to meet her.

With the reins held loosely in her gloved hands, Rosa heard the jingle of bridle and the snort of a horse before she saw him. She spun her head round abruptly, like a young deer aware of danger. Her heart gave a sudden leap when she saw Lord Ashurst emerge from the shadows of the trees. He was riding a big brown hunter, with a rippling black mane and tail. The horse's sleek coat gleamed. Rosa saw how he looked at one with the environment, as if he had been born to this wild terrain. He wore a tight-fitting dark blue riding coat, cut away at the front to show a matching waistcoat, the cloth of both of good quality. A snowy-white neckcloth and gold pin enhanced his tanned face. She tried to imagine him in military uniform and thought he would have looked equally as fine. He looked lean and hard, exuding virility and a casual, lazy confidence. Sunlight burnished his thick dark hair.

Meeting his calm gaze, she felt an unfamiliar twist of her heart, an addictive mix of pleasure and discomfort. His light blue eyes looked at her in undisguised admiration as he drew alongside, a smile curving his firm lips. Thinking how handsome he looked and how nice it would be to run her fingers through his wind-tousled hair, she could feel a flush tinting her cheeks despite all her efforts to prevent it. She did not want to feel that way—not about him. They held each other's eyes for far too long. Rosa was the first to lower her gaze, for there was something about him that was different to any man she had known. And that something was affecting her deeply.

'Good day, Miss Ingram. My apologies. I didn't mean to startle you.'

'You take me unawares, Lord Ashurst. I was just admiring the view.'

William shifted his horse closer. His face was grave, though Rosa noticed one eyebrow was raised in a whimsical way.

'It is impressive, I agree.' His gaze swept the landscape, settling for just a moment on his home, before coming to rest on the young woman once more. With her honey-gold skin and large green eyes, which were as wide and solemn as a baby owl's, she had an ethereal quality. Like a free spirit she confronted him, her head poised at a questioning angle, her hair spread over her shoulders like a cloth of autumn colours, watching him approach as if she were some forest creature. Every time he saw her she tweaked and teased his baser emotions.

'You appear to make a habit of riding to Ashurst to take in the view. The last time you did you saved

Dhanu's life so I will not arrest you for trespassing on my land.'

Rosa slanted him a laughing glance. 'That is extremely generous of you, Lord Ashurst. If this wonderful vista is the only part of Ashurst Park you are willing to offer me, then I suppose I shall have to be content with that.'

He laughed at her light-hearted remark. 'Who knows, Miss Ingram. I may be prepared to offer you more—for a price, of course.'

Rosa laughed in turn. 'Of course. I would expect no less.'

William gazed at her for a moment in silence, his eyes sweeping and appreciating her lovely face. 'The colour of your hair, all shades of autumn, is unusual— beautiful like your eyes.'

Rosa stared at him, somewhat taken aback by his reference to her eyes, then she decided he'd meant nothing by it. 'I think you flatter me, Lord Ashurst.'

'No. Flattery is nothing but empty words without true feeling. I meant what I said.'

There was something in his expression that made her feel more than she wanted to feel. Her pulse raced. In that moment, Simon and Antigua seemed very distant. In fact, every time Lord Ashurst looked at her, Antigua felt more and more distant. His tall and lean, yet athletic, stature had a splendour to it with which few other men of her acquaintance could compete. He rode with an air of utter assurance, exuding a strong masculinity she imagined few women could resist, giving them the impression he was a man of lusty, unashamed appetites—with merely a look and a cynically humorous smile she suspected he had the ability to charm his way into the most rapidly beating heart. Listening to the steady rhythm of her own, she looked away, unable to prevent a certain excitement from sweeping over her, making her realise that she was not as immune to his powerful masculine personality as she had thought. She must not let him affect her like this.

'How is Dhanu settling in at Fountains Lodge?'

She laughed. 'Very well. He is adored by one and all—especially Clarissa—and keeps everyone on their toes.'

'I can't pretend that I am not concerned about him.'

'Don't be. He is fine but you must call and see for yourself.'

'I will.' A gentle expression spread over his face.

'We didn't get off to a very good start, you and I,' he said softly.

'No.'

He looked at her. 'I find I have to reconsider my options.'

Tilting her head, she returned his gaze. 'Do you have any?'

'It would appear not. Can we talk about it?'

'What—here?'

'Ride back to the house with me. We will talk there.'

'Oh—I don't know if I should.'

'If you are afraid that your reputation is in danger of being ruined should you be seen riding alone with me, then do not be concerned. There is no one to see.'

Rosa smiled. 'It is considerate of you to be so concerned for my reputation, Lord Ashurst.'

His blue eyes twinkled merrily. 'I am well aware that once a young woman's reputation is lost it can never be retrieved, Miss Ingram.'

'Then my reputation must be protected at all cost. We must see to it that we keep away from prying eyes.'

'Does that mean you agree to come back to the house?'

'How can I refuse?'

He looked at Thomas hovering some yards away. 'Send the boy back. I will ride with you when you return to Fountains Lodge.'

Rosa did as he asked, instructing him to go to the house and explain to Clarissa where she was and to tell her not to worry, before riding with Lord Ashurst down the hill to the road that skirted the lake. He rode with the casual ease that could only come with a lifetime's acquaintance with horses.

'You ride well,' William said, with an admiring smile. She was light and lovely in the saddle. Earlier he'd watched her ride at breakneck pace, taking each jump with an effortless, breezy unconcern for style that William had never seen before. 'I'd been watching you for a while. You are one of the most skilled female riders I've ever seen.'

Glancing sideways at him, she laughed lightly. 'That is praise indeed from you, Lord Ashurst. I started to ride before I could walk. I love horses. My father kept a fine stable on Antigua.'

William looked at her with unconcealed appreciation as he surveyed her perched atop her mount. She lifted her head and the sunlight glistened on a chestnut curl that fell to her neck. She was smiling broadly, her generous lips drawn back over perfect white teeth, and her colour was gloriously high.

'Do you normally dress in breeches?' he enquired.

'Not all the time, but I hate riding side-saddle and I

find breeches are so much more comfortable and offer more freedom. Of course, Grandmother didn't approve. She was forever chastising me over one thing or another.' She cast him a conspiratorial glance. 'When I ride out I try to keep away from the village. I am not unaware that I am supposed to be dressed in mourning and behaving with more decorum, but I'm afraid I did not conform to the idea of a proper English miss.'

William laughed. 'I have to say, Miss Ingram, that I agree with that.'

On reaching the house, William swung himself out of the saddle and went to assist Rosa, but she'd already leapt from her horse as sprightly as a young athlete and was handing the reins to a groom who seemed to appear from nowhere. They entered the house.

'Have you eaten?' William asked.

'No. I usually eat after my ride.'

'Then join me for breakfast. I would appreciate the company.'

'Thank you. I would like that.'

'Come,' William said, taking her elbow in a firm grip. The conversation was not going to be easy for either of them. 'We'll eat in the garden where we are less likely to be interrupted and there are no staff within earshot to carry tales back to the village. Besides, it's too nice a day to sit inside.'

Instructing one of the maids to have breakfast sent out to the terrace, he escorted her through a set of large French windows out on to a raised veranda which offered a splendid view of the gardens. Seating her at a wrought-iron table, William took a chair across from her, resting one booted foot atop his knee. For a moment he observed his companion. There was a subdued strength and subtleness that gave her an easy, almost naïve elegance that she was totally unaware of as she sat. Few women were fortunate enough to have been blessed with such captivating looks. Her eyes were clear and calm as the waters he had seen lapping a stretch of hot sand in India and were an exquisite mixture of green and brown. In fact, Rosa Ingram was blessed with everything she would need to guarantee her future happiness. Yet here she was, prepared to marry a penniless earl for reasons that he failed to understand.

Breakfast was carried out to them on silver platters—eggs, mushrooms, bacon and delicious warm bread and butter. Rosa was strangely content as she ate and drank her tea, gazing out over the gardens and to the orchards beyond. The gardens were beautiful in their wild and wonderful state of neglect, with roses and honeysuckle climbing and tumbling in profusion. With the sun warm on her face she felt its calmness and tranquillity. Everything was so still that not even a leaf moved, only the heady scent of flowers hung in the air. Aware of Lord Ashurst's scrutiny, she managed to control her emotions. She watched the swallows swooping low and looked at the patches of blue sky between the branches of the tall trees.

At length, William spoke, breaking into her reverie. 'I think we should both put our cards on the table, don't you? We have both had to leave the place of our birth to come to England, no matter how reluctant we were. You were happy on Antigua?'

'Always.' She looked at him. 'I imagine you felt the same when you left India, having lived there all of your life.'

'Yes, although I did come here for my education. I am the only issue of a second son. My father's older brother, who became the Earl on my grandfather's demise, had two sons. My father had no reason to believe he would inherit the estate and was allowed to make his own way in life. He qualified as a doctor. With a desire to see the world he became employed by the East India Company. He met and married my mother in India. When my uncle died, followed by his eldest son in the Peninsula War, Charles, my cousin, inherited the title and the estate. His death was a great shock to me,' he said, pain at the remembrance of his passing in his eyes for Rosa to see. 'We were close—like brothers. Being his heir and duty-bound to take up the reins at Ashurst Park, I had no choice but to leave India.'

'That must have been difficult for you. Are either of your parents still alive?'

'They died when I was in my youth. Had my father still been alive, he would have taken the title. Like my father before me I forged myself a successful career and pledged my life to the Company. Something of India remains deep inside me and will course through my blood for ever—distant memories—the smell of the soil, the fragrance of the desert sands.'

As they talked he seemed more relaxed. He clearly loved the land of his birth and it was not the first time Rosa had met a man who was truly committed to the land of his adoption. There had been many on the Caribbean islands. She realised that despite the antipathy he had aroused in her on their previous encounters, William Barrington was remarkably easy to talk to and it surprised her how much she enjoyed talking to him.

'But they were dangerous times,' William went on

quietly. 'The states were constantly at war with each other. When the letter came informing me of the death of my cousin I was unprepared. Now, as heir to Ashurst Park, my place is here. I quickly learned from my cousin's lawyers that the estate had been left in dire financial straits. In fact, it is bankrupt. Not having seen either my uncle or my cousins for several years, I had no idea of the extent of the debts. I regret not keeping in touch more. Perhaps then I would have been able to help in some way before things became so bad.'

'How did that happen? I remember Grandmother telling us it had something to do with the Battle of Waterloo, but I didn't pay much attention at the time.'

'She was right. Rumours reaching London that Wellington had lost the battle at Waterloo ignited panic in the financial markets and caused the Stock Exchange to crash. In their desperation, London stockholders wanted out of their investments immediately, believing they would need the money to survive. The market panic was halted when news of Wellington's victory at Waterloo arrived. Unfortunately, it was too late for the countless innocent people who lost their investments and hundreds of reputable merchants and noble families were ruined—including my own.'

'And your cousin?'

'Unable to live with the loss, Charles committed suicide.'

Rosa was unable to conceal her shock. This was something she did not know. 'How dreadful. I am so sorry. Mrs Hope told me he drowned in the pool below the cascade. I—I thought it must have been an accident.'

'I'm afraid not. Initially I was of the opinion that

he could have managed his affairs with a little more finesse, but when I learned the full extent of what had happened, I realised he was unable to live with the guilt he felt over his haste to sell off his shares. It was too painful for him to bear. Sadly, he wasn't alone. As a consequence the estate is bankrupt. It costs a king's ransom to run. I am beginning to realise the weight of the responsibilities heaped on me. They have become like jewels too heavy to carry, too valuable to neglect and too enormous to ignore.'

'I can see that.'

'My solicitor has pointed out that if I do not come up with a solution very soon, I will lose the estate. The many creditors are becoming impatient. They could foreclose on the estate. My cousin was a gambler, which does not help matters.

Not only are there gambling debts to be settled but the estate has been mortgaged up to the hilt and the tenant farmers are suffering very badly.'

'Accept my offer and all the debts will be cleared,' she said softly.

'That is a hard offer to refuse. Maybe I was a trifle hasty in dismissing it initially. Circumstances have forced me to reconsider. It could work out to be beneficial for us both. I realise that although it galls me to do so, as a solution to my problems I will have to marry a rich woman. Unfortunately, I do not have the time to go hunting for a wife.'

'Then why did you refuse me when you knew you had no other means of settling the debts on Ashbury Park?' she retorted, unable to remain calm when faced with such contradictory behaviour.

'I didn't realise the urgency of the situation. I cannot

rest knowing others are owed because of my cousin's folly. It is not right. It should not impact on the livelihood of others.' His lips curled in a thin smile. 'Lord knows what my father would make of it all. When he died he thought my life was all mapped out with the Company.'

'Were you close to your parents?' He nodded. 'My own father was such a strong force in my life, my mother such a loving support to all of us. Things began to fall apart when she died. It would seem the cards haven't turned out the way we wanted for either of us.'

'It would appear not. So, Miss Ingram. Do you still wish to live at Ashurst Park?'

'As your wife?'

'What else?'

Slowly she let her thoughts dwell on what he was saying, realising just how uncertain her future was. She did realise that with the death of her grandmother and no longer forced to marry anyone if she did not want to, she was free to go to her Aunt Clara and try to coerce her into letting her work with her on her charities and put her wealth to some good. But the temptation to marry Lord Ashurst and make this beautiful house her home beckoned.

'What else! you say.' She sighed deeply. 'What else is there? What else will there be when Clarissa has married and gone back to the Caribbean? I have lost most of my family and am about to lose Fountains Lodge. I realise that I don't need to marry anyone.'

'What else is there?'

She smiled. 'You might think me quite mad but I have considered helping my aunt with her many charities—

not just putting some of my father's wealth to good use but to take an active part.'

'I don't think that's a bad thing. It's very noble of you to consider others in that way and I am sure that with all the misery I see every time I go to London your money will be welcome to whichever charity you decide to support. Of course it is something you can take up when you are married.'

'Yes—yes I could,' she remarked, uplifted by his suggestion. 'And you wouldn't mind?'

'Of course not. Why would I?'

'I can't tell you how much that means to me. I won't have to go to London after all—where my wealth will make me a target for unscrupulous fortune hunters.'

William's lips curved in a cynical smile. 'Better the devil you know.'

Chapter Five

Rosa looked at him, her senses dazed, snared by the light blue eyes that roamed leisurely over her features, pausing at length on her lips and then moving back to capture her eyes. They glowed with a warmth that brought colour to her cheeks. Compared to Simon and the numerous men of her acquaintance, William Barrington was as near to perfect as she had ever met.

A calm came over Rosa. Thinking back to the day she had come to Ashurst Park to propose he marry her instead of Clarissa, when he had refused her she had been swamped with regret that she had been foolish to come to humiliate herself before this penniless Earl of Ashurst. She had reached the conclusion that no one could push him into any decision not of his own making, and for the first time since she had devised the wild scheme, she had known the feeling of failure. Yet here he now was, telling her he was willing to accept her offer. She realised how much such a decision was costing him in both pride and self-respect.

'I do understand how difficult this is for you, Lord Ashurst. I think I would feel exactly the same in your shoes.'

'Believe me, Miss Ingram, you can have no idea.' Sighing resignedly, he held out his hand. 'Come, let's walk. I'll show you the garden.'

Rosa ignored his hand and got to her feet.

'Ashurst Park needs some money injected into it right away and the creditors have to be paid what they are owed to keep it from being sold.'

'Then it would seem my offer is timely. Console yourself with the fact that the money that will come to you on our marriage will outweigh your concern at marrying a sugar planter's daughter.'

'Your background is not an issue—or how your father came by his wealth. Although my Christian upbringing taught me that it is not acceptable to enslave an unconsenting individual. There is nothing noble or honourable in that. It is against all humanity and reason.'

Rosa looked at him steadily. 'I told you that I share your abhorrence for the trade—in fact it's refreshing to find someone who shares my views. I was raised in a world where slavery was commonplace, a way of life, and I never thought to question it or paused to consider how others might feel. I led an insular existence in a loving home with loving parents, totally ignorant of who kept the wheels turning in that privileged world. It was only when I was older that I began to realise the true nature of the evils of slavery, that it was maintained by force and people were treated as pieces of property.'

'And you were shocked.'

'Yes. Unlike many other plantation owners, my father abhorred unnecessary brutality where the slaves were concerned—and you are going to tell me that that still does not make it right and I would agree with you. But right or wrong it is a state of affairs that exists— one, which I am certain, can be changed. The plantation owners insist that slaves are necessary for the plantation system to survive. I am not very knowledgeable with the British political system but I have read a great deal about it and I am aware that there are anti–slave trade activists. When you take your seat in the House of Lords, as a peer of the realm you will be in a strong position to influence bringing about changes. It would be marvellous if you could use some of the money that will come to you through me to do that—and it will make me feel that I am compensating in some way.'

Giving her a long speculative look, William nodded slowly. It would appear Miss Ingram had hidden depths. 'I see you have it all worked out.'

'Not really but I do feel rather passionate about it.'

'There is strong opposition to the trade and at this time the Anti-Slavery Movement is too weak to overcome the system. The people who trade in slaves are an influential group because the trade is a legitimate and a highly lucrative business.'

'It will not always be that way. The argument should be carried through the press and any other means to attract public opinion. Then you can work with the activists to change that. I know a politician called William Wilberforce frequently introduces a motion in favour of abolition. Have you heard of him?' she asked purposefully, watching his reaction to her question, asked in a casual manner, carefully, but, apart from a slight tightening of his jaw, his expression remained unchanged.

'There are few who have not heard of the illustrious Member of Parliament for Yorkshire, Miss Ingram.'

'Total abolition will take time, I know, but the issue will not go away if people like him remain active in persuading members of parliament to back the parliamentary campaign.'

'The trade is a legitimate form of commerce that only an Act of Parliament can put an end to.'

'Then Parliament must be lobbied. Feeling as strongly as you do, Lord Ashurst, I am sure you would find it a worthwhile and—hopefully—rewarding cause.'

'I'm afraid it is not that simple,' he said, smiling at her. 'However, I do not intend on debating the moral aspects of it just now—not on so fine a day as this.' William glanced at her with interest. 'You are forthright, Miss Ingram.'

'You look surprised that I speak out. Do you find fault with that?'

'Not at all. It is refreshing to find a woman who speaks her mind with such conviction. You speak brave words. Such sentiments are highly commendable and admirable to say the least. Should I become involved in the cause, I see I shall have your full support—should you become my wife.'

'Of course. I would support you as much as I am able to do so.'

'As I will do when you are involved with your charities. I see you are your own woman.'

'I try to be. I like to think of myself as a free thinker. My mind from an early age has been impressed with question and analysis. Unfortunately, it is not always easy for a woman to be free and independent. My father's view was that women cannot handle the physical rigors—or possess the mental ability that men have—

and should be content with home, husband and child. In which case they have to work so much harder to succeed. You're lucky to be a man. Women don't get the same opportunities.'

'Perhaps they will one day. Things change.'

'Very slowly. In the meantime men will continue to make the rules for a good many years, just as they have always done. Many men think it unnecessary and im-pudent for females to be tutored beyond the basics of womanly duties, that anything more intellectual than learning how to run a house efficiently would be too taxing for our poor feeble minds.'

'That doesn't trouble me. Does it trouble you, Miss Ingram?'

'Not in the slightest, but many men are prejudiced when it comes to women who are opinionated—which is something, I suppose, that husbands would frown on.'

'Surely that depends on the husband,' William said quietly.

When Rosa met his gaze she experienced a shock of something between recognition and a kind of thrilling fear. Those eyes, light blue and narrowed by a knowing, intrusive smile, seemed to look right past her face and into herself. For that split second she felt completely exposed and vulnerable—traits unfamiliar to her, traits she did not care for.

'Yes—I suppose it does. So where do we go from here? I realise I should respect a period of mourning for my grandmother but here is an urgency that cannot be ignored. Goodness knows how many times she called me headstrong and too spirited for my own good, but I know she wouldn't want us to wait.'

'If you are certain marriage to me is what you want,

then our solicitors will meet and finalise the agreement. In the meantime we will arrange the ceremony.'

'Given that I am in mourning, I must insist on it being a quiet, private affair. I want as little fuss as possible'

'I understand. I will speak with the rector in Ashurst.'

'There is something I would like to ask you. Does it matter to you that you will be marrying out of your class? When word gets out the gossips will have a field day and the scandal could be enormous.'

'Personally I don't give a damn what people say. What does concern me is if the scandal hurts you.'

Rosa laughed. 'Please don't concern yourself. I am strong and will weather the storm.'

'And you will become the Countess of Ashurst. You get the title—I get the money.' Rosa winced a little at his words, even as he pressed on. 'There will be difficulties at first, but I will try to make the situation as comfortable as possible—for both our sakes.'

They walked on a little way in silence.

William looked at his companion, the sun shining on her bright head. Her hair rippled and lifted in the gentle breeze and he found himself imagining how it would feel to run his fingers through the silken strands. Sensing his eyes on her, she turned, met his gaze and smiled, her teeth gleaming white between her softly parted lips, before averting her eyes once more.

William was a man not unaccustomed to the attractions of a beautiful woman, having admired and loved many in a casual way, and because of his looks and his rank in the Company he had never had to work very hard at getting them to part with their favours, for those assets alone made him desirable to them. But he had never been impressed with emotions of the heart. Until he had met and fallen in love with Lydia, romantic love was something he was unaccustomed to, and she had betrayed him without a care.

He had never met a woman who had impressed him with her intellect, wit and dignity, a woman who possessed an agility of mind enough to make him want to spend the rest of his life with her. But that was before he had met Rosa Ingram. For the first time in his life he found himself responding to a woman's intelligent individuality, making him both captivated and intrigued. He wondered how long it would be before he succumbed to her irresistible beauty which he had secretly come to love.

He studied her profile, noting that her cheeks were tinted pink, her expression one of melting softness as she took pleasure in seeing the garden. The longer he looked at her he reluctantly faced the fact that Miss Ingram was a far cry from being an ordinary woman. In reality she was intelligent, spontaneous, courageous and naturally sensual.

At length, William said, 'Have you ever been in love, Miss Ingram?'

The question took Rosa by surprise. She stopped and turned to him. 'Why do you ask? What has that to do with anything?'

'A great deal, I would say. You see, young ladies of my acquaintance dream of love and marriage.'

'I am not like other women, Lord Ashurst.'

'No, I'm beginning to see that.'

'I'm too outspoken—too independent. My father

was always telling me. He also said I needed someone to tame me.'

'I would not do that.'

'I would despise you if you did.'

William laughed. 'So? Have you?'

'Have I what?'

'Been in love.'

Flustered, Rosa averted her eyes and walked slowly
on. 'Why—I—yes,' she confessed quietly.

'He lived on Antigua?'

'Yes.'

'And was he handsome?'

'Yes—at least, I thought he was. He had the warmest
laugh and bright blue eyes. To my romantic, seventeen-
year-old imagination he was Lancelot and Apollo all
rolled into one. No legendary hero could compare.'

William was surprised to find himself resenting and
thinking jealously of the young man she had known
before. 'He sounds like the answer to every maiden's
prayer.' He glanced sideways at her downcast face.
'What happened to this prince among men?'

'I—I really don't think—'

'If you want to be my wife, Miss Ingram, there must
be honesty between us. I don't like secrets.'

The question seemed to discomfit her. As if stalling
for time she looked straight ahead, fighting a sudden
mistiness in her eyes. She waited a moment before answering, and when she did her voice was low, almost a
whisper. 'He—he died.' Her eyes welled up with tears.

'I see. And you have leftover feelings.'

'Something like that.' Rosa didn't want to enter into
any discussion about Simon and turned her head away.

'Tell me.'

'Our feelings for each other grew out of years of friendly proximity. I—I was in love with him. He made me feel extraordinary—special. We were both young with our future spread out before us.'

'What happened?'

'He drowned on a fishing trip when the boat he was in capsized in a sudden storm. Two of his friends died with him. I was devastated.'

'You must miss him.'

Memories of Simon knotted somewhere deep in her chest and she had a feeling of not being far from tears. But, as she always did, she swallowed her emotions and nodded. Having never discussed her feelings, it was incongruous that she was opening up to a total stranger.

'So you have told yourself you will never love again and thought you had nothing to lose when you decided to change places with Clarissa and asked me to marry you instead. Loving your sister like you do, you do not want her to experience the same kind of loss as yourself.'

Wiping her cheeks with the back of her hand, Rosa stared at him. 'You are very perceptive.'

He smiled. 'Oh, I understand perfectly. You will always have feelings for the young man who stole your heart. That is natural. But you must move on with your life.'

'That is what I am doing and why I am here now.'

'Thank you for being honest with me.'

'And you, Lord Ashurst? You say there must be honesty between us so tell me about yourself. I suspect I am not the first woman you have considered marrying—you mentioned marrying someone when we spoke after Dhanu fell into the lake,' she explained when he gave her a sharp look. 'Who was she?' His eyes became guarded and he turned from her. 'Please,' she murmured. 'I have just opened my heart for you. Will you not do the same?'

William was still for a moment, clearly affected by her question. Then he turned to face her, a resigned look on his face. 'Her name was Lydia Mannering. We met in India.'

'I realise how difficult it must be for you but please tell me. Was she connected to the army?' Rose prompted gently.

'No. Her father was an Englishman living in Bombay. He went out to India to make his fortune. He succeeded.'

'What was she like?'

'Popular, beautiful... She dazzled everyone she came into contact with.'

'And—you loved her?'

He nodded. 'At the time I worshipped her. Whatever it was that bound me to her was so powerful that I was in danger of losing my mind. We spoke of marriage. She gave meaning to my life and I thought she felt the same, but beneath her skin she was deceitful and treacherous as sin.'

Rosa stared at him. 'What did she do to you? Tell me, so that I can understand.'

'It ended badly. She was ambitious, you see. She wanted more than I—as a common soldier—could possibly give her. While I was away on a long tour of duty she met someone else—a man higher up the social scale. She could no longer countenance marriage to a common soldier. I chided myself for ever having been tempted by her, for having believed she felt as I felt.'

Rosa had a sharp, painful vision of how he must have suffered and her heart went out to him. He must have been devastated. He was a man of pride and she realised how much his pride must have suffered by what Miss Mannering had done to him. When she had come to Ashurst Park to propose marriage he had told her he didn't want to marry anyone. Now she could understand why.

A lump in her throat, she struggled to find words which were neither foolish nor hurtful, for she sensed in him a raw and quivering sensitivity. Drawing a shaky breath, she smiled. 'Thank you for telling me. Perhaps if she had not been so hasty to wed while you were absent, with your new status as the Earl of Ashurst, she might well be your countess.'

'Maybe—but perhaps she did me a favour. Whatever I felt for her, had I married her might well have been destroyed when I got to know the true nature of her.' What Rosa said was true, but when William had left India Lydia was already dead to him. It had taken a concentrated effort to eradicate her from his heart and mind, but he had done it. But it had left scars and hardened his heart against forming any kind of loving relationship with a woman.

'I can understand your reluctance to marry after what happened. You are very brave to consider taking me on.'

He laughed, his tension easing. 'I still cannot believe that you could come here to confront a perfect stranger and propose that I marry you instead of your sister. I do believe it to be the most outrageous proposal of marriage I have ever heard of. You really are

the most unprincipled young woman, Rosa Ingram,'
he said with a wayward smile.

'Which you obviously find amusing.'

'You have to admit it is a little unusual.'

'At the very least,' she agreed. She looked at him
steadily. 'I suppose it does take some understanding.
But suppress your pride, Lord Ashurst, and see it for
what it is. Your debts are insurmountable unless you
acquire money to sort them out. I am not ignorant of
the fact that everything a woman possesses at the time
of her marriage belongs to her husband as a matter of
common law. I know you will use it wisely. As for
me—well—it would seem I am in need of stability.'

'You could always live with your Aunt Clara in London until something—or someone—turns up.'

'It already has, Lord Ashurst. You.' she opened her
arms wide to embrace the garden, 'here I could by
happy.' Letting her arms fall she thought about what
marriage to him would be like. Her face became sombre, her eyes wistful.

'I am under no illusions as to what to expect. I accept the fact that I am nothing more than a commod-
ity to you and, in all fairness, that is what I have made
myself. With so many differences between us our marriage will not be like other wedded couples.'

Reading panic overlying her inner feelings, William's expression softened. 'Few couples know each
other really well before they marry. You will have to
take me on trust.'

Rosa raised her chin a notch, looking directly into
his eyes. 'As you will me, Lord Ashurst.'

Taking a step back he gave her a hard look, his jaw
tightening as he stared into her bewitching eyes. She

might look fragile, but he was beginning to suspect she was as strong as steel inside. When he next spoke his expression was resolute and inscrutable.

'You know nothing about me, Miss Ingram, nothing about my character. I think I should enlighten you before we finalise our plans. You must have no illusions about me. I am arrogant—which I am sure you have accused me of being. I am also a battle-hardened soldier given to moods, temperamental and difficult to live with. I am telling you this because when we are married I never want you to look back with any kind of regret.'

Rosa tilted her head and held his gaze. 'Are you trying to discourage me, Lord Ashurst?'

'I am merely pointing out the flaws in my character and trying to establish some ground rules of my own. As long as we are totally honest with each other in advance and make sure we have no false illusions or unrealistic expectations, it should not be a problem. My name is William, by the way—Lord Ashurst is far too formal in the circumstances.'

'Very well, William. My name is Rosa.'

'We neither of us know what the future holds, but if we are to have any kind of life together we must strive for an amicable partnership. Initially you will accept that marriage between us is considered a business arrangement. Our marriage will not be that extraordinary. Many marriages are transacted purely for their monetary benefits—to join lands and money, irrespective of the feelings of those involved. I need money and you need a home and respectability.'

'It will be a complicated matter of working out a strategy that will benefit us both.'

'I realise it will not be a romantic matter—more an affair of convenience—a marriage in name only for the time being.'

'I see,' Rosa replied, feeling more humiliated and degraded than she cared to admit. 'You appear to have thought of everything.'

'I ask you to be patient. I am determined that this time I will get it right—that there will be no repetition of what I went through with Lydia. Had things been different I would have sought your grandmother's permission and there would have been acceptance followed by a long betrothal and finally marriage, but because of the circumstances there was no time for that, which is why I want to take things slowly at first. Do you understand?'

Rosa nodded, too disappointed to reply. William Barrington was marked with a proud arrogance and an indomitable will. Lydia Mannering must have hurt him desperately. She felt that it was not a subject he talked about, and that since that time he had held virtually every woman he had come into contact with with contempt, regarding them as being irrelevant—both dispensable and replaceable.

'I will be blunt. The arrangement will not be permanent. You don't love me and I do not love you. We have not known each other long enough for that. In truth, I don't need you—I don't need any woman—but I do need what you will bring to our marriage—your money and in time a son.'

'A son? And if the child is a girl?'

'I shall love our child irrespective of its gender. In fact, I would love to have a daughter.' Aware of her unease, he smiled. 'Don't look so worried. I am sure the arrangement is one that you can live with. I want an heir to continue after me, to carry on the Barrington name, so I have no intention of living the life of a monk.'

Rosa had given little thought to the intimacies of marriage he would be entitled to. Speechless with dismay that he would come up with this unthought-of condition of his own, that he had considered everything with the cold and calculating brain of a man who was used to making his own decisions and doing everything his way, Rosa stared at him, her cheeks flushed, as he continued to hold her gaze. The thought of having children with him shocked her—but also, in a strange way, it touched her heart.

'Do you like children, Rosa?'

'Of course,' she replied without a second's thought. 'I like children very much.'

His eyes locked on hers. He did not doubt for one minute that behind her demure exterior hid a woman of passion. He wanted her, despite the conditions he had set down. When the time was right he meant to capture her, to turn this calm young lady into a tantalising creature of desire, who, when aroused, would breathe a sensuality she was not even aware of, to take her to the very heights of passion.

He ran a gentle finger down her cheek, relieved that she did not pull away. 'Eventually you will be my wife in every sense, Rosa. That I promise you. Do you agree with what I have said?'

Rosa's heart gave a little leap in answer to the sheer, powerful masculinity he emanated. She looked at him, not with acquiescence, but she was determined not to let her emotions get entangled with being his wife. She hesitated before giving him an answer as she thought

of the enormity of what she was committing herself
to. Dazed by confusing messages racing through her
brain, driven by the need to make this beautiful house
her home and by something less sensible and completely inexplicable, she conceded.

Her hesitation to answer brought a slight smile to
his lips and he fixed her with a look, and for a fleeting
moment, Rosa felt they were bound together, as if she
was being inexorably drawn towards him.

'I think a kiss would not go amiss to seal the deal.'

Unable to tear her eyes from his, she froze to stillness as he lifted his hand and ran his finger along the
line of her jaw and down the column of her throat. Rosa
caught her breath as a shot of heat surged through her,
for it was an oddly sensuous and erotic gesture. There
was a silence as he gazed down at her flushed face and
time stood still.

'Please don't look at me like that,' she whispered,
her voice quavering. 'It makes me feel uneasy.'

He smiled. The light fell upon her face, glinting on
her hair and outlining her small head.

'You are very lovely. Has anyone ever told you that?'

'Yes—once.'

Gently, he touched her cheek with the back of his
hand. 'You are blushing.'

'Yes—I suppose I am.'

He looked at her for a long moment and then very
slowly moved closer still and curled his hand around
the back of her neck. Suddenly the garden seemed to
close in on them, making each aware of the closeness
of the other, of the warmth, the intimacy. The pull of
William's eyes was far harder for Rosa to resist at that
moment than the frantic beat of her heart.

'Oh…' she whispered, hardly trusting herself to speak. 'Are you sure you want to kiss me?'

'Absolutely. Would you like me to?'

'Yes,' she whispered, her eyes fixed on his lips. 'I do believe I would.'

'Then we are in accord.' He took her chin between his thumb and his forefinger and lifted it, forcing her to meet his steady gaze as he quietly said, 'I promise you that it will not hurt. A little kiss here and there is quite harmless. You might even enjoy the experience.'

'A little kiss here and there could be dangerous,' she countered, thoroughly convinced of that premise where he was concerned.

She turned her head away. The powerful force of sensual persuasion that he was capable of launching against her could reap devastating results. She must guard her heart. She was very susceptible. But when he placed a finger against her cheek and brought her face back to his, when his eyes delved into hers, he all but burned her heart inside out and touched at its inner core.

There was something in his eyes, something intense and passionate. They were clear and nothing had prepared her for the thrill of excitement that gripped her now, beginning in the middle of her chest where her heart lay and trailing delicately through the whole of her body. She was aware that this was an important moment in her life and a great revelation, but she could not comprehend it.

With aching tenderness he reached out and took firm hold of her, drawing her close and slipping his arms around her. 'It's all right, Rosa. I'm not going to hurt you,' he murmured, his lips against her hair. 'Try to relax.'

As if awakening from a deep trance, Rosa began to do just that. She was too vulnerable, too inexperienced to object to his embrace, and besides, he felt so warm and strong, his arms comforting and his voice soothing. She made no effort to free herself—and William seemed to have no intention of letting her go while she was content to remain there. She could feel the hard muscles of his chest and smell his maleness and the spicy scent of his cologne. A tautness began in her breast, a delicious ache that was like a languorous, honeyed warmth.

Recognising the change in her, William slackened his arms. His senses were invaded by the smell of her. It was the soft fragrance of her hair—the sweet scent of roses mingled with a musky female scent that made his body burn. Curling his long masculine fingers around her chin once more, he tilted her face up to his. Her eyes were large, dark and soft. It seemed a lifetime passed as they gazed at each other. In that lifetime each lived through a range of deep, tender emotions new to them both, exquisite emotions that neither of them could put into words. As though in slow motion, unable to resist the temptation Rosa's mouth offered, slowly William's own moved inexorably closer. His gaze was gentle and compelling, when, in a sweet, mesmeric sensation, his mouth found hers. Rosa melted into him. Although his lips were soft and tender, they burned with a fire that scorched her. The kiss was long and lingeringly slow. Closing her eyes, Rosa yielded to it, melting against him. A strange, alien feeling fluttered within her breast and she was halted for a brief passage of time.

William tasted the sweet, honeyed softness of her mouth, finding himself at the mercy of his emotions, when reason and intelligence were powerless. Savouring each intoxicating pleasure, he gloried in her innocence, her purity, painfully aware of the trembling weakness in her body pressed against his own.

As his mouth moved against hers, Rosa could not have anticipated the rush of sensation that took her breath, nor the frantic beating of her heart. The kiss was long and lingeringly slow.

When William finally lifted his head and stared down at her flushed face, he was stunned by his unprecedented reaction to one virginal kiss from an inexperienced young woman who hadn't seemed to have the slightest idea of how to kiss him back. It had proved what he suspected, that she had not the least idea of the mechanics of sexual intimacy between men and women. He had sensed her ignorance in such matters. He had seen it reflected in the shocked expression on her face when he told her he was going to kiss her and had sensed it in her body's lack of response when he had. So much for the young man she had known on Antigua—it was evident that Rosa Ingram hadn't had much practice at kissing.

But he was encouraged by the fact that her lips had answered his kiss. They had been soft and sweet and pliable beneath his own and he would have liked to educate her further, but seducing Rosa Ingram was not in his immediate plans. The warmth of affection he was beginning to feel for her was too disconcerting for his peace of mind. He was attracted to her by the sincerity in her gaze, sensing that her charm and personality made her unlike any other woman he had known. She had a distinctive beauty of which she seemed totally unaware and a natural femininity which remained un-flawed by self-interest.

But his instinct told him that he must be wary, oth-erwise he would find himself drawn deeper into some-thing over which he would have no control. For the time being, somehow he would have to cool the lust gnawing at his very being and try to forget how soft and sweet she had felt in his arms, to ignore that she had set her hooks into him and to control the attraction that seemed to bind his heart and mind to her.

Kissed and caressed into almost unconscious sen-sibility, Rosa let her slumberous dark green eyes flut-ter open.

William smiled down at the incredibly desirable young woman who had the power to set his body on fire. He had only wanted to kiss her, then walk away. Instead he'd ended up wanting to make love to her. Her magnificent eyes were naked and defenceless. His tanned features were hard with desire. 'Well, Miss In-gram,' he murmured, his voice a purr of pleasure, 'you have hidden talents I knew nothing about.'

Rosa trembled in the aftermath of his kiss, unable to believe what had happened and that she desperately wanted him to repeat the kiss that had stunned her with its wild sweetness. William was still holding her gaze and she looked with longing at his lips.

'Don't look at me like that unless you want me to kiss you again, Rosa,' he murmured huskily, his eyes dark with passion.

With her heart beating hard against her ribs, slowly she raised her eyes to his and, leaning forward, again boldly touched his mouth with her own, feeling her breath sucked from her body as, unable to resist what she so innocently offered, he pressed his mouth to hers once more, causing the blood to pound in her head and her senses to reel as her mind retreated down an unknown, forbidden path, plunging her into an oblivion that was dark and exquisitely sensual.

Drawing a shattered breath, and out of sheer preservation, an eternity later William raised his head, astounded by the passion that had erupted between them, astounded that this woman had the ability to make him lose his mind completely.

Rosa felt almost drugged as she stared at him bemused, her eyes large and luminous. As reality began to return and she came back to full awareness, she was shocked by the explosion of desire she had felt, shocked by what she had done. What had happened surpassed anything she had ever known.

With her eyes aglow with passion and her lips trembling, he smiled down at her. 'Well, Rosa' You are full of surprises. Perhaps the arrangement I spoke of will become void sooner than either of us thought. I don't think either of us will be disappointed when we are wed.'

Her cheeks flushed and her heart beating quickly, Rosa turned from him, wanting to conceal how deeply she was affected by what had just happened between them. Marriage to him was no longer straightforward. Considering what he had told her about his failed relationship with Lydia Mannering and her ultimate betrayal, she understood how his trust in women had been shaken and his reluctance to form a serious relationship with another. But when she thought of the kiss, how it had stirred her feelings, her desire, and how she had wanted him to go on kissing her—his desire equalling her own, then she didn't expect either of them would be disappointed.

Turning to face him once more, she was anxious to run from the truth of what had just happened. 'I—I really do think I should be getting back. Clarissa will be concerned that I have been gone so long.'

'Of course,' he said, taking her elbow.

When they stepped into the hall the butler was opening the door to a visitor, who sailed forward. A tall confident woman, about thirty-five, was attired in a stylish vermilion riding habit and matching hat perched at a jaunty angle atop her warm, ash-blonde curls. She was not beautiful, or even pretty, but tall and stately, handsome, alarmingly lively and arresting. She had everything a woman could ask for, in a physical sense at least. Rosa noted her plump lips, parted to show small perfect teeth, and how her eyes sparkled like dark sapphires as they passed over them, coming to rest on Lord Ashurst.

William stood watching her in silent fascination, then he smiled as their eyes met and he excused himself to Rosa and stepped forward to meet her. Much to Rosa's surprise, he embraced the newcomer warmly.

'Lady Willoughby! It's good to see you. It's been too long.'

'It certainly has,' she replied in a deep, husky voice that was curiously fascinating. 'I came as soon as I heard you had arrived at Ashurst Park. So much has happened here—we have much to talk about.'

Rosa watched the meeting between these two, strangely resentful and fascinated at the same time. Just moments ago she had commandeered William's attention and now felt forgotten as she surrendered the centre of the stage to another woman. Nothing could have prepared her for the remarkable presence of Lady Willoughby. Rosa imagined she could enchant the company about her with her sophisticated presence and charm with no effort at all.

Recollecting himself and remembering his manners, William turned to Rosa, who stepped forward. 'Allow me to introduce Miss Ingram. She is also a neighbour of mine. Rosa, this is Lady Caroline Willoughby.'

Interest kindled in Lady Willoughby's eyes. 'You are Amelia Ingram's granddaughter from Antigua?'

'Yes—Rosa Ingram.'

'I see. I was sorry to hear of your grandmother's demise. My condolences. She was a good woman—well liked and respected.'

'Thank you. It is kind of you to say so.'

'Not at all. It's the truth.'

'Miss Ingram is just leaving,' William said. 'What can I do for you, Lady Willoughby?'

'Forgive my impropriety and bad manners for calling on you like this without an appointment and unannounced, but good lord! How tiresome good manners can be where there is something to be done, something one has to say. I have a proposition to put to you, Lord Ashurst and since I am to leave for London shortly I would like to talk to you about it if you can spare the time.'

William was intrigued. 'Of course.' He turned to the butler. 'Show Lady Willoughby into the study. I'll be with you shortly.'

'Please don't worry about riding back with me,' Rosa said, stepping out of the house. 'Go and see to your visitor. I'll be quite all right alone.'

'I won't hear of it,' he replied, signalling to the boy bringing her horse from the stable. 'Escort Miss Ingram to Fountains Lodge, Martin.'

'But I really don't need an escort—'

'Not another word. I insist,' William said as the boy hurried back to the stable to get himself a horse.

Before parting William reached out and placed his hand over hers as she was about to mount, turning her to face him. Relief flooded ridiculously through her. He had not forgotten her after all. She could still gain his attention even though Lady Willoughby, on instant acquaintance, seemed to treat him as if he was her special passion.

'Have we reached an agreement that is satisfactory to both of us?'

She summoned up her spirit to try to bewitch him, her eyes glowing with brilliance and fire. 'Yes, I believe we have.'

'Even though I may prove to be a purchase you will regret?'

'I agree to the arrangement. I will not renege on it. You may have many failings, but so do I, and what good is wealth if one cannot use it to one's advantage?'

As Rosa rode away from Ashurst Park she could not shake off the unease she felt on leaving William alone to entertain his visitor. Lady Willoughby was unlike any woman she had met. She had the magnetism to seduce and enchant and had the power to hold any man in the palm of her hand. Rosa felt vulnerable and gauche and, worst of all, very young and strangely inadequate, knowing she could never compete with the fascination and worldly experience of the older woman.

* * *

William returned to the study, curious about Lady Willoughby and what she wanted to discuss with him. She was pacing the carpet with an impatience that seemed inbred in her. Her very manner was purposeful and he suspected that everything Caroline Willoughby did was done in a hurry.

'Now, Lady Willoughby, what can I do for you?'

'I'll come straight to the point. It's not my way to beat about the bush. I have a proposition to put to you, Lord Ashurst, and owing to your circumstances—you are in dire straits, I believe—it cannot wait.'

William cocked a brow. 'You are well informed, Lady Willoughby.'

'I make a point of keeping abreast of what is going on. I have spoken to my lawyer, who has spoken to your lawyer. The proposition I am about to put to you will be beneficial to us both—if you agree to it.'

'Then I will be happy to hear what you have to say. Please, take a seat.' William was wary, his guard up.

As soon as she was seated, Lady Willoughby chose directness, saying, 'I have come to ask if you would consider selling your estate—to me.'

Riding back to Fountains Lodge, Rosa didn't know what to think about what had happened to her when William had kissed her. She wasn't certain of his feelings, or hers, either. All she knew was that when she looked at him, at his hard, handsome face and bold light blue eyes, it made her feel tense and alive. She knew she had liked it when he had kissed her. Added to his other attractions it was something else that drew her to him. She sensed that behind his hard, knowing façade and rugged vitality, William Barrington had a depth that most people lacked. Could she ever love him? she asked herself. Her heart gave a gentle leap.

'Yes,' she whispered. Yes, she could. Over time it would be nurtured by appreciation and shared experiences and a knowledge of each other. She smiled, feeding her imaginings of future bliss. A rosy blush spread over her cheeks and everything that was in her heart was shining in her eyes. She was unable to believe her good fortune.

In an agitated state Clarissa was waiting in the drawing room by the window for Rosa to return. Clarissa turned when she entered the room, her face ashen.

'Rosa, what on earth were you doing with Lord Ashurst?'

'We met while out riding,' she replied, flopping into a chair and proceeding to pull off her riding boots in a most unladylike fashion. 'He's an early riser like me and it seemed perfectly natural for us to ride together.'

'That is all very well, but it is not what I asked. What were the two of you doing together—and to send Thomas home… It was not the proper thing to do.'

'For heaven's sake, Clarissa, not proper? What are you talking about? I suppose you think I am shameless—and you may be right. What do you imagine we were doing?'

'Don't be obtuse, Rosa. Grandmother hasn't been dead two minutes and already you are gallivanting about the countryside without a care for anything.'

'Please stop it, Clarissa—and I wasn't gallivanting. You're beginning to sound like Grandmother. If you must know Lord Ashurst invited me to have breakfast with him at Ashurst Park. I've also agreed to marry him—as soon as it can be arranged.'

Clarissa stared at her with disbelief. 'Marry him? But that's ridiculous! You can't! Goodness! It's all too soon. A period of mourning has to be respected before either of us can think of marrying. And besides, I was hoping you would return to Barbados with me.'

'No, I won't do that,' Rosa said firmly. 'I refuse to live with you and Andrew when you are married. As much as I miss my home I don't want to go to Barbados. It wouldn't be the same. I have decided to remain here.'

'But everything has changed now. Neither of us has to marry a title any more. Lord Ashurst would be marrying you for your money and nothing else.'

'I am not stupid. Do you think I don't know that?' Rosa replied sharply. 'And before you go jumping to conclusions, Clarissa, I asked him to marry me, not the other way round.'

'Oh, Rosa!' Clarissa exclaimed with distress. 'How could you? You are too rash for your own good. Some day your impetuosity will get you in trouble. You never take the time to think a situation out before rushing into things. You'll be so unhappy.'

'Like you would have been, had you married him?'

'Yes. I love you, Rosa. I am the elder and with no one else—except Aunt Clara, who is too far away in London to be of any help—it is my place to protect you.'

Rosa opened her mouth to protest that she didn't need to be protected from William and then changed her mind. She thought it incongruous that Clarissa, who was usually so reticent and was prone to tears at the slightest provocation, should suddenly take on the role of her guardian. Rosa didn't want to argue with her. Standing up and picking up her boots, she padded across the room in her stocking feet to the door. She was unhappily aware of how upset Clarissa was by what she was doing, but she was going to stand by her decision to marry William, no matter what she said, but she loved her sister very much and she hated the distress she was causing her.

'It's done now, Clarissa,' she said, looking back at her sister. 'I am sorry if it upsets you, but I have made up my mind. I want to determine my own future. Where is Dhanu?'

'In the garden with Mishka. Don't worry. We haven't let him out of our sight for a moment. He's a lovely child. I'm going to miss him when I leave.'

'We all will when he has to return to India. I'll join him in the garden when I've changed my clothes.'

Marching out of the room, she almost bumped into Margaret with her arms full of bed linen. With William's visitor still very much on her mind and curious about her, Rosa stopped.

'Margaret, I want to ask you something. Do you know Lady Willoughby?'

'Lady Willoughby—Caroline Willoughby of Hampton House?'

'Yes. What can you tell me about her?'

'Well, she's wealthy in her own right, that I do know—spends a good deal of her time in town. Her husband was a lot older than she was when they married. He died a few years back, leaving her to bring up their son alone—Rupert, he's called. The Willoughby estate adjoins Ashurst Park to the north. It's no secret that they have coveted some of Lord Ashurst's land for years. Why do you ask?'

'Oh—no particular reason—curiosity, I suppose. I met her at Ashurst Park earlier.'

'No doubt she's heard of Lord Ashurst's circumstances. I wouldn't put it past her to put an offer in for the estate. By all accounts she can afford it.'

'But he won't sell.'

'No? Then as a very wealthy widow—and not an unattractive one if my memory serves me well—she might put herself forward. She won't be averse to marrying him herself to get her hands on Ashurst Park. As his wife it would enable him to hold on to the estate— and if she were to bear a child, a son, then he would be the next to inherit the title and Ashurst Park.' She laughed suddenly. 'Imagine what a feather in her cap that would be. One son the Lord of Hampton House and the other the Earl of Ashurst.'

Rosa stood and watched Margaret climb the stairs, balancing the pile of linen in her arms. She wondered if she should be worried. Had Lady Willoughby approached William with a proposal of marriage—exactly as she had done? And if so, how would William have responded?

Rosa saw little of William during the days leading up to the wedding that was to be a small ceremony in the chapel at Ashurst Park. Both had much to occupy their time. The demise of the old mistress was felt by all the servants at Fountains Lodge. As they went about their work with heavy hearts, Clarissa and Rosa made preparations for the arrival of Antony Ingram and his family and their own departure. Antony wrote informing them that he would be leaving Scotland with his family a month hence and asked that unless they had made other arrangements the servants were to be kept on.

Clarissa wrote to Andrew in London to tell him she would be leaving for London the day following the wedding. Rosa instructed her solicitor to inform him of her forthcoming marriage and the financial settlement to Lord Ashurst.

Clarissa was finding it hard to believe that Rosa was serious about marrying Lord Ashurst.

'If you had asked me to name the last man on earth I would have expected you to marry, it would have been Lord Ashurst—although I have long passed the point where anything you do surprises me.'

'I have to confess that in the beginning I felt exactly the same,' Rosa replied as they strolled arm in arm in the garden. 'But I have got to know him better of late. Be happy for me, Clarissa.'

'If it is truly what you want then I am, Rosa. I am going to miss you terribly. I hope Lord Ashurst makes you a good husband. Even though he seems very civilised on the surface, when I met him I thought there was a ruthlessness about him, a forcefulness. When he wants something I believe he will stop at nothing to acquire it. At this moment he wants your money, but I can't help worrying what he will do when he has it.'

'William is embarrassed by his lack of finances, Clarissa. I do not know him well, but my present impressions are favourable. I trust him so please don't worry about me. It is what I wish to do.'

And with that end to the conversation Rosa prepared to become the Countess of Ashurst at Ashurst Park.

Chapter Six

Rosa and William were to be married three weeks hence in a small ceremony in the chapel at Ashurst Park.

William managed to find his way to Fountains Lodge most evenings before Dhanu's bedtime. These were light-hearted occasions when games that involved everyone were played and Dhanu's laughter rang through the house. William's gaze would collide with Rosa's pleasure-filled eyes. It was amazing how easily she had bonded with Dhanu—she was amazing. A game was in progress when each of them had to pretend to be an animal and the others had to guess what it was. Rosa's dreadful imitation of a tiger had been guessed by Dhanu and now it was William's turn. He had everyone guessing and whatever he was meant to be he was very convincing. Unable to make out what he was supposed to be they gave up—all except Dhanu, who went to him and said in a very low voice, 'Are you a monster?'

William dragged him onto his knee, fighting back a laugh as he made the scariest monster face and spoke in a deep voice. 'I certainly am and I am going eat you up.'

Dhanu made a sound that could be described as either a scream or a giggle and scrambled from his knee, racing across the room to Rosa and hiding behind her, his laughing face appearing every few seconds from behind her skirts.

His eyes warm with humour, William watched him, before focusing his attention on Rosa. Something in the way she bent down and hugged Dhanu, telling him he need not be scared of the monster while she was there to protect him, so charming in her laughter, so naturally generous with the boy, made him achingly aware of her as a woman.

When Dhanu left with Mishka to go to bed, Rosa walked with him to the door.

'I'm happy to know monsters are welcome at Fountains Lodge.'

She laughed softly. 'Happy monsters are always welcome. Dhanu loves your teasing and he gets so excited when he knows you are coming.'

'I look forward to coming. The evenings have a tendency to drag and I look forward to the company.'

Rosa's heartbeat quickened as she watched him ride away, disappointed that he hadn't tried to repeat the kiss that had sealed their betrothal.

The day before the marriage ceremony was to take place, William received a weary traveller from India, who had arrived that morning. His name was Ahmet Pandit, Tipu's most trusted servant and well known to William. He had been born in the palace and claimed privileges accorded to none other of Tipu's servants.

His dark face and the sound of the swift, familiar speech revived memories of the country William would always look upon as his home. William received him with some concern, for he knew he would not have travelled to England unless it was of a serious nature.

'I don't understand what you are doing here, Ahmet,' he said when they were comfortably ensconced in the drawing room. He looked at him with some concern. His face was drawn, his eyes bloodshot. 'You look tired. Are you feeling well?'

'It's been a long journey, Sahib. I am not a good sailor, I'm afraid.'

'Then you must rest here. How is my good friend Tipu? Well, I hope.'

'It grieves me to tell you that I am the bearer of sad tidings. My master fell ill of a fatal sickness soon after you left. He did not live more than two days.'

William stared at him in shock. This was indeed a bitter blow. Everything wavered before him. He gripped the back of the nearest chair to steady himself and spoke in a breathless whisper. 'Dead? Tipu? It's not possible. Good Lord! He was perfectly all right when I last saw him.' The words were barely audible, but the horror in them and the shock was unmistakable. 'How?'

'It was poison.'

'Poison?' William repeated, unable to believe it. 'But—who on earth would want to poison Tipu? For what reason?'

'The Rajah is quite beside himself with grief over his brother's death. It was his wife, the Rani, who poisoned him. Because of his closeness to her husband, she hated Tipu and the fact that he was against her.'

William tried without success to hide his shock, horror and dismay. 'And the Rani?'

'Although the poison may not have been administered by her hand, it was certain that she contrived it. She wept—swore she knew nothing about it. The Rajah did not believe her—not when it came to the murder of his brother.'

'What was her punishment?'

'Banishment. The Rajah sent her back to her father in shame.'

'And her sons?'

'They are his sons, too. They will remain at the palace.'

'So, Ahmet, you came all this way to tell me this.'

'No—not exactly. I have come for the Prince, Dhanu. His father misses him. He realises why Tipu did what he did—how he feared for the boy. The Rajah was so blinded by his devotion for his wife that he could not see what she was doing.'

'He never was capable of distinguishing between friends and enemies.'

'Now the danger has been removed he wants him to return. With three sons his succession is secure.'

'While the Rani was at the palace her arms were far reaching. If anything had happened to the Rajah, she would no longer have enjoyed the high status as his wife. To secure her position further, Dhanu had to be replaced by one of her own sons. She knew Tipu had asked me to take Dhanu away. She sent two of her henchmen to England to kill the boy. I believe one of them to be her brother Kamal Kapoor. Already one attempt has been made on Dhanu's life.'

'This I did not know, but it does not surprise me. I know Kamal Kapoor. He is a cruel, ambitious man who will stop at nothing to achieve his aim. If you are correct and he is one of the men, then Dhanu's life is in grave danger. Where are these men?'

'Unfortunately I have no idea. They were seen briefly in Ashurst village. I have made discreet enquiries, but they seem to have vanished into thin air.'

'Will you let me take Dhanu back to India?'

'I cannot stop you, Ahmet—nor would I want to. If his father has summoned his return, then that is what he must do.'

'I have letters for you—one from the Rajah and one from Tipu. It was important to him that he wrote to you before he died. You will read them. Everything is explained. The Rajah is grateful to you for keeping his son safe—you will see how grateful when you read the letter.' Getting to his feet, he passed the letters to William.

William quickly scanned the Rajah's letter, unable to believe his generosity when he saw the large amount of money he had gifted to him as his gratitude for taking care of his son at a difficult time. The letter from Tipu was an emotive one. With not long to live and knowing of his friend's struggle to save his estate, he had bequeathed an equally astounding sum of money.

Waiting a moment for it all to sink in and what it would mean to his future, raising his eyes, William looked at Ahmet, meeting his quiet gaze. 'Do you know what is written in the letters?'

Ahmet nodded. 'Tipu and the Rajah did me the honour of reading them to me before they were sealed, so that I should realise how necessary it was to reach you quickly. I have further papers that you must take to your bank—and for you to instruct your solicitor accordingly.'

'But—I cannot possibly accept this. I look for no reward for taking care of Dhanu.'

'Please, Sahib, you must accept it. Your father saved Tipu's life when he was a boy. The Rajah and his father before him owe him a great debt.'

'My father was a surgeon, Ahmet. He asked for no reward.'

'Please—it is a token of his esteem and gratitude. It is a great service you have performed. You must accept it. Our ways are sometimes not the same, but I hope you will allow me to convey my master's gratitude to you. He begs that you will accept his offering in token of the thanks which he cannot adequately express himself. He realises just how foolish he has been, how blind to Dhanu's needs, so it is fitting that I, on his behalf, place myself at your feet.'

To William's surprise this most dignified messenger went down on his knees and put his forehead on William's shoes. William was well used to this form of expressing gratitude from the Indians and always found it embarrassing, although he knew it was custom.

'Please, Ahmet, get up.' William helped him get back on his feet.

'It would offend the Rajah deeply for you to refuse his gift.'

'Then what can I say? Suddenly I have much to think about. In the meantime you will stay here, Ahmet, and enjoy my hospitality. I will make arrangements to return to London with you and see you safely on board ship for India.'

'Thank you. That is most generous of you. How is Dhanu? I imagine he finds England very different from India.'

'He does, but he's settled down well. I had my doubts at first, wondering how it would affect him—dispossessed of his home and his father and cast adrift in an alien world. His nurse, Mishka, is much attached to him. He is an inquisitive child—and mischievous. I have to keep a guard over him at all times since he has a habit of wandering off when something of interest catches his eye.'

'I look forward to seeing him—and I, too, will keep an eye on him.'

When Ahmet had been shown to his room, in the silence of his study William thought about his friend Tipu. With his fists clenched in anger, he dwelt on the cruelty of the woman who had taken Tipu's life. He fought to control the churning whirlpool of emotion that his loss had wrought in him. Bittersweet memories of the happy times he had spent with his friend came to mind, and sadness rose inside him that he had not been there for him in his hour of need. Tipu's death, coming so soon after his cousin's, was hard for him to accept, and he grieved for them both.

Forcing some order to his thoughts, he considered what the astoundingly generous gift from the Rajah would mean to him. It changed everything. There was more than enough money to cover the debts on the estate. He no longer needed Rosa's money. With cool logic he realised he had to put an end to it—and to reverse his decision to marry her. She wasn't in love with him any more than he was with her. He told himself he would be releasing her from entering into a love-less marriage and she would be free to follow her de-sire to help those underprivileged children in the city.

But he knew he would be unable to dismiss her from his life or his mind so easily. His passion for her was torn asunder by guilt. In the past hard logic and cold reason had always conquered his lust—with Rosa it was different. At that moment he realised that reject-ing her, as he must, was the hardest thing in his life.

On arriving at Fountains Lodge, William was di-rected to the garden where he was told he would find Rosa.

The sky was pale blue and cloudless with the gentlest of breezes, the garden filled with the scent of roses and laughter. He paused for a moment to watch Rosa and Dhanu throwing a ball to each other, Mishka seated in a rose arbour peeling an orange, happily watching her young charge at play. William's heart swelled as he ob-served the happy scene and listened to Dhanu's childish laughter, the leaves casting shadows on his happy face. He was clearly at home at Fountains Lodge, respond-ing to all the fuss and attention with a startling vital-ity, which poured from him like heat from the sun. He watched him drop the ball and run into Rosa's arms. She swung him round and round before putting him down. She ruffled his dark hair and stroked the curve of his cheek. The gesture was tender, which brought a constriction of emotion to William's throat, making him hate himself more for what he was about to do.

On seeing William, with a cry of delight, Dhanu ran

to him. William swept him off his feet, laughed when Dhanu told him he was playing ball with Rosa, before setting him back on his feet.

With an apron wrapped around her waist, Rosa was a beguiling picture of industrious femininity. When he was close she gazed up at him, a broad smile of welcome stretching her lips and her eyes shining bright.

'Why, William. This is a pleasant surprise. We weren't expecting you.'

'No. We have to talk, Rosa.' Placing a gentle hand on Dhanu's shoulder, he looked at Mishka. 'Would you take Dhanu in the house, Mishka.'

Without a word Mishka got up and took Dhanu's hand. William's eyes followed them, smiling when Dhanu turned and cheerfully waved back at him. Watching him, William felt the dependency of Dhanu. It awoke in him a protectiveness for the boy that made his body ache. Not until they had disappeared into the house did he speak.

'Dhanu seems happy.'

'He is. He's a happy, bright child, charged with energy and a playful devilment. I shall miss him when he has to return to India.' She gazed up at him, seeing how his dark hair gleamed in the sunlight. She experienced a rush of feeling, a bittersweet joy. His being there sent a message of warmth. The morning breeze tugged at her chestnut curls, freed from their restricting pins and falling in loose tresses about her shoulders. With numerous tasks to attend to this day before her wedding, wearing a plain green gown with her sleeves rolled up to the elbows and a stained apron, Rosa was not looking her best. She regretted him seeing her in such attire, little realising that she made the simple clothes seem stylish and almost elegant. He had been there for just a few seconds, but Rosa had the distinct feeling that he had been watching her for much longer and she felt at a disadvantage.

'And what brings you to Fountains Lodge, William?'

'To see you. The maid told me you were in the garden.'

His tone of voice made her look more closely at him. She detected some indefinable, underlying emotion in it as his eyes gleamed beneath the well-defined brows.

'I am deeply honoured. But you see I am not in any proper state to receive you.'

He smiled. 'You could be wearing sackcloth and ashes for all I care. I assure you, Rosa, that apron is most provocative at this time of day.'

Rosa was unaware that her hair, tumbling unfashionably about her shoulders, was a hundred different shades and dancing lights. 'I didn't expect to see you today. The wedding is tomorrow. You cannot be aware of the impropriety of such a visit or you would not have ventured to see me. I believe it is bad luck for the bride and groom to meet the day before the wedding.'

Despite her words, Rosa was genuinely happy to see him. She felt herself being drawn into his gaze, into the vital, rugged aura that was so much a part of him. Being this close to him and the memory of their kiss, which was never far from her mind, was having a strange effect on her senses. She was too aware of him as a man, of his power, his strength.

William was obliged to smile as he looked at her candid gaze, her face suddenly alight with expectation, yet trying hard to be patient as she waited for him to speak. He paused a moment before stating his business, hesitating to say the words which, in the presence of those clear eyes, seemed suddenly out of all proportion, monstrous and cruel.

'I have come to see you on a matter of some importance.'

Rosa saw a grave look lurking in his eyes. She felt his tension and a stirring of alarm began low in her chest. Something about him filled her with misgivings. He looked at her in silence. His tight-fitting riding coat emphasised the breadth of his shoulders and the tan of his complexion. She felt a wave of desperation as she strove for control and to calm her mounting fears. For a moment she did not speak, she could only hold her breath in anticipation, hoping desperately it was not bad news.

William banished her suspense by coming straight to the point. 'There will be no wedding, Rosa,' he said with controlled directness. 'I am not going to marry you.'

Confused, she stared at him, scarcely comprehending, too overwrought by what he had said to wonder about the sharp tug of loss she felt at the realisation he wasn't going to marry her. A great wave of disappointment filled her heart. Her world tilted crazily and with her heart fluttering wildly, she said, 'Oh, I see.' What was this? Why was he saying this? Her mind was in such turmoil she didn't know what to think any more. Everything seemed to spin around her and though her clarity was missing, a cold sensation on her flesh told her that there was certainty in what he said. It was like a slap in the face. For a moment she thought her legs might give way, but she didn't give him that satisfaction. She raised her chin and steeled her spine. 'And you won't change your mind?'

'No. I won't do that,' he said firmly, unprepared to refute it. 'I'm sorry, Rosa.' His tone was brusque.

'So am I.'

'I know how you must feel.'

'No, you don't,' she was quick to retort, her fists tightly clenched as she struggled to contain her rioting emotions. 'You couldn't possibly know how I feel.'

'I do know how insecure you must feel about your future.'

She stared at him, her eyes, which had been soft and welcoming on first seeing him, hard. 'Insecure?' She could feel her heart beating in slow, heavy beats. 'What do you mean? I am a very wealthy woman, so I shall never be insecure, and as for my future, that is entirely my own affair.'

'I'm sorry, Rosa—truly. Had things been different I would have been honoured to marry you.'

'I'm sure you would,' she responded sharply, her tone heavily laced with sarcasm. She could feel her resentment growing.

'I need to explain,' he said. 'We need to talk about this.'

When he was about to explain she held up her hand to silence him. 'No, we don't. Please don't tell me. There's no need—really.'

'Yes there is,' he countered quickly. 'I want you to understand and I think you will. A messenger has arrived from India with news and letters from the Rajah—Dhanu's father. I have also received the Rajah's commendation for taking care of his son at a difficult time, which he felt called upon to make a handsome gesture of gratitude. Suddenly I find I have more than enough wealth to take care of the estate.'

Surprised, Rosa stared at him. 'Oh—I see. That is indeed generous of him. And Dhanu?'

'The Rajah has asked that he be returned to India. Much has happened since I left,' he told her, thinking of Tipu and feeling the pain of his death. 'Be content when I tell you that it is safe for him to do so and the Rajah is eager to see his son.'

'I see. Then there is nothing more to be said.'

Bowing his head slightly, he stepped away from her. 'As you wish.'

'I do. How could you do something so utterly diabolical to me—on the eve of our wedding? Your timing could not be worse.'

'It was not my intention to hurt you.'

'Hurt?' She stared at him. 'I am not hurt, William. We have not known each other long enough for me to form any kind of feeling that would result in hurt. I am just thankful that it was to be a small affair and we don't have to go to the trouble of informing anyone. What about the rector?'

'I called on him before coming to see you.'

Raising her brows, she nodded. 'I see. You really have thought of everything. And Dhanu?'

'He will have to return to Ashurst Park. I will send someone over later on to collect him and Mishka.'

Anger seared up within Rosa, the anger of betrayal, an anger which gave her an inner strength to survive. Drawing herself up proudly, Rosa showed him that she too could be hard and cold. He would never know how much she was hurting. She also knew how unsettling it would be for Dhanu to leave.

'Rosa, I am grateful to you for making it possible for me to retain the estate—you will never know how much. With the arrival of the messenger from India, in all moral decency I find I cannot act in any other way. I am relieved to be able to release you from entering into a marriage that threw up difficulties for both of us.'

'Yes,' she agreed tightly. 'I'm relieved you've found another way to retain the estate.'

William had accepted her offer and agreed to marry her, and now, on the eve of their wedding, he had jilted her. What shocked her was how willingly and suddenly he had given her up. It was hard to understand. After their shared embrace and the kiss when she had melted against him, she had wanted to believe he was beginning to feel something for her, which was clearly not the case. She did her best to hold on to the resentment she felt, to be dignified, while feeling terribly let down and hurt, despite what she had said to him a moment ago.

'We both understood the nature of our relationship. It was an arrangement that suited us both.'

Rosa's chin came up. At least he didn't utter words of sentiment he didn't feel. 'At the time.' She moved her head in a slight, helpless gesture that was an acceptance of his rejection.

Something in that small despairing movement hurt William with a savage pain that was entirely physical. 'Yes. Things change. It is over.'

Rosa could hear the absolute finality in his voice that told her it would be futile to argue—and she wouldn't humiliate herself by doing so. Making a concerted effort to hide her regret and disappointment that Ashurst

Park and its owner were both lost to her, she looked at this cool, dispassionate man standing before her. He seemed powerful, aloof and completely self-assured. Why did he adopt this remote, almost hostile attitude towards her? Her eyes met his proudly and her tone when she spoke to him, her very posture, was cool and aloof.

'Then there is nothing more to be said.'

'No, it appears not. Whatever happens, Rosa, I wish you well and I am sincerely grateful to you for making your offer.' William looked down at her, aware of the futility of saying anything further. What was the point? The thing was done. Turning on his heel, as he walked away, he felt his heart move painfully in his chest, aching with some strange emotion in which regret and sorrow were mixed. She had made a strong impact on him and he told himself he was a fool to let her go.

Of all the women who had passed through his life, he hadn't wanted any of them the way he wanted Rosa Ingram. What was it about her? Her touch? Her smile that set his heart beating faster, like a callow youth in the first throes of love? Her innocence? Her sincerity? Whatever it was, she affected him deeply.

He was a man who, when he had made a decision, seldom changed his mind. He had accepted what Rosa had offered in a logical and precise mode of thought, but all that had changed with the arrival of Ahmet.

Rosa's face was a pale, emotionless mask as she watched him go. She felt totally incapable of moving as she stared at the sun-drenched garden. The day had taken on a strange, unreal quality and suddenly the heat had become oppressive. Her mind shied away from delving too deeply into the exact nature of her feelings for William. She had little faith in trying to judge her own emotions. But she had come to care for him, there was no use denying it. Suddenly her heart and mind felt empty, and she was chilled to the marrow, and even now, when she was desperate with the thought of everything falling apart, she had to ask herself why it should hurt so much and to question what was in her heart.

In the tearing, agonising hurt that enfolded her, she was ashamed at how easy it had been for him to expose the proof of her vulnerability.

The security that she had hoped for in the years to come was gone. Tears blinded her vision. Lowering her head, she moved towards the house, scolding herself for entertaining a misguided infatuation due only to her own youth, inexperience and ignorance of the world.

It had all been a lovely, glittering dream, but now it was over and for the first time in her life she knew the real meaning of isolation. She had no choice but to try and survive. With Clarissa going back to the Caribbean and her grandmother dead, there was no one she could turn to now, only her aunt Clara.

Riding back to Ashurst Park, William was contrite and disgusted with himself. What he had done had been cold and callous and he wasn't to know that what had just passed between them had been the most humiliating and humbling event of Rosa's young life. She had looked so small, so vulnerable, he felt sickened with himself and his conscience wrenched. But at the last moment, when he had turned to leave, seeing how her head had lifted and she had squared her shoulders, he had felt admiration for her stubborn, unyielding refusal to cower before him.

How well he had come to know her. He could still feel the fragile warmth of her body in his arms when he had kissed her, in his senses he could recall the delicate fragrance of her flesh, the taste of her on his lips, and see the luminous green eyes that had gazed into his with such soft, trusting candour. If things had been different, if she hadn't sought him out and proposed marriage, offering her money like a carrot to a donkey, he would have married her. He had never known a woman like her. But his visitor from India had brought him the means to survive without her money. Everything had changed and, as far as he was concerned, it could only be for the better.

As soon as Clarissa saw Rosa's dejection when she entered the house she knew something had gone badly wrong. Rosa's unaffected warmth was absent and Clarissa noted that her current attitude of proud indifference was a façade to conceal a deep hurt.

'What is it, Rosa? What did Lord Ashurst want?'

When Rosa looked into her sister's sympathetic eyes, she lowered her eyes to hide the shine of her tears. 'There will be no wedding, Clarissa. Lord Ashurst has called it off.'

With the ties of family and long-standing affection tightening around them, Clarissa sat down next to Rosa on the sofa. 'But—I don't understand. How could he do that on the eve before you were to wed? What has happened to make him change his mind?'

'Apparently he has found another way to retain Ashurst Park so he no longer needs my money—or me.'

'But—how?'

'Dhanu's father has made him a gift—a large one obviously—for taking care of his son.'

'And Dhanu?'

'He is to return to Ashurst Park. William is to send a carriage for him and Mishka so we must get him ready to leave.'

'Oh, dear! He won't want to leave but I suppose he had to at some time. What will you do now? You can't stay here.'

'I know. I wouldn't want to anyway. I'll go to London and stay with Aunt Clara for a while. Something will turn up.'

It was an emotional moment when the time came for Dhanu to leave. The child couldn't understand why. It was with a heavy heart that Rosa watched the closed carriage drive away, removing one more person she had come to love from her life.

Rosa and Clarissa along with Dilys, who was to remain with Rosa as her maid, left Fountains Lodge when the sun came up.

Determined to face her future with dignity and courage, the closer they got to London Rosa's resilient spirits began to stretch themselves once more. She began to feel human again and resolved not to think about William Barrington. What she needed was to rejuvenate herself. She had money—a lot of money. How well could a rich girl entertain herself in London? She smiled to herself. She would soon find out now she no longer had to think about marrying a stranger.

But she was determined that now she had the opportunity she would put her wealth to good use. Taking care of Dhanu and the loving relationship that had developed between them made her wonder if she could help less fortunate children in some way. A new future was opening up to her. Even though she was still hurting over William's rejection, she grudgingly had to thank him for this new direction her life had taken.

Aunt Clara and her husband Michael resided in Bloomsbury. Aunt Clara lived an enviable life. She was energetic and vital, always bright and cheerful, with a positive attitude to life. If there were things to be done, she wasn't one to rest on her laurels. Her vivacity and enthusiasm were contagious. She was constantly busy with her charities and knew so many people and had connections to help her.

Her husband, Michael Swinburn, was a successful businessman in the city. He was a pleasantly mannered, quiet man, with a direct and simple view of life, a man who adored his wife and lavished his attention on her, happy to go along with whatever she planned and to attend his club. They had travelled to Antigua for two extended visits over the years and Clarissa and Rosa had become extremely fond of Aunt Clara and Uncle Michael.

Aunt Clara swept into the hall to welcome them. She was taller than Rosa, with a generous figure. Her resemblance to their mother was so strong that it made Rosa's heart ache.

She had been expecting Clarissa to arrive alone, so Rosa's appearance was unexpected and Clara's reaction was filled with disbelief and pure delight. When condolences had been made for the death of their grandmother, she ushered them into the drawing room and ordered refreshments. They sat chatting companionably for a while and then Clarissa excused herself, saying she would like to rest before dinner.

'I can't tell you how delighted I am to see you back in London,' Clara said, taking a seat beside Rosa and arranging the skirts of her gown. 'It was so good of you to stay and take care of me when I was ill, instead of going to Berkshire with Clarissa. Now tell me about Lord Ashurst. I thought your grandmother was considering him a match for Clarissa and now here she is, back in London and about to marry the young man from Barbados. And the Earl of Ashurst? What happened to him?'

Rosa sighed. 'It's a long story, Aunt Clara, and not a very happy one.'

'Tell me. I'm a good listener.'

Clara listened patiently to what had transpired between Rosa and Lord Ashurst and when Rosa fell silent she squeezed her hand with sympathy and compassion while feeling a duty to bolster her niece's spirits. 'Dear me, Rosa, what a time you have had.'

Rosa nodded. Her eyes held a deep sense of sadness, but she raised her head with pride. 'Yes. There is no point in crying about it. I'm not the first woman to be jilted on the eve of her wedding. So you see, Aunt Clara, in the end he didn't want my money—or me. The source of my wealth is abhorrent to him—his rejection humiliating and degrading for me. He must have had a better offer than my own. I can only feel relief that we didn't go through with the wedding.'

'Then you must let him go. No good will come of brooding over what might have been. You have your whole life to consider. What you need,' she said, her voice softening as she sipped her tea, 'is something to occupy your time—and a little light entertainment. I shall so look forward to introducing you to my friends. With Clarissa returning to the Caribbean—and I know how you will miss her dreadfully—I will see to it that you are never bored. Lord Ashurst will cease to matter.'

Rosa laughed. 'I'm sure you will.'

'No one need know of your association with Lord Ashurst. If it becomes known that the two of you were engaged to be married and he jilted you on the eve of the wedding, it will do your reputation no good. From what you have told me it would appear that he has too much on his plate right now to divulge it himself and if he were to do so it would not show him in a favour-able light.'

'I don't think he will do that. Besides, it is hardly likely we will see each other again.'

'Possibly not. I am engaged in so many interesting charities and projects that I do not have too much time on my hands—I know I was against you helping me when you broached it before, but since your grand-mother's demise, I have decided to let you help me. The two small institutes we opened five years ago for destitute children we struggle to keep open. They are inadequate for the number of children we take in and we are constantly short of funds and must find ways to raise more. Taking care of the children has become an important part of my life. I would so like to find bet-ter premises and even to open an orphanage but…' she smiled wistfully '...all that is for the future. You have a lot to offer and there's so much you can do to help.'

Rosa was happy to comply. Aunt Clara had always been a source of common sense and good advice. She was all about living and being engaged in life, and was passionate about all she did. She was just what Rosa needed now and perhaps the wealth William Barrington had turned his back on could be put to good use after all. She would not say anything to her aunt just now, not until she had seen what it would entail.

Clarissa and Andrew were married in a quiet ceremony by special licence two weeks after Clarissa arrived in London. They were to travel to Portsmouth, where they would board ship for Barbados. Rosa's heart was heavy with sadness when the time came for Clarissa to leave—it was the first time they had ever been apart. It was difficult for Rosa to watch her go. The separation would leave a huge hole in her heart. They were both tearful, but Rosa was happy for her sister: a new island, a new home—a new life.

At Ashurst Park William poured himself a large brandy. His mind occupied with financial matters, he settled himself in a comfortable chair near the hearth, propping his feet on the brass fender. During the day he gave himself up to adjusting to life at Ashurst Park and the day-to-day running of the estate. Bailiffs were called in to give an account of their management, accounts gone into and meetings with his tenant farmers, which always made him feel that Charles was looking over his shoulder. The tenants had held Charles in high regard and his tragic death and near bankruptcy had

affected them all, making William even more determined to make things right.

He stared into the shifting flames, but his mind was
wandering far afield as an image of Rosa entered his
thoughts—of dark-fringed eyes, glowing with their
own light, the colour in their depths forever changing
like a roughly hued gemstone. She was seared into his
memory. He could see the way her hair blew in the
wind when she rode her horse, the sway of her hips
when she walked. She filled every inch of his mind.

Casting this image aside, he brought a more favourable one to mind, of moments when her eyes had
been bright and full of laughter, expressive and alive,
of a pert nose, gently curving lips—then he held the
image in his mind, where it burned with the memory
of their incredible softness beneath his own. When he
had kissed her he had not been driven by lust, but he
had wanted to kiss her, very much. He thought of the
rounded grace of her body, which possessed a subdued
strength and honesty that lent her a naïve elegance.
She was unaware of how lovely she was and she dwelt
firmly in his mind.

The truth was that neither time nor distance had
blunted the feelings he had for her. As he continued to
gaze into the flames they leapt high, then died back, the
coals snapping as if with a stoic purpose. Just thinking
of her he felt a protectiveness so profound that it shook
him to the depths of his being. Yes, he missed her but
maybe the best way of protecting her, not to make her
a target for the gossips, would be to stay away from
her. Looking back, the sweet memory of her response
to his kiss touched him deeply. She had been so open
and generous in her response, as she was in every as-

pect of her life. What he was feeling stunned him. So, what was to be done to fill the gaping emptiness of his life her departure from it had left?

When the clock chimed the hour, he rose, having reached a decision.

Refusing to wallow in self-pity, days merged into weeks that passed in a blur of activity for Rosa. Aunt Clara left her no time to brood and refused to let her be still for a day. She was happy to work alongside her aunt on her charities and could not believe the poverty and destitution that she saw. The children touched her heart. They had nothing and very little hope. She was swamped with guilt when she thought how she had lived a life of privilege, taking all she had for granted, while children all over the world were living in such abject poverty. A great many of them were orphans, others unwanted, having been turned out by parents who had too many mouths to feed already, and others had been sold to chimneysweeps and the like for a few shillings. She could not help all the children but she would do her utmost to make a difference for as many as she was able. She made a generous donation to the charities but they were always short of funds.

The long summer days slipped almost unnoticed into autumn.

When they weren't occupied with charity matters, the days were filled with a frenetic round of social activities. With Uncle Michael and Aunt Clara acting as chaperons, Rosa was escorted to soirées and any social event to which they were invited. She loved attending the theatre and the opera and she was often to be found seated beside her aunt in an open carriage when they would join the elegant traffic to promenade through Hyde Park during the fashionable hour. The park was a rendezvous for people of quality, fashion and beauty, with splendid, shining carriages and high-stepping horses.

Under Aunt Clara's instruction, Rosa blossomed into an extremely attractive and desirable young woman, who was refreshingly unselfconscious of her beauty. She was a new distraction and London welcomed her and embraced her. She drew the admiring, hopeful eyes of several dashing young males displaying their prowess on prime bloodstock.

There were few people in Aunt Clara's elevated circle of friends and acquaintances who didn't know of her background, and all the unattached males at the social events she attended clamoured to be introduced. It was not just her charming self and her beauty that drew them to her, or the mystery of her tropical-island background, but what she had always feared, the enormous wealth the man fortunate to win her would receive when he placed a wedding ring on her finger.

William had taken up residence in his London town house in Grosvenor Square. He had no love of the city—it was much too noisy and too many people wanted to encroach on his time. He had much to occupy himself with and his forays into society had gone well. The buzz of curiosity he had aroused in the *ton* he could have done without, but nevertheless it amused him.

He was to book Ahmet, Dhanu and Mishka a passage on one of the East India vessels sailing for India. Kamal Kapoor still posed a threat to Dhanu so he would continue to keep the boy safe until he could leave. Today William was enjoying some leisure time riding in Hyde Park with others whose acquaintance he had made, when his attention was caught by one of the occupants in a carriage parading in the ring.

Chapter Seven

Since Rosa had come to London, the onset of winter had forced a knife-edge to the colder weather, but today the sun was shining and did not deter people from parading in the park. It had filled up with its usual array of rich and famous when Clara told the driver of their carriage to head for home. They were to attend a fund-raising event later and she wanted to make sure they had ample time to prepare.

Rosa's attention was drawn to a group of young gentlemen on the grass close to the ring. They were a melee of horses and riders moving and shifting, the air around them filled with noise and laughter. Having just run a race, they appeared in jocular mood. She was surprised to see a woman in their midst, totally at ease in masculine company. A tall, handsome woman, she was dressed entirely in sapphire blue, her blonde hair arranged in flattering curls beneath her hat set at a jaunty angle. Infected by their fervour, Rosa smiled to herself, her eyes idly drifting over their shining faces. One gentleman in the midst of them seemed familiar.

She watched him dismount and say something to the

woman, which she obviously found amusing, for she threw back her head and laughed hilariously. Rosa's eyes were drawn to back to the gentleman. He turned so that his face was in full view. Rosa's gaze became riveted on the scene and a sick paralysis gripped her when she recognised William. A shock tightened itself about her heart. He wore a dark green riding coat and a pristine white neckcloth and was so tall that he towered over his companions. His narrow hips and muscular thighs were encased in buff-coloured breeches and his gleaming black boots came to his knees. His dark hair was brushed from his brow and his high-planed cheekbones gave his handsome face a harsh expression. In the surrounding haze Rosa was no longer aware of anyone save him. Her heart gave a sudden leap of surprise and consternation. How positive his presence was. She was aware at that moment of a sudden pang in her breast.

Despite her efforts to try not to think about him, he was never far from her thoughts. His appearance here in London was completely unexpected. She stared at him fixedly, with a strange sensation of fatality, and the tidal wave of emotions caused by his presence almost overwhelmed her. For a moment she was thrown into a panic. Her first instinct upon seeing him was to climb out of the carriage and hide, yet at the same time she was unable to move.

Looking at the woman once more, she now recognised her as being Lady Caroline Willoughby. Beautiful and vivacious, her red lips parted in a wide smile of sensuality, she dominated the scene. A pain like she had never experienced before almost severed Rosa's heart in two. She suspected that it was no coincidence that William and Lady Willoughby were here together.

Unable to tear her eyes away and hoping they could drive past without William seeing her, she tried to compose herself. Unfortunately there was a congestion of carriages and their driver had no alternative but to stop.

Clara, noticing her niece's strained profile beside her and sensing that she was not enjoying the outing, leaned towards her. 'Rosa, are you all right? You're not ill, are you?' she enquired softly.

'No. No—I'm quite well, Aunt Clara,' she replied with a weak smile. 'I'm a little tired, that's all.'

Unable to ignore his presence, wide-eyed, Rosa looked directly at William, as did Aunt Clara, whose sharp eyes had observed his interest in her niece.

'That gentleman staring at you, Rosa—is he familiar to you by any chance?'

'Yes. It is Lord Ashurst, Aunt Clara, the Earl of Ashurst.'

Clara's eyes narrowed on the gentleman in question. 'Is it, indeed? Then I would like to be introduced.'

Rosa's eyes hadn't left him. She became like a senseless inanimate object, mindless, and she thought she might have remained this way for ever, with the crowd milling around them. Although there was noise, laughter, the conversation of people who came to the park to absorb the atmosphere and socialise, there was stillness and silence about them.

Excusing himself to his companion, William ducked under the railing that separated them. With cool composure Rosa watched him approach. Clara ordered the driver to stop the carriage.

William's eyes lingered on Rosa. Her presence had taken him wholly by surprise. She was as beautiful as he remembered, a radiant sunburst among the colourful throng. She was innocence and purity, and worth far and above all the other young ladies on show in the park. Warmly dressed against the cold, the mass of her chestnut tresses was swept up in a sleek and sophisticated arrangement beneath a fetching little hat. Small diamond droplets dripped from her ears.

All his attention was focused on her, each conscious of the anger, the argument and the strife of their parting at Fountains Lodge. Rosa displayed none of the frivolity that was present in the others in the park. Her eyes were wounded and cold. She wasn't the same Rosa who had come to Ashurst Park to propose marriage to him. There was an unspoken message about her now that said, *Don't come too close.* Had he done that to her? If so, he was deeply sorry. It was plain to him that what had transpired between them had stripped all humour from her, for she was as cool and aloof as an ice queen.

Unsmiling, Rosa returned his gaze. Her lips curling a little, she inclined her head in acknowledgement of his presence, but his rejection still burned in her heart. His expression was hardly contrite. She tried to temper the pleasure she took on seeing him with the coolness appropriate to his behaviour.

'Lord Ashurst,' she said, greeting him with cool composure. 'It is indeed an extraordinary coincidence to see you in London. I am surprised. I would have thought affairs in Berkshire would have kept you from town.'

He acknowledged her graciously, bowing his dark head in acknowledgement, his magnificent eyes mov-

ing over her easily and familiarly before returning to
her eyes. He saw that she was looking at him frankly,
openly, and with a dispassion so chilling that he was
intensely moved by it, yet he sensed that beneath it all
was a heartbreaking dejection.

'Make of it what you will, but it is a pleasure to
see you here. My estate can do without me for a short
while. I have important business commitments to discuss first-hand with my bankers and solicitor that need
my personal attention. I also considered it time that I
showed my face at Westminster.'

'I see.' The tone of his voice was as natural as if
they had met the day before and nothing untoward
had passed between them. Its very ordinariness struck
Rosa with ire. His eyes remained fixed on her. It unsettled her. It was weeks since she had last seen him, but
she had not forgotten how brilliant and clear his eyes
were. In a strange, magical way they seemed capable of
stripping her soul bare. Every fibre of her being cried
out for him, but her betrayed spirit rebelled. 'We were
about to leave the park, but before we do I would like
to introduce my aunt, Mrs Clara Swinburn.'

William turned his attention to her companion and
bowed his head graciously. 'My pleasure, Mrs Swinburn.'

'I am happy to meet you, Lord Ashurst. My niece
has told me so much about you that I feel I know you
already.'

William looked at Rosa, a slight smile curving his
lips. 'Has she? All good, I trust.'

'But of course,' Clara replied, laughing lightly.

'And your sister?' he enquired of Rosa. 'Is she here
with you?'

'Clarissa is married now and on her way to Barbados with her husband.'

'You will miss her.'

'I do. Very much.'

'And you will not be returning to Berkshire?'

Her answer was sharp and to the point. 'No. There is nothing there for me any more. My aunt has generously invited me to spend some time with her here in London.'

'Of course,' he said, amused by the note of indignation in her voice. He glanced at her aunt, who was looking from one to the other with a secretive smile playing on her lips.

Another carriage drew up alongside them. The occupants were well known to Clara and she immediately made introductions before falling into conversation.

'Mrs Swinburn,' William said, seizing the opportunity to have a moment alone with Rosa. 'May I have your permission to walk with your niece for a while? There are one or two matters I would like to discuss with her.'

'Why—no, of course not. Rosa? Is that agreeable to you?'

Rosa glared at him. She didn't want to walk with him anywhere, but to refuse him would probably cause a scene. Smiling tightly, she took his proffered hand and climbed out of the carriage. They did not speak until they reached the edge of the crowd and William led her into the privacy of some trees. She turned and faced him, almost overawed by his nearness and trying to break the connection he was beginning to stir inside her.

'I don't know what you hope to achieve by this, Wil-

liam. I think we have walked far enough,' she uttered
frostily, coming to a standstill. 'Everything has been
said between us before I left Berkshire.'

'Has it?'

'Yes. And I must thank you for being so frank with
me.'

'I came to London to see you, Rosa. Yes, there were
other reasons that brought me, but my main reason was
to see you. We can't leave things like this between us.'

Without emotion, Rosa stood perfectly still as William came closer. There was an aura of calm authority
about him. His expression was now blank and impervi-
ous, and he looked unbearably handsome. The sight of
his chiselled features and bold blue eyes never failed to
stir her heart, but she was resolved to keep him at arm's
length. She would not humble herself at this man's
feet, and pride—abused, stubborn, outraged pride—
straightened her back and brought her head up high as
she met his steady gaze.

William stood looking down at her, deep into her
eyes. At that moment she was the epitome of a stubborn, prideful woman. And he had not ever seen anyone more beautiful.

He was seized by a passionate longing to protect and
revere this lovely young woman who had crept into his
heart. He ached to treat her as she should be treated,
to tread the hesitant steps of courtship and woo her as
she deserved. He gazed down at her pale face, looking
deep into her entrancing green eyes, and he felt himself overcome and gripped by the same coldness that
had flowed out of her when they had parted in Berkshire. He observed with sorrow that the pink bloom he
had adored so much had gone from her cheeks and the

aching sadness dulling her lovely eyes dragged at his spirit. Never had his heart felt so heavy.

Rosa looked at the forceful, dynamic man standing before her. He looked powerful and aloof and disgustingly self-assured. 'We should not be here. After everything that has happened, how dare you try to manipulate me as if I am yours to direct—just as though you have a perfect right to.'

Beneath the dappled light of the tall trees, her unparalleled beauty proved a strong lodestone from which William could not drag his gaze. Quietly, he said, 'All I wanted was to speak to you alone.'

Rosa did her best to hold in the resentment she felt, to be dignified, but it was very hard and her expression was icy. 'Nothing you can say can undo what you have done to me.'

'I would like to try. You look tired,' he said quietly.

'My state of health need not concern you.'

'But it does. I feel that I am responsible.'

'Please don't flatter yourself.'

'I don't. It was not my intention to cause you pain. There is something I have to say to you.'

'Really? Tell me.'

'I want to say that I am sorry. Can you possibly forgive me for—?'

'What?' she interrupted sharply. 'Jilting me? No, William, I don't think I can. I understand perfectly why you did, but it doesn't lessen the disappointment. Although I suppose we should be thankful your visitor from India arrived before you made the mistake in marrying me. I would not have been so easily got rid of then. And what flight of fancy leads you to suppose that I will forgive you?'

'I can but live in hope.'

'Please don't bother. What you did hurt me deeply, humiliated me. If you cannot see that, then you are more insensitive than I realised.'

'But I do. I knew it the moment I told you the wedding would not take place.'

'Forgive me if I do not believe you. I have no other recourse but to consider myself entirely free of any commitments to you. You owe me nothing, William—no explanation—nothing.'

'You were engaged to be my wife. Please allow me a little of your time?'

'No—better not. Since you left me I have thought long and hard about my future. Aunt Clara has been a godsend. I enjoy what I do—helping her with her work. For the first time in my life I have something to focus on, a purpose in my life. I feel needed—useful—and I have found a way to make use of my wealth. When people are starving and children don't have a family or a roof over their heads, children who are bred to dirt, disease and grinding poverty, they don't question the source of their good fortune when I put food into their bellies. I don't expect you to understand that and I don't really care. At this present time marriage is not on my agenda.'

Her sharp reply brought a tight smile to his lips. 'I don't suppose it is, but if you change your mind then it should not be a problem. You have plenty of money to buy yourself another husband and you have other assets to your credit besides your money.' He spoke with suave brutality, his insolent gaze raking over her.

William's jibe, savage and taunting, flicked over Rosa like a whiplash. Stung to anger by his harsh words, hot colour flooded her cheeks and her soft lips tightened as she exerted every ounce of her control to keep her temper and her emotions in check. 'I apologise for approaching you in the first place. It would seem there had been some misunderstanding on my part.'

William sighed, his anger beginning to dissipate. He had not meant to speak so harshly or so brutally, but her persistent resentment had provoked him. 'No, Rosa, there was no misunderstanding, although I think your actions are indicative of your character.'

'And you know me well enough to have made a judgement of my character, I suppose?' she said acidly.

He nodded slowly. 'I think I have known you long enough to make a fair judgement of your temperament. You are intelligent and generous, which are both noble assets. But you are a stubborn young woman and you have a quick temper and a sharp tongue. You also have a propensity to recklessness and to jump to conclusions. I fully understand why you offered me your money as well as yourself, and for what it's worth it touched me deeply. But when I marry I will do the asking. It will be on my terms and it will not have anything to do with money.'

'Then you should have told me that in the beginning.' With a great effort she made her voice cold, implacable and determined. 'The fact is that no matter what has happened between us, you will always be Lord Ashurst, the Earl of Ashurst, whereas I will always be the daughter of a plantation owner. So taking that into account, how could I possibly have imagined for one moment that I—or Clarissa, for that matter— would make you a suitable wife? All things considered, it would have been best if I had never met you.'

William stood gazing down at her, looking deep into her eyes. 'Don't be angry, Rosa. I have no wish to argue with you. Have you come to hate me in so short a time?'

A deadly calm settled over Rosa, banishing everything but her hurt and disappointment. Her small chin lifted, her spine stiffened, and she stood before him looking like a proud young queen, her eyes sparking like twin jewels.

'Hate? I don't hate you. Let us be honest, you had no interest in me as your wife. I never saw any evidence of that.'

'I didn't realise you wanted me to. Ours was a business arrangement—that was how you wanted it. I confess that I did not like the idea of being bought.'

'It wasn't like that—at least not the way I saw it. Did you have to wait until the eve of our wedding to realise it—to tell me? What you did was cruel.'

'I'm sorry. But from the first time I laid eyes on you I knew you were different. You intrigued me. I wanted to know you better.'

'Nevertheless, your actions led me to believe otherwise—that you were unwilling to accept me as your wife. I don't know why you are here or what it is that you want from me, but if it is because you have come to tell me that you have made a mistake, that you have changed your mind,' she said, even though she suspected he might already have accepted Lady Willoughby's suit, 'then I feel I must tell you that I have a reluctance to consider you as my husband. I think what you did was altogether reprehensible and your actions unforgivable. You are the most selfish man I have ever had the misfortune to meet. That I should be forced to this opinion of you after all I expected of you is—is painful to me. What we had is gone, past retrieving, so please save us both from embarrassment and refrain from speaking of it and visiting me again.'

'I am sorry you feel like this. I shall not be happy until you tell me I am forgiven. What can I do to redeem myself in your eyes?' He smiled crookedly at her, willing her to respond, but there was no answering spark in her eyes.

'Nothing,' she replied coldly. 'It was wrong of me to approach you in the first place. I see that now. There has to be more to marriage than a business arrangement.'

William raised an eyebrow enquiringly, the corner of his mouth twisting wryly. 'Such as love?'

'I can't answer that. I have experienced something like it once—but I strongly suspect that love is a contradiction of emotions which should be given freely and has nothing to do with marriage.'

'And desire? Passion?' he asked, regarding her closely, his gaze narrow and assessing.

'At least desire and passion are honest emotions.'

'And all-consuming,' said William.

'And I would say that there speaks a man of experience,' she said coldly. 'But I would think those kinds of emotions are not as consuming as love—which you must have experienced before with the lady you were to have married before she betrayed you with another.'

He nodded gravely, his eyes darkened. 'You remembered.'

'Yes. You must have loved her for her betrayal clearly affected you to the extent that you found it impossible to trust another woman. I would also say that when passions are spent they are easily appeased and forgotten,' she remarked drily, referring to the kiss that had ignited passion between them, a passion they both knew would have flared into something more and run out of control had it not been checked. 'But I forget, you were a soldier—tough and invulnerable. No doubt your training has taught you that a man need trust none but himself—and use women for naught but pleasure.'

'You are beginning to sound like a romantic. I agree that lust, desire, passion—call it what you will—is good while it lasts. But it is fleeting—extinguished by the boredom of familiarity.'

It took Rosa a moment to answer, for he could not have made his feelings clearer, which made her even more determined to guard her heart. 'You have an uncommon honesty about such matters,' she said quietly.

'I do not always find it easy to say what I think and feel. I am not accustomed to baring my soul.'

'I suspect that it might have something to do with you being a military man. I strongly regret what happened between us—when you kissed me. Believe me, William, I am not the kind of woman to go around kissing just anyone—although I don't suppose the same could be said of you.'

William's firm lips twisted in a morose smile, while inwardly admiring her perception. 'I have kissed many women I have been attracted to, but that does not mean to say that I wanted to marry any of them.'

'Only one,' Rosa was quick to remind him. She was conscious of a sudden surge of anger, realising just how stupid and naïve she had been. How dare he treat what had happened between them casually, as if the kiss was insignificant and meant nothing at all? But clearly this was nothing out of the ordinary and he was used to kissing ladies all over the place. After all, she thought bitterly, how would she know?

Mortified and humiliated, she nevertheless managed to lift her chin and look at him directly. 'I do not have your experience. Now, if there is anything else you wish to say to me, please say it and then leave.'

Her words, spoken with simple honesty, gave William further insight into just how truly innocent she was. The coolness faded from his face, replaced by an expression so intense, so profoundly gentle. 'You are a beautiful woman, Rosa,' he said, his gaze lingering on her lips, remembering what it had felt like to kiss them.

Rosa gave a hard, contemptuous laugh, stiff with pride and anger, the humiliation and the hurt she had suffered at his hands never far away. 'The passion that flared between us was enchanting while it lasted—but I soon realised that the magic was just an illusion.'

'It needn't be.'

'Yes, it does. But I have much to thank you for,' she said, her eyes shooting green sparks of anger and not wavering from his. 'You see, from now on, if I ever find myself in a similar situation, I shall be too distrustful, too much on my guard against men's wiles, to allow myself to be deceived by charm, soft words and a handsome face. I am my own woman now, William, and answerable to no one.'

'And there is no prospective husband in the offing?'

'No. I can't tell you how grateful I am to you for ending our short engagement. I like my freedom and independence—which is something a husband isn't likely to give me.'

'That depends on the husband.'

'Maybe. But for now you can leave me alone, knowing that you have at least achieved something. You can forget you ever met a stupid woman who quite shamelessly threw herself at your head.'

Halted abruptly in the midst of this unpremeditated outburst of feeling, William knew she was trying to punish him, but behind the hard expression and glib words, the real woman, the warm and passionate Rosa, was still to be found. His ill-considered treatment of her when he had cancelled their wedding that had driven a wedge between them had been replaced with this angry young woman who was being extremely careful at keeping him at arm's length.

For a long moment, his eyes probed the dark depths of hers. He was profoundly aware of the enchanting young woman's body standing close to him and her intoxicating perfume. His entire personality was pervaded by a shrewdness that had never taken principles into account, but only the fluctuations of human nature. He was clever, and he knew that when he held a woman in his arms he was very powerful. There was always a moment when the woman's self-defence yielded before the lure of sensual rapture and he knew how to turn that moment to his advantage.

Unable to prevent himself, he reached out to touch her, taking her arm and drawing her further into the shelter of the trees, away from prying eyes.

'That I can never do,' he said, drawn by the softness in her bewitching eyes. Forgetful of where he was and mastered by a passion almost beyond his control, he took her face between his hands, his clear blue eyes penetrating as they probed hers. Desire was in his own and something more, something so profound that it held

Rosa spellbound. 'I haven't handled things particularly well, have I, Rosa? When I saw you on the eve of our wedding I wasn't considering your feelings.'

'No, you were not.'

'I came here because I couldn't help myself,' he said fiercely. 'I do care about you. I don't want to hurt you.'

Like a magnet William's eyes were drawn to her mouth and he became lost in the exciting beauty of her. He watched the bright rays of the sun slanting through the trees strike gleams from her hair—the play of light on her face and lips, the soft lustre of her dark green eyes, held him in thrall.

'William—please stop it,' Rosa said, recognising the desire in the smouldering depths of his eyes and trying to push him away. He was much too close and she was beginning to feel distinctly uncomfortable. The tight tension of regret was beginning to form in her chest that she had not sent him on his way sooner. With wide, disbelieving eyes, she stared at him, not knowing what to think or how to feel. He really was the most arrogant, outrageous man. 'This is not a game.'

'Pity. It was just getting interesting.'

Before Rosa could guess what he meant to do, an iron-thewed arm slipped about her waist and brought her against that broad chest. With her head reeling, she found herself imprisoned against him.

'Please don't do this,' she murmured. 'Not here— someone might see.'

'To hell with them,' he whispered thickly, ignoring her request as he purposefully held her chin firm and lowered his mouth to hers. '

'Have you any idea how much I want to kiss you? —and I think you want me to. Is that not so?'

'Oh—I—I…' She expelled her breath on a long sigh.
'Yes,' she whispered, 'maybe…'

He smothered any protest she might make with a
hungry, wildly exciting kiss, temporarily robbing her
of her resistance, which fortified his determination to
have her melt in his arms.

Rosa could not free her mouth from his. She thought
to remain passive in his embrace and did not struggle
as his mouth pressed upon hers, but her lips flamed
with a fiery heat that warmed her whole body. It was
as though she had never felt the touch of his lips or his
arms around her. That was when she realised the idea
was ludicrous and a gross miscalculation of her power
to deny him, for the kiss went through her with the
impact of a broadside. He ruthlessly laid siege to the
defences of an inexperienced, virginal young woman
until her traitorous body lost its power to struggle. The
cry of warning issued by her mind was stifled by her
pounding heart and the absolute pleasure of being in
his arms.

The scent of his spicy cologne and his tender assault
were more than she could withstand and with a silent
moan of despair, she melted into his kiss, her lips parting beneath the sensual pressure and, at that moment,
his tongue slid between them, invading her mouth and
taking possession of her. Pleasure engulfed her as she
became caught up in the moment. It was an extraordinary sensation to feel the heat of his body so close
to hers, to feel the muscles in his chest and arms, his
slim hips pressed to her own. Her eyes closed and the
strength of his embrace and the hard pressure of his
body made her all too aware of the danger she was in,
that he was a strong, determined man and that he was

treating her as he would any woman he had desire for. Her head swam and she was unable to still the violent tremor of delight that seized her, touching every nerve until they were aflame with desire. Her world began to tilt and she was lost in a dreamy limbo where nothing mattered but the closeness of his body and the circling protection of his arms.

When he eventually raised his head there was fire in his eyes. Once more he proceeded to kiss her lips long and deep and hard, with a hunger that alarmed her. Such was Rosa's own desire, the sudden, awakened fires, the hungering lust, the bittersweet ache of passion such as she could never have imagined, that she little realised the devastating effect her soft lips were having on him as he crushed his mouth to hers, invading, demanding, taking everything with a sensual, leisurely thoroughness, aching to sample the woman more meticulously.

William's hand slid from her waist to her breast and Rosa gasped when he caressed none too gently the tender mound of flesh beneath the fabric of her coat. Instantly her sanity returned. Some stubborn, protective instinct warned her to have a care. She was irritated by the way in which he had skilfully cut through her defences, but she could not deny the magnetic attraction that still remained beneath her irritation. After all that had been said between them she could not let this happen. She struggled furiously when he bent his dark head and his lips took possession of hers once more. Placing her hands against his chest, she pushed herself away with all the strength she could muster. She stood glaring at him, breathing hard, her green eyes burning, completely unaware of the vision she presented to William's hungering eyes.

'No more, William. Nothing can come of it.' Trembling visibly, she moved away from him. She had been reduced to confusion for a moment, probably deliberately, but she had recovered herself quickly. 'I don't think I shall ever understand you.'

'There is nothing to understand. I am but a simple man.'

'You are not,' she said vehemently.

'I disagree.' He was tempted to take her in his arms once more, but, seeing that she was struggling to control her rioting emotions, he restrained himself. 'Come now, Rosa,' he managed to say, smiling, though he himself was shaken by the moment. 'It was only a kiss—an innocent kiss, nothing more sordid than that.' Even as he uttered the words he was not convinced he was telling the truth. The lingering impression of that firm young body pressed to his own had done much to awaken a manly craving that had gone unappeased for some months.

'A kiss that could have led to other things—which was what you had in mind had I not had the presence of mind to end it,' she flared, furious with herself for not only responding to it, but *liking* what he had done to her. 'You forced your will on me, forced me to kiss you. I did not invite you to do that. I am not one of your common women to be tumbled between the sheets and left to bear the shame. This was a mistake—one which I regret. Now I would like you to take me back to the carriage.' She turned from him, trying hard to control her rising temper.

'It was a mistake for you, maybe, but not for me.

You see, I know you, Rosa. I know how you react to my kiss, to being in my arms. The next time you may not be so eager to leave.'

She whirled in a flare of rage. 'Why, you conceited, arrogant beast! There won't be a next time. We are no longer affianced, William. You mean nothing to me and never will.' As she spoke the words a picture of the self-assured, beautiful Lady Willoughby came into her mind and she almost shouted her suspicion of his relationship to the noble lady—which were totally groundless—but she managed to hold her tongue. 'I am no longer the slip of a girl who rode to Ashurst Park to propose marriage in exchange for my wealth. I left her behind when I left Berkshire.'

'My eyes confirm what you say, Rosa,' he murmured, his eyes probing with flaming warmth into hers. 'You are what any man would desire. You have whet my imagination to such a degree that my pleasure would be to make you my wife—despite your will to fight me.'

She stepped back. Behind her lovely face she was outraged. The red blushes on her cheeks had settled into a dark glow, the flush of sudden battle in her face. Her retreat was necessary to cool her burning cheeks and to ease to some degree the unruly pacing of her heart. 'Your wife? Have you taken leave of your senses? After all that you have done to me, how dare you say that? Because of you I have been hurt and humiliated. At this time my future is uncertain. Because of my sheltered upbringing I am a rather limited person, not given to over-optimism.'

'It won't always be so.'

'I know. I will not allow it to be. It is not in my nature to simply sit and do nothing. But for now I am secure enough living with Aunt Clara, so leave me in peace.'

William did not seem surprised or insulted. He looked at her for a long moment. He appeared to be deep in thought and contemplating whether or not to voice his thoughts. All the conflicting emotions that Rosa had always aroused in him flooded over him again with the knowledge that, although she had outwardly given the impression she had not been happy to see him, the eagerness of her kiss told him otherwise. Undaunted, he lifted his brows quizzically, a twist of humour about his beautiful lips. But never had he looked more challenging.

'Come, I will return you to your aunt. She will wonder where we have got to.'

Rosa was glad of the long walk back to the carriage. It gave her time to compose herself.

Mrs Swinburn's friends were just driving away when they reached the carriage and William helped Rosa inside. He turned when he saw Lady Willoughby sauntering over to them, brandishing her riding crop like a sword in front of her.

Introductions were made and for a moment Rosa was completely at a loss for words.

'I am happy to see you again, Miss Ingram,' Lady Willoughby said. 'I'm so sorry we didn't become better acquainted when I met you at Ashurst Park, but time was of the essence. Berkshire certainly has its full complement of visitors in town.'

'My appearance seems to have surprised Miss Ingram somewhat, Caroline,' William said, his gaze passing meaningfully over Rosa's calm features. 'I can't think why.'

'Perhaps that's because she didn't expect to see you here,' Lady Willoughby replied.

'Then I am pleased that she didn't know,' William said, his eyes gleaming wickedly as they continued to hold Rosa's wide-eyed gaze. 'Had she known it might have caused her to stay at home and then I would not have had the pleasure of renewing our acquaintance.'

Rosa glared at him. Acquaintance! Was that all she had been to him? An acquaintance? They were to have been married, for goodness' sake! Her expression tightened. Until she could sort out her feelings, the kind of feelings she had never had to cope with before she was bewitched, weakened and challenged by William Barrington and his kisses, she was determined to remain calm, to brazen it out. 'Forgive me, Lord Ashurst, but I think there has been a misunderstanding, for I am baffled as to why you would want to renew our *acquaintance* at all. Lord Ashurst and I were neighbours for a while,' she explained to Lady Willoughby, 'and have met only occasionally. Is that not so, Lord Ashurst?'

He smiled at her with cynical amusement. 'Our encounters may not have been frequent, but you cannot deny that they were by any means ordinary, nevertheless. I think we know and understand each other well enough.'

'I'm sure you do,' Lady Willoughby said with a throaty laugh, glancing curiously from one to the other. 'Oh, look—I can see Lord Marchant beckoning to me. Tiresome man. It's a good thing his wife isn't with him. As a widow and still in my prime, Miss Ingram, all the ladies suspect me of flirting with their husbands.' She chuckled throatily. 'In some cases they are not wrong,' she said, a wicked twinkle dancing in her eyes. 'My husband found me a bit forceful while declaring he loved me dearly, but he took every opportunity of getting out of the house on some pretext or other—usually to do with horses. I think he preferred horses to people.' Casting her eye over the twittering throng, she said, 'I have to confess that I am sometimes of the same inclination. Tell me, Miss Ingram, is there a man in your life?'

'No, not at all,' Rosa replied, surprised by the question and trying not to look at William. 'I have come to London to keep my aunt company—and I enjoy helping her with her many charities.'

'A noble occupation. A young lady who prefers to involve herself in charitable works instead of useless activities—I can only extend my sincerest admiration.'

'I am no saint, Lady Willoughby—far from it. My father was forever telling me I am not ladylike, for I have this awful habit of doing the opposite of what I am told to do and arguing when I should be agreeing.'

Lady Willoughby laughed throatily. 'Then you are a girl after my own heart. None of us is perfect, Miss Ingram—but I dare say one day soon you will get married. A good-looking, sensible girl like you won't remain single long with all these handsome bucks around.' She gave her a direct stare. 'It's a pity you left Berkshire. I would have enjoyed calling on you.'

'It's kind of you to say so.'

'While we are both in London I will make a point of inviting you and your aunt to one of my evenings. Be sure of it.'

'Why—I—thank you. That is most kind. How is Dhanu?' Rosa asked, addressing William.

'He is very well.' William looked at Lady Willoughby, who was looking from one to the other with interest. 'Miss Ingram dived into the lake to save Dhanu when he tumbled in from the cascade. If not for her quick thinking, I shudder to think what would have happened to the boy.'

'Goodness!' Lady Willoughby exclaimed. 'That was a brave thing to do. As far as I recall the pool below the cascade is very deep and I imagine incredibly difficult to get out of. You were right, Lord Ashurst, when you said your meetings with Miss Ingram were somewhat out of the ordinary.'

'Miss Ingram swims like a fish,' William said, his gaze settling on Rosa with a quiet admiration.

'I am all astonishment. Unfortunately, I never learned. I wish I had. I would like my son to learn.' Turning her head, she gave a snort of disapproval. 'Lord Marchant is still beckoning. I really must go and see what he wants.'

Rosa watched her go, unable to quell her admiration for the older woman. Since she could see nothing detrimental about Lady Willoughby, she could feel no resentment. Confidence simply oozed out of her.

'And is your young charge with you in London?' Clara enquired.

'Yes. Dhanu is a lively, child and has the infuriating habit of escaping the watchful eyes of his nurse and finding his way out of the house at the first opportunity. Unfortunately,' he said, addressing Rosa, 'the problems that followed him from India remain.'

'Then I hope you manage to keep him safe. How

fortunate that you and Lady Willoughby are in town at the same time,' Rosa remarked. 'I'm sure you two will get on famously and find you have much in common.' If she was hoping that her comment would draw William on his relationship with Lady Willoughby, she was mistaken. But when she caught the look of total absorption on William's face as he gazed after his retreating neighbour, she felt she had been correct in her assumption that William and Lady Willoughby might have something going on between them after all.

But she was totally bemused. When she had parted company with William Barrington so many weeks ago now, she had thought he intended severing all contact with her, yet here he was, going out of his way to see her. Why did he insist on this contact when he had no interest in her? What could it possibly mean?

When William Barrington was lost in the crowd, Rosa rallied as best she could, hiding her sharp disappointment. For her, something had gone from the day, something elusive, exciting and vital.

Clara put out a gentle hand and laid it on her niece's arm. Rosa turned and looked at her aunt, who was reading her face so clearly.

'How I wish that things had turned out different for you, my dear, or that your dear father had found some other way to obtain his wealth,' Clara said, her understanding of the situation complete.

She never ceased to amaze Rosa, showing an ability to see in others what they kept to themselves. There were aspects to her nature that were gentle and hesitant, with a wisdom that became more profound the

older she got. Rosa studied her aunt with the relief of
one who does not have to explain anything.

'I know you and Lord Ashurst parted with bitterness, Rosa, but, oh, my dear, how I do approve of your
choice. I pride myself on being a good judge of character and I have formed a favourable opinion of that gentleman. He is just the man for you and it is the greatest
pity he did not marry you. However, I admire a man
who lives by his principles. Call me an interfering old
woman, if you like, but I am not ashamed to say that
I consider you and Lord Ashurst to be right for each
other, and despite what has gone before between the
two of you, if anything should come of it I would be
extremely happy.'

'I cannot ignore what he has done to me, Aunt Clara.
It would be too difficult. How can I possibly overlook
such humiliation?'

Chapter Eight

A week went by and Rosa caught neither sight nor sound of William Barrington. Clara came bustling into the house after a day doing her charity work. Rosa met her in the hall, having spent the day at home.

'You look harassed, Aunt Clara. Have you had a busy day?'

'Extremely,' she replied, handing her hat and coat to the hovering maid. 'I've just come from the institute in Ludgate. One of the women from Soho brought in an older child. She had some interesting information about a young boy who had been brought in earlier—a foreign child apparently, probably Indian. According to the quality of his clothes, he comes from a good home.'

Rosa looked at her sharply, all her senses alert. 'An Indian boy? How old is he?'

'Young—about five years old, I think. The trouble is he is clearly traumatised and extremely distressed. He hasn't spoken a word so we can't find out anything about him.'

Rosa frowned. 'Five years old, you say. Where was he found?'

'Close to Green Park, I believe—huddled behind a pile of rubbish. He was trembling and frightened, poor little mite. I'll go and see him tomorrow—first thing. Perhaps he might have found his tongue by then and we'll know more about him.'

Aunt Clara and Uncle Michael were visiting friends in Richmond that evening and would not be back until the tomorrow afternoon so Rosa was left alone. There had been so many social events of late and she had put in long hours at the institute. She had intended on catching up on some sleep and having an early night, but she couldn't settle. She felt a peculiar hollowness in the pit of her stomach.

'Is something wrong, Rosa?' Clara asked as she was preparing to leave the house. 'Since I told you about the young boy you've been distracted.'

'It's just a suspicion I have. It is possible that the child is Dhanu. It's probably just a coincidence but I am uneasy. I must go and see for myself.'

'But is that wise? It will be dark soon.'

Rosa was already ordering the carriage. 'I'll not rest until I know. Would you send someone to Lord Ashurst and tell him to meet me at the institute—just in case it is Dhanu. He lives in Grosvenor Square. I'm sure it won't be too difficult finding him.'

It was almost dark, the lamplighters lighting the oil lamps to illuminate the streets, when Rosa climbed into the closed carriage and told Archie, the driver, to take her to the institute in Soho. Nearing her destination, the streets were thronged with pedestrians. Caught up in the congestion the carriage paused. Looking out of the window to see what the holdup was, she had a peculiar sense of being watched. A man was leaning on a lamppost, looking directly at her. Her heart skipped a beat. The man was of Asian origin and there was something in the unswerving gaze of his yellowed eyes, some hint of expression in his face that struck fear in her heart. That it was Kamal Kapoor she had no doubt.

Immediately she pressed herself back against the upholstery with a terrible sense of foreboding. Fear instilled itself into her heart—fear and desperation. If the boy at the institute was Dhanu, was it possible that they had seen him and followed him?

The institute was situated close to Soho and Seven Dials. The building stood in what was little more than a narrow passage. It had no lamps so it was shrouded in darkness. It was also congested with carts and barrels and crates of every description stacked high against the buildings so Rosa had to leave the safety of the carriage some distance away and proceed on foot. The institute was a well-built but grim-looking building in a small yard situated in an area where poverty and disease ran side by side.

Aunt Clara found the time she spent at the institute and the one in Ludgate highly rewarding, particularly so when she found situations for the older children. Rosa had been to both several times, but the condition of its young inhabitants never failed to shock her. This institute in Soho had been brought into being ten years earlier, paid for by donations from wealthy donors with the intention of providing aid and provision for destitute children—a place of Christian charity. But it was always difficult to afford the necessities— coal and food.

Inside, a score of undernourished children dressed

in rags, their legs bowed and eyes enormous in pinched faces, were quietly sitting or lying on small makeshift beds or standing about. The windows were small, the furnishings stark, but it was warm and everything was scrubbed clean. The air was tinged with the aroma of cooked food, plain but appetising, and two women with aprons fastened about their waists passed among the children, doing what they could to make their lives more comfortable and lessen the fear that lurked in their eyes—fear of the world outside and the dangers it posed to those alone and very young.

Rosa looked around, her eyes searching for the boy her aunt had described. Beth Penworthy, one of the women who came in to do what she could, pointed towards a bed in the corner of the room. A child, his forlorn little face watching what was going on around him, turned and looked at the new arrival. At first he just sat and stared, and then, giving a low mewling sound, he threw himself off the bed and darted across the room as fast as his legs would go and wrapped his arms about Rosa's legs, clinging to her for all he was worth.

Rosa gasped, horrified. How could it be? 'Dhanu! What on earth has happened to you?' Leaning down, she gathered him into her arms. Going to the bed, she sat and tried to comfort him. He was clinging to her with the desperation born of enormous fear.

'Well, glory be! You know him, Miss Ingram?' Beth said.

'Yes, yes, I do, Beth, but as to how he came to be wandering the streets on his own I have no idea.'

'His family's clearly well to do. If they've missed him there could be a hue and cry.'

'I'm sure there might very well be. I'm hoping his

guardian—Lord Ashurst—will meet me here. If not I shall see he gets home to Grosvenor Square. I have the carriage at the end of the street.' She looked at Dhanu. 'What happened, Dhanu? Did you leave the house by yourself?' He nodded, his expression one of profound fear. 'It's all right, Dhanu. You are quite safe. No harm will come to you now, I promise.'

'I wanted to go to the park to see the bears I saw yesterday.'

Whatever had happened to him, his mute shock seemed to have passed. 'They prompted you to go out. I see.'

'Mishka wouldn't take me,' he whispered, tears welling in his big dark eyes.

'So you thought you'd go by yourself.' She sighed, her arms tightening about him. 'Oh, Dhanu. What are we going to do with you? You know you shouldn't wander off on your own. Did you get lost?'

He shook his head. 'No,' he mumbled. 'Two men chased me—those bad men.'

Immediately Rosa understood. Her mouth set in a grim line and she held him in a firmer grip as though the very fierceness of her protective instincts would keep him safe, for there was no doubt in her mind that the men he spoke of were the same men who had been hounding him ever since he had arrived in England. Her emotions were scattered amid twisted layers of fear, sadness and outrage that the people who were supposed to be taking care of this five-year-old boy had once again failed in their duty.

It was mid-afternoon when Mishka alerted Lord Ashurst to Dhanu's absence. Having gone to check on the boy she had left him having his nap in the nursery and finding his bed empty, frantic, she searched the house but he was nowhere to be found.

'Lord Ashurst, something has happened.'

William looked at Mishka hard as he listened. He felt a peculiar hollowness in the pit of his stomach. At first he stared at her wordlessly, distinctly feeling his heart almost stop beating in his chest as he tried to comprehend her words, but then, understanding that she was telling him that his worst fears had been realised, that Dhanu had disappeared, his eyes sprang to life.

'How long has he been missing?' he demanded.

'I don't know. Perhaps half an hour—no more,' she told him, distraught.

'He must be hiding somewhere.'

'I don't think so. I put him down for his nap and went to check on him but he had gone. With Ahmet I've looked everywhere but he is nowhere to be found. Oh, Lord Ashurst,' she cried wretchedly, wringing her hands in her wretchedness and despair, 'I am so worried that something terrible has happened to him.'

One of the footmen, alerted to Dhanu's disappearance by Mishka, came to tell them that a child had been seen leaving the square a short while before.

The hollowness inside William deepened. His eyes were ice-cold and shining with a light that seemed to come from the depths of him. He flung himself towards the door, his formidable anger bursting from him and vibrating around the walls of the room. It was directed at Kamal Kapoor, who had been sent to end Dhanu's life.

He immediately instructed the footman to inform the

constables and with Ahmet at his heels he left the house
in pursuit of Dhanu, thinking he might have headed for
the park. The thought that something dreadful had happened to Dhanu after all the efforts he had taken to keep
him safe tortured him. It consumed him and filled him
with a torment worse than any soul could.

Giving up on William, thinking that perhaps he was
away from home when Aunt Clara's messenger reached
Grosvenor Square, Rosa decided to take Dhanu home.
Opening the door of the institute, Rosa scanned the
shadows before venturing out, holding Dhanu's hand.
She was aware of the danger they faced from the two
men she was certain were somewhere close by. Keeping Dhanu close, she looked right and left. The passage-
way was quiet and dark. Stealthily they made their way
along. Hearing a footfall, she ducked behind a cart, her
eyes fully adapted to the darkness, her mind racing. The
street was redolent of smoking chimneys and the sour
scent of the garbage-filled gutters, where dogs scav-
enged for a meal. Above her own breathing she heard a
soft footfall, then another, growing momentarily nearer.
Dhanu wriggled against her at being held so tight. He
kept his eyes closed, too afraid to look in the dark recesses where menace lurked. Rosa shushed him calmly
and, to her astonishment, now that she was closer to
absolute peril than ever before in her life, she felt com-
paratively calm. Every sense was alerted and quivering
with sensitivity. Never had her senses been so acute.

She waited, holding her breath as the footsteps
halted close by. Hearing words spoken in a strange
language, she knew without doubt it was the two Indians. Fear clamped its cold hand over her heart, con-

centrating her mind and adding steel to her spine as she held her breath. Through a small crack between the boards of the cart, she saw the two men silhouetted in the dark. Her eyes widened as they came closer. She dared not breathe for fear of being heard. A sigh of relief passed her lips when the men turned and became absorbed into the shadows.

Shocked into full alertness as she held the small boy close to her, she waited a few seconds before creeping out, holding on to Dhanu's hand. Suddenly, without warning, disaster struck. When something small and live ran over Dhanu's foot, to Rosa's dismay he stumbled and cried out, alerting the men to their presence. Immediately they rushed menacingly towards them. Cringing against the stacked barrels, Rosa watched them come closer and in a moment of fear and desperation, letting go of Dhanu's hand, she placed her hands on the barrels and gave them an almighty push. Not only did she dislodge the barrels but also a vast amount of debris, showering them in dust and garbage she could not and would not care to put a name to. Grabbing hold of Dhanu's hand once again, she jumped aside and watched as they came crashing but the two men dodged the barrels and moved menacingly towards them.

Dhanu whimpered with fear. Rosa held him tight, tenderly placing her hand on his frozen cheek, her heart seized by a terrible anguish. Hopelessness at her situation traced through her body. Dhanu seemed to shrink inside himself. Rosa shoved him behind her, praying hard for a miracle.

The servant sent by Clara Swinburn arrived at the Earl of Ashurst's residence in Grosvenor Square. When he entered, an agitated Lord Ashurst was pacing the floor in his study. His face was set and grim. Seeing his strained features, sensing his tortured frame of mind, his grief and fury which he kept in abeyance, the servant was aware that beneath the gentleman's remarkable self-control, which unbeknown to him his military training had taught him to employ, he was a man in the grip of a nightmare.

On hearing what the servant had to say he took no time in ordering the carriage to take him to the institute, hoping and praying that the boy taken there earlier was indeed Dhanu.

The miracle Rosa prayed for came in the form of William. Like Rosa earlier, he'd been forced to leave his carriage at the end of the street. The sudden noise Rosa had created when she had toppled the pile of barrels had brought people onto the street, along with beggars who appeared out of dark recesses. Adjusting his eyes to the dark, he proceeded with stealth down the alley, seeing a woman pressed against a wall, her determined stance like that of a tigress defending her cub as she tried to protect with her life the small boy. He was labouring under all the effects of considerable terror, clinging to her leg as two men bore down on them. One he immediately recognised as being Kamal Kapoor. William was oblivious to everything but that small group. Other images were blurred, voices faded. His hands were clenched into fists so tightly they ached, and there was hate in his eyes as they settled on Kapoor. He hurried on, careful to keep to the shadows until he was behind Kapoor and close enough to reach out and grasp his arms in brutal hardness, pulling him back.

Taken by surprise, a cry escaped Kapoor and he struggled. His accomplice, seeing what was happening, made a dash for it, disappearing into the dark streets of St Giles.

The noise had attracted more people into the alley. Some carried lanterns, holding them high to throw some light onto the scene, which had become one of devastation. Two women came out of the institute and the two carriage drivers appeared with Mishka close behind.

A tirade of curses in Urdu issued from Kapoor's lips as he made vain attempts to disengage himself from William's iron hold on his arms.

'Try to get away, Kapoor, and you're a dead man. Here,' William said, thrusting Kapoor towards the two carriage drivers. 'Hold on to him and for God's sake don't let him go. Take him inside the institute. I'll follow.'

The drivers were only too happy to oblige. Dragging the Indian to the open door of the institute, they disappeared inside.

William took in Rosa's appearance, realising what she must have been through. He was deeply concerned and afraid for her in many ways. The obvious danger of injury or even death when confronted by two assassins was only a part. There was also the vulnerability of her mind to the seriousness of the situation.

He frowned, showing his concern, clearly moved at the tenderness and compassion she showed for the child clinging on to her. 'What about you, Rosa? Are you hurt? Are you harmed in any way?' She shook her head. 'And Dhanu?' Dhanu, frightened by the suddenness of it all and the terror he had been subjected to, began crying loudly. William scooped him up into his arms. 'Thank God! Thank God you're all right.' The ragged note of relief in his voice was apparent as he held the boy tight, offering strength and comfort to the trembling child.

Rosa watched him, her throat tight with emotion. She could see Dhanu's need of him as he wrapped his short arms around his neck, the man who had promised to protect him against all things, and she was struck by the various emotions playing over William's features, the love reflected in his eyes could not be concealed. She must have trembled perceptibly because she felt William's fingers tighten on her shoulder and drew some comfort from the warmth of the contact. She could only look at him, her eyes shining with the unbelievable comfort of knowing that they were safe.

Having no wish to linger in the street, they went into the institute, closing the door behind them.

Kamal Kapoor, stood beside a bed, guarded by the two carriage drivers. In no hurry to confront him, Dhanu's plight more important just then, William turned to Mishka, whose relief on finding Dhanu safe, was evident on her face.

'I want you to take Dhanu home, Mishka. This is no place for him.' He looked at his driver. 'Take them home—send for the constables while you're at it. And, Rosa,' he said, taking her arm. 'Go with them. This is no place for you.'

'I work here, William—doing what I can for the children.'

'Nevertheless—'

'No,' she said firmly. 'I'm staying.'

Rosa turned and looked at Mishka, who had tears of relief swimming in her eyes as she checked Dhanu over for any injuries. 'Take him home, Mishka. Apart from being frightened he doesn't seem to have suffered too much from what has happened to him. When he gets back to the house a hot bath and a good night's sleep will do him good, although he should not be left alone. After today's unfortunate escapade, even though Mr Kapoor has been apprehended it might be wise to have someone with him at all times.' She knew her advice sounded like a rebuke, but she could not help herself. It was the third time she had come to Dhanu's rescue. The next time he might not be so fortunate when Mishka left him alone.

Rosa watched them leave, the driver saying he would direct the constables to the institute, before turning her attention to what was happening around them. When Kapoor had been brought in, Beth had gathered the children together and ushered them into another room, closing the door so they could not witness what was happening.

Face-to-face with Kamal Kapoor at last, William had to make an intense effort to control himself, even to keep his voice from shaking when he spoke. 'Kamal Kapoor, we meet at last.' He moved closer. His jaw was rigid and a muscle twitched dangerously in the side of his neck. It took a physical effort to maintain his calm and stop himself going to Kapoor and wringing his neck. 'Your accomplice appears to have fled.'

Kapoor's thin face broke into a reptilian smile, and the hiss that he emitted was more venomous and more fearful than any snake. He stared at William with eyes

that were like ragged holes in his face. There was loath-
ing there and contempt, not fear. Kapoor feared no man
and was renowned for his prowess with a blade, but
William Barrington's reputation as a military man with
both pistol and sword was an enviable and well-known
fact. William approached him. There was something
ugly beneath Kapoor's skin. William knew the man
had no scruples and would sell his own mother for the
right price, and kill her for more.

Kapoor tried to lunge at him, a murderous lunge,
but Archie jerked him back. William wanted to hurt
him. He had suffered all sorts of hell knowing this man
and his accomplice would kill Dhanu if he dropped
his guard. William prepared to defend himself and to
ward off the threat. Refusing to accept defeat, a gut-
tural sound rumbled from deep in Kapoor's chest and
crimson hate filled his sight. Instead of backing away
Kapoor drew a short bladed knife and launched himself at William, his thrust like lightning. Unable to
avoid the forceful assault, the blade nicked the back
of his hand. Kapoor was not quick enough to inflict
more injury. William grabbed his wrist with both
hands, turned and pivoted his back into him, using
his arm as a lever. Kapoor was smaller than William.
The arm could not stand such torsion. With grim satisfaction William watched as the knife fell from his
hand and clattered to the floor. William kicked the
knife away and pushed him back against the wall,
where he slumped onto a stool. A terrible, consuming hatred flared in his eyes when he looked up at his
powerful assailant. He was defeated, he knew it, and
it came as a crushing blow.

'Why don't you finish me?' he hissed, breathing

shortly. 'While ever I am alive I will pose a threat to you and yours. This is a stay of execution, not a reprieve.'

The words were uttered with a hard, bright stare that seared William to the backbone. It was chilling, the way he said it so matter-of-factly. It worried William more than he showed, and he knew that Kapoor meant it. 'I am sorely tempted—and had I any sense I would. You have escaped your fate—and you have been a burden on my flesh from the moment I set foot on English soil. You sought to end Dhanu's life with nothing more than a fat purse from your sister—and the promise of more when the deed is done I don't doubt. I should tell you that Anisha has been banished. Apparently she is responsible for the death of the Rajah's brother and she is no longer in favour.'

The news brought Kapoor's head up sharp. 'Tipu is dead?'

William nodded. 'By your sister's hand. She was lucky to survive with her head intact. The Rajah has asked for Dhanu to be taken back to India and if he is harmed in any way his wrath will know no bounds.'

'Then what now? What will you do with me?'

'The constables will deal with you. You are in England now and subject to English law.'

'I have committed no crime.'

'Not through want of trying. In England I am a powerful man. I will see to it that you rot in gaol.' And he would. The resolve inside him was set like steel.

Kapoor smiled, a knowing smile, and his eyes became hooded, as if he held a secret. 'If you are able,' he said, his words holding a hidden meaning. 'Things happen when you least expect them to.'

William looked at him hard, wondering what he

meant by that. Unable to concentrate his mind on Kapoor any longer, he handed Archie a small pistol. 'Watch him. Shoot him if he tries anything.' William turned to Rosa, taking her arm and drawing her aside. 'You should go. Dhanu is safe now. There is nothing else you can do here.'

Rosa looked at him, her face set and white as she turned her eyes blazing anger and defiance on the man she held responsible. Without a bonnet and with her hair dishevelled and full of debris and streaks of grime on her face, she knew she must look a sight, but never had she been so uncaring of her appearance as she was then. Her emotions came rushing to the surface and the tension of the last few hours was released in one sweeping moment.

'How on earth did this happen?' she fumed. 'For goodness' sake, who is supposed to be looking after the child?'

William stiffened, brought up sharp by her words. 'He is in my charge,' he said, having recovered from the shock of Dhanu's disappearance and objecting to Rosa's accusing manner while trying to remain calm. But he had been negligent and he was shamed to the core.

'Precisely, and for that reason alone you should have more control over his movements.'

'I do realise the gravity of the situation. I admit I should have taken stronger action to keep him safe. I failed. You are right to put the blame on me. I knew my responsibilities and I should have taken better care of him. I have had so many commitments of late that I have neglected my duties. I should have honoured the pledge I made to Tipu.' His voice was harsh with self-recrimination. 'I promised him I would take care of Dhanu. I gave him my word and I broke it.'

Rosa found it somewhat satisfying that he experienced guilt, but it did not lessen her anger. 'Yes, you did. Thank goodness Aunt Clara made me aware of the situation and I managed to bring him home. But I do not want to be put in a situation again when I might have to save his life. It is your responsibility to do that. He was entrusted to your care. You have an obligation to take care of him. He has been through a dreadful ordeal today. Thankfully he appears to be unhurt. But when I think what those two men who followed him from India might have done to him—well—it doesn't bear thinking about.'

William's eyes narrowed and his expression tightened. 'How did Kapoor know where you were. What were they doing here?'

'Dhanu encountered them in the park and ran from them. It was fortunate that someone who looks out for destitute children on the city's streets found him and brought him to the institute. When he arrived he was a very frightened little boy. Indeed, he was so traumatised he could not speak. When my aunt told me a small Indian boy had been brought in I thought it could not possibly be Dhanu—I was horrified to find I was mistaken. Those men were watching the institute. They must have seen where he was taken. I shudder to think what might have happened had they got their hands on him.'

'Thank God,' he murmured hoarsely, overcome with emotion and putting a hand to his suddenly aching head. 'Hopefully everything will be all right now.'

Looking at him now, seeing how affected he was by

this whole sorry business and the death of his friend he had told her about, Rosa's attitude softened. 'Yes—yes it will,' she uttered. 'I—I am sorry to hear about your friend. You must feel his loss terribly.'

He nodded. 'Something like that. He was a good man. He did not deserve to die the way he did.'

Two burly constables appeared. William gave them an account of what had happened. 'I can rely on you see this man is put under lock and key?'

'Aye, sir—we'll see to it.'

After speaking to Beth, who was relieved the situation had been resolved with no one hurt, William and Rosa left the institute. He had almost reached the carriage when a haze appeared in front of his eyes and he stumbled.

He shook his head. What the devil was the matter with him? The night was dark and there was a haze that was thickening around him and voices came to him from down a long reverberating tunnel.

'William? Are you all right?' Rosa asked, having left the institute in his wake and seeing him sway and reach out to the wall for support.

He turned his head and looked at her. Suddenly there was something strange in his sensations and indescribably new. He seemed to be losing all identity. Trying to bring his mind back to the present he thought of the cut Kapoor's knife had inflicted on his hand and cursed. The confusion, the giddiness—the knife must have been dipped in one of Kapoor's concoctions. This was what Kapoor had been referring to when he had said—things happen. That had to be it. He shook his head to try and clear it, and looking through the haze he saw that Rosa was watching him closely, her eyes dark with concern. Her face swam before him and he heard her voice coming from somewhere a long way off.

'William? Speak to me. Are you ill? What is wrong with you?'

'Get me away from here, Rosa,' he managed to gasp, his words slurred. 'I don't care how you do it—but for God's sake get me to a bed. The knife—Kapoor's knife—something on it… A drug, poison—God only knows what it was. It's the only explanation I can think of. That damned Kapoor… I don't want anyone to—to see me like this… Take me somewhere—anywhere—soon…'

'A doctor. I must get a doctor to look at you.'

'Just get me to a bed… I have to lie down.'

Rosa was incredulous, but she felt the urgency of the situation. Shouting for Archie to help her, the two of them managed to get him to the carriage and inside. It was a long way to Grosvenor Square, the distance not so great to her aunt's house in Bloomsbury. In a state of indecision she looked at William. He suddenly became restless, pulling at his cravat as if it was too tight and muttering something unintelligible beneath his breath. The decision was made for her. On impulse she shouted to Archie to make for home.

Archie helped him out of the carriage and walked him to the door. 'Shall I come in with you, Miss Ingram?'

'No—no, Archie, I'll manage. He's still upright and seems able to walk—if unsteadily, although for how long I cannot say. I don't know what it is that's made him like this. Fetch Doctor Walsh, will you—Aunt Clara's doctor. Tell him it's the Earl of Ashurst and that he needs urgent attention. It's useless trying to talk sense to him while he's in this state. When you've fetched the doctor go to Grosvenor Square and inform them Lord Ashurst is here and for them not to be concerned. I am sure he will feel much improved in the morning, although I suspect he's going to have an enormous headache.'

Sick with dread, inside the house she did consider waking Mrs Loxley, the housekeeper, but her room was on another floor and at the back of the house. She was also a heavy sleeper—as was Dilys, who slept in the next room to Mrs Loxley. Her aunt and uncle were not expected back until the following afternoon. She turned to William, who was having to hold on the newel post to keep from falling over. Looking at his handsome face with his hair tumbling in disarray over his brow, at that moment she had no wish to dwell on what had made him so ill, or the sinister implications of it.

Time for that later, when she had got him to bed and the doctor had taken a look at him. Taking his arm she forced him to look at her. 'William, can you understand me?' He nodded, trying hard to concentrate on her face. 'We have to get upstairs so come along. I will show you to a room.'

William tried to allay her fears by pushing himself away from the newel post and, with difficulty keeping his eyes focused, he gripped the balustrade as he followed her up the stairs. Opening the door to one of the guest bedrooms, Rosa crossed to the window and closed the curtains before lighting a couple of candles. Turning to William, who was about to collapse onto the bed, she helped him out of his jacket before turning down the bedcovers. He had the presence of mind to remove his cravat and open the neck of his shirt before dropping onto the sheets. She removed his boots and stood looking down at his face, the sweep of his long lashes as they rested against his cheeks, the little creases at the corners of his mouth, the black hair curling on his brow. There was nothing more she could do.

Thankfully Doctor Walsh came straight away. He lost no time in examining William, lifting his eyelids and feeling his pulse. William moaned, muttering incoherently. The doctor looked at the cut on his hand. With Rosa's assistance he cleaned and dressed it. Seeming satisfied he stepped back.

'I don't think it's poison—there's no vomiting. I think it's probably a narcotic of some kind. Hopefully he'll sleep off the effects before morning. He should feel better by then—although his head will ache considerably.' Picking up his bag he walked to the door.

'Thank you for your time, Doctor Walsh. I'm most grateful.'

'Not at all. If he gets any worse send for me. I'll see myself out.'

Left alone with William, Rosa looked at his head resting against the pillows, his hair ruffled and his eyes closed. She was reluctant to leave him. Following all that had happened since finding Dhanu, all her senses were heightened and she was in a very strange mood.

As if he sensed her confusion, William's eyes flickered open. Raising his arm, he took hold of her hand, pulling her down until she was sitting on the bed facing him.

'Stay,' he whispered, raising her hand to his lips. 'Don't leave me.'

His lips were soft on the back of her hand. She did

not pull it away. His half-open eyes held hers like a
magnet, drawing her to him and doing strange things.
Suddenly she felt a throbbing heat creeping into her
body and everything began to change. She was not
immune to him. He was making her feel things she
didn't want to feel. An alarming, treacherous warmth
was creeping through her body. Dazed by the confusing messages her body was sending to her brain, and
afraid that if she didn't withdraw her hand things could
take a dangerous turn, she gently removed it from his
grasp and rose. Once again his eyes flickered closed
and he began to breathe deeply. In the partial darkness
of the room she stood perfectly still, gazing down at
him with trembling disquiet, mesmerised by the partial uncovering of his magnificent body. Her gaze caressed his strong shoulders, his open shirt revealing
the upper part of his furred chest.

Time seemed to stand still. She was conscious of
her increased pulse rate—due to her nervousness and
trepidation, no doubt—but what to make of the weakness in her legs and the warm, glowing feeling low in
her belly she truly did not know.

As if he sensed her continued presence, William's
eyes again flickered open. With some difficulty they
focused on the shape of the woman peering down at
him. Her features were indistinct. Through his confused, drug-clouded mind his thoughts strained for
clarity, but it was no use. Everything struck him as odd
and his brain refused to register things. But the memory of a face he adored fluttered through the caverns
of his mind like a butterfly and penetrated his torpor.

Somehow he managed to say, 'Rosa...'

Surprised to hear him speak her name, she whispered, 'Yes?'

His eyes gleamed bright. 'I want to hold you.'

She stared at him, wanting so much for him to do just that. When he reached out his hand she felt something stir within her—something she had never felt before. A flicker, a leaping, a reaching out. She found herself moving towards him, slowly, her eyes fastened to his.

Through the lingering effects of the drug clouding his brain, William drew her once more onto the bed so that she was half sitting, half lying beside him.

'Thank you for not leaving me,' he uttered hoarsely.

The closeness of her body whetted his appetite, and with a surge of lust and desire he wanted her—wanted to fill his mouth with the taste of her and draw those inviting hips beneath him.

Rosa studied him in the dim light. He was staring at her, breathing hard and fast, and behind the haze and confusion she saw in his eyes, mirroring her own, was hot, burning desire. It shook her to the core of her being. She wanted to feel the broad expanse of his chest pressed to hers, to kiss again those beautifully moulded lips. Looking into his half-shuttered eyes, she found her gaze held in a wilful hungry vice of blue. They had a fixed, unnatural brightness and were without expression. She knew that somewhere in his fuddled mind he knew who she was, but he didn't really see her. She shivered, but it was not from the cold. Suddenly she was warm—far too warm.

Something was happening to her. It was as if a spark had been lit that could not now be extinguished. A need was rising up inside her—a need to be close to this man, to wallow in the desire that had suddenly taken hold of her, to saturate herself in passion. Pulling her head down to his, he found her lips with his own, moving hungrily, twisting and demanding, warming her to the very core of her being. His tongue passed between her lips to probe and taste the honeyed sweetness within with a ferocity that drew a moan from her throat, breaking her resolve and lacerating her will, causing every one of her senses to erupt in a ball of flame.

Rosa knew she could not withstand his persuasive and unrelenting assault for long—and she knew what he was doing to her could be a prelude to other pleasures. At that moment she wanted to experience every one of them—and why shouldn't she? Encouraged by his mouth and his caress, the thought took root and began to grow. Desire swept through her, warm and hungry, gathering force until it became a storm of passion. An inner voice inside her head said, *This is wrong. It is not right—stop now before it is too late.* And yet she could not pull away from the grip of whatever had her as its prisoner. Nor did she want to.

The thought of what she was about to do flashed through her mind, but she rejected it quickly. There had been no vows said between her and William and there never would be. She knew it was a sin for a woman to give herself to a man in carnal lust outside wedlock and that she must learn to exercise the strictest discipline over the demands of the flesh. She had always regarded her virginity as something infinitely precious, but she hadn't realised that desire could be so powerful and all-consuming. The feelings she carried in her heart for William she could not put a name to, but he occupied her heart and mind. If she could just have this one night of happiness to remember, to savour and memorise in the years ahead, then surely God would forgive her this one weakness. She realised that in the cold light of dawn the pain of what she had done might be intolerable, but regardless of this and what came after, tonight she wanted to belong to him completely.

Shoving William's arms away, she stood up, pulling off her clothes until she was completely naked. Seeming to sense what she was doing, William sat up and rid himself of his shirt. His trousers proved to be more of a problem, but with Rosa's help he managed to remove them and flung them aside.

Rosa's hair tumbled down to her waist and her heart was pounding in her breast. Carried away by desire she lay beside him. Coming into contact with his flesh, she relaxed against him with the familiarity of the most successful courtesan, little realising the devastating effect her naked body had on him. He was vital and strong, all rippling sinews.

With desire burning fiercely in his veins, William held her to him, his arms strong and protective, his lips claiming hers. They were sweet and moist and parted eagerly beneath his own. Sliding his tongue between them, his arms tightening possessively around her, he groaned and his long-starved passions flared. Their bodies bent in the ardour of their embrace. The kisses became fierce and stirring, devouring and all-consuming.

'You are wanton, my love—and how perfect you are. I must have you.'

'Shh…' Rosa whispered against his lips in the warmest tone, thankful for the shadows that covered them both. Her body was burning and she wanted more of him. 'Don't talk.'

When she felt the bold, insistent pressure of his body she realised that the reckless path she had chosen was where she wished to go. He cupped her breast in his hand. She had never been touched like this by a man before and the feel of his hand almost melted her bones. It was when her thigh brushed the scorching heat of his manhood, throbbing with life, that she was shockingly made aware of her innocence.

Suddenly primeval fear mixed with the awesome pleasure of his body. Less sure of herself, she felt fear take over and panic set in. She shouldn't be doing this. It was wrong—totally wrong. She felt her body tightening, and she felt cold, as though her blood had turned to ice. She wanted to cry out, to tell him to stop and push him away, but having lost his sense of reality, with his mind reeling and filled with the scent of her, his lips were on her demanding more.

In desperation she tore herself free and rolled away from him. How could she possibly give herself over to him in his drugged state, when he would be unable to remember anything of what he had done? But, not to be cheated out of what he desired and what he believed she wanted to give, he laughed and pulled her back with a strength she had not thought possible. Her body was pale and lustrous, his hand moving up her calf warm, encircling her knee, then spreading and caressing her aching thighs. Sensing her capitulation, his ardour increased and he kissed and caressed her with a hunger he saw no reason to control. Covering her with his body, growing more purposeful, his hungering lips were insistent. With his mouth against her flesh his tongue teased the soft peak of her breast, his hand spreading, caressing the soft flesh of her inner thigh that began to tingle and to glow.

Like magic her fear was gone. Incapable of reason and drowning in a flood of pleasure, she felt her body respond as if she were another person. And though her mind told her this was wrong, lost in that wild and beautiful madness, her female body told her mind to go to the devil. Her body became alive with pleasure, unfolding like the petals of an exotic flower. Never in her imagination had she experienced anything so erotic as this. There was nothing she wanted more than to let herself go. What was happening to her? What was he doing to her? Every fibre, every pulse, every bone and muscle in her body came alive. All her senses became heightened and focused on William and what he was doing until nothing else mattered. A shuddering excitement swept through her and the strength ebbed from her limbs as his lips travelled over her flat belly, hips and thighs. She strained beneath him. They were entwined—and a burning pain exploded in her loins as the delicate softness was penetrated. She cried out softly and for a moment he stilled, locking his gaze with hers, until her body eased around him.

Joined with him in the most intimate way imaginable, crushed beneath his strength and able to feel the beat of his heart against her breast, Rosa became aware of a sense of fullness as he plunged deep within her. With lips and bodies merged in a fiery fusion, she gasped. His hungering mouth searched her lips and he kissed her with a slow thoroughness, savouring each moment of pleasure before beginning to move.

And then she felt something new and incredible as she began to respond to his inner heat.

Never would she have believed that she could feel such fierce pleasure, nor that she could respond so brazenly as she yielded, giving all her desire and passion, as if an ancient, primitive force were controlling her, driving her on. Operating wholly on instinct since her wits had flown long since, she craned her neck back and her fingers laced through his thick hair as she abandoned herself to his lips, his hands. They were no longer two separate entities, but one being. Then his control shattered and, as though he were seeking a much-needed release for his mind and body, he claimed her fully, filling her with an urgent desire until he collapsed completely, his shuddering release over.

Still in a drug-induced state and unable to keep at bay the oncoming forces of sleep, with his rock-hard body glistening with sweat, William drifted away in a heavy slumber, losing all contact with reality and the young woman in his arms.

Rosa was aware of nothing but an immense, incredible joy, beyond which nothing was comparable. Her body was aglow, her limbs weighted with contentment. Sated and deliciously exhausted, her body and lips tender from his caresses, she slipped away from him. Gathering her clothes in her arms, she crept to the door and let herself out.

Chapter Nine

William opened his eyes and closed them quickly when pain stabbed through his eye sockets. He tried lifting his head, but there was a regiment of soldiers tramping through his skull. Completely disorientated, he lay without moving. He tried to remember the events of the night before that had rendered him senseless.

He remembered being at the institute with Rosa and Dhanu. Kapoor was there. He remembered the constables coming and taking him away and very little after that.

Images presented themselves one after another, pictures vibrant and strange. Dear God, what had possessed him? Carefully opening his eyes, he glanced about the room, seeing his clothes strewn over a chair, forcing himself to remember, to concentrate on certain things. Rosa's face came to mind. Had she brought him here? Yes, he remembered climbing the stairs—and there was something else he had to resurrect, something to do with Rosa, something that was deliciously warm and passionate. Images of what had happened between them began to infiltrate his mind, images of how, even in his drugged state, he had made love to her. A mixture of incredulity and amazement worked slowly across his face. His heart pounding with disbelief, he experienced a wrenching pain of unbearable guilt and a profound feeling of self-loathing. Had she given herself willingly—in all truth he really could not remember—or had he forced himself on her? If he had, then how could he ever forgive himself? In a fit of lust he had robbed that beautiful, laughing girl of her innocence.

Rosa had informed Mrs Loxley of Lord Ashurst's presence. She was clearly shocked to learn that Miss Ingram had brought a gentleman back to the house and allowed him to stay without her aunt and uncle's permission, but apart from a few disapproving tuts she kept her opinions to herself. When Lord Ashurst appeared on the stairs and asked to see Miss Ingram, she directed him to the drawing room.

When he entered, Rosa rose from her chair by the window, where she had been flicking through some magazines. Surprisingly calm, she looked at him for a long moment, her face serene. All the way down the stairs he had been rehearsing in his mind what he would say to her and now he was with her he couldn't remember a thing.

'Good morning, William,' she said, moving closer to him, trying to maintain a strong semblance of control while feeling somewhat weakened and vulnerable after what had happened between them. When she looked at the harsh, lean planes of his face, his jaw set and rigid, a vision of the tumble of dark hair against the white sheets, and the long, powerful limbs sprawled alongside her own invaded her mind. The growing ache in her heart attested to the degree of her feelings, of her love. To her at that moment, never had he looked so handsome—so unattainable. 'How are you feeling this morning? Better, I hope, now the effects of the drug have worn off.'

'All things considered, I am remarkably well,' he assured her drily, fixing her with a level stare, 'for a man who has made love to a woman and is unable to recall little of the incident. Do you mind telling me what happened last night?'

'Don't you remember?'

'Some of it and I have to tell you that it does nothing for my male ego, my self-esteem or my pride. Only the remembrance that the woman I made love to was passionate, warm and responsive acts as a balm of sorts. You are right, I was drugged, that I do know. Why did you not take me to Grosvenor Square?'

'I brought you here because you told me you didn't want anyone to see you in that state. You were most adamant. Besides, you were on the verge of total collapse. This house was much closer than Grosvenor Square and I thought while you were able to walk at least I could get you into the house and put you to bed. Archie fetched Aunt Clara's doctor to take a look at you. He was certain you had been administered a narcotic of some kind and that you would sleep it off.'

'I see. You have gone to a lot of trouble. I am grateful.' Remembering that this was what had happened he looked at her in appalled silence as a vague memory of this woman, naked and warm with desire lying in his arms, took shape in his memory. 'When I awoke this morning to a small degree I was still under the influence of the narcotic. I was in a somewhat nebulous state. My memory of the night was unclear, with disjointed, faceless shadows flitting about in my mind. I was certainly not myself so tell me exactly what happened.' When she didn't reply his voice was quiet and controlled when he spoke. 'You *did* stay with me, didn't you?'

Inhaling deeply and raising her chin a notch, she nodded. 'Yes.'

'Did you have control over what so obviously happened between us?'

'Some.' A little smile played on her lips. 'You can be very persuasive.'

'Did I hurt you?'

Rosa considered his question. Her body ached and still throbbed with a strange kind of tenderness. But she had wanted him to make love to her and he had been as eager as she had been—even if he couldn't remember any of it. 'You didn't hurt me.'

'There was a trace of blood on the sheets. You were a virgin.'

Rosa winced at the fierce tone of his voice. 'Yes. Does it matter?'

A muscle flexed in his jaw. 'It does—to me. It should also matter to you.'

'Please don't feel any sense of guilt.'

'How do you expect me to feel? I have wronged you—dishonoured you.'

'I don't feel in the least wronged or dishonoured. If that is how you feel, then that is unfortunate and for you to deal with. You needn't worry. I have no intention of demanding that you do the honourable thing.'

'Do you bear malice towards me—for what I did before? Is that why you remained with me last night.'

'Malice?'

Briefly Rosa closed her eyes. It was painful to re-count his rejection of her, especially when she had become so accustomed to burying her thoughts—or trying, for no matter how hard she had tried she had not succeeded. Secretly she had missed him more than she would have believed possible, for how could she ever forget how volatile and rakishly good-looking this man was. She recalled the pain she had felt when told the wedding would not take place, the hurt and humili-ation of it. Never again would she allow herself to be so treated. Besides, how could she be certain of any-thing with Lady Willoughby hovering in the wings?

Reaching deep inside herself, she pushed thoughts of his rejection away. Thinking like this served no pur-pose. 'I don't bear malice. I can understand why you did what you did and as far as I am concerned it is over.'

'And you are sure about that, are you? Don't you think that what happened between us last night has changed matters somewhat?'

'What are you saying—that you have had a change of heart and will marry me now?'

'The way I see it we have no choice.'

'I disagree. I do have a choice and I see no reason for us to marry.'

'And if there is a child from our union? What then?'

Dear Lord! Rosa had not thought of that. Her hand immediately went to her abdomen and something stirred inside her—a wistful hope and fear. 'I will not have my destiny or that of my child—if there is one—

dictated by circumstance.' As she made a move to turn away, he reached out and placed a hand on her arm. Looking down at his hand, she shook her arm free. 'Please don't touch me.'

William dropped his hand as if he had been burned.

'I think you should leave now, William.'

She crossed the room and opened the door, only to find it slammed shut when William came up behind her with the sure-footed skill of a panther. She stood there, anchored between his strong arms. Unable to turn, she could feel his closeness, the muscular hardness of him, the vibrant heat of his body pressed close against her back and his warm breath on her hair. She didn't move as he shoved her hair aside and ran a finger down the back of her neck, trailing it round to her chin and along the smooth curve of her jaw. It was a smoothing caress that awoke tingling answers in places she tried to ignore.

The betrayal of her body aroused vexation in her. His touch burned her flesh and seared into her heart, reminding her how deeply she had come to love this insufferable man. It was a hard fact for her pride to accept, especially after he had rejected her so coldly. She trembled as she felt his mouth on the soft warm flesh on the back of her neck. Her heart was pounding and for a moment she was tempted to turn and let him capture her lips with his own, but she must not. She must be strong.

'Please don't do this,' she said tightly, trying to control the beat of her heart, which was thundering in her ears.

'Why? The damage is done, Rosa. What are you afraid of?'

You, her mind screamed. *You, and what I might let you do to me.*

William had come to London to try to win her back and he was not prepared to let her go so easily—especially not after what had happened between them last night. With desire crashing through him in waves, he looked down at her bent head, his lips brushing her shining hair. Slipping an arm about her waist, he drew her tight against him, feeling a shimmering tremor in her slender body.

'This is a mistake. Take your hands off me and don't ever touch me again.'

'Don't fight me, Rosa. You are emotional.'

'I am not emotional. I am angry, while you are the most ill-mannered, arrogant, inconsiderate man I have ever encountered,' she upbraided him coldly, 'and I thank my lucky stars that I did not become your wife. Now please do as I ask and let me go.' Without waiting for him to do so, she violently thrust his hand away.

William's eyes narrowed and his lips tightened. Reluctantly he stepped back. 'I dare say I am all you accuse me of being. It goes with the title.'

Rosa was in no mood to be mocked and when she turned to face him she could see by the gleam in his eyes that he was doing exactly that. 'Then with you as an example, I can only hope that Dhanu will soon be back in India. When you left me in Berkshire I fervently hoped and prayed I would never have the misfortune to set eyes on you again. Unfortunately that did not happen. Despite what has happened between us, nothing has changed. Such an outward display of temperamental frustration I regard as a sign of ill breeding...'

'I think I have the picture,' William drawled.

'Good. Then I needn't go on—but how I wish I'd never come to England and met you.'

William's eyes, which had been soft and full of passion a moment before, now held a feral gleam. 'Really! How easily those words trip off your tongue and how ready you are to insult me. Perhaps I am an uncivilised being marked by the life I have led in India—but how would you know what such a being is like, raised as you have been in the privileged, cocooned world of genteel drawing rooms you have inhabited all your life. Trained as a soldier, I do all manner of things you would call ungentlemanly and ill bred, things you disapprove of. And you are the most infuriatingly outspoken woman I have ever met. How dare you say these things to me— things you know nothing about?'

Rosa's eyes sparked with anger as she faced him. 'I did not realise when I brought you here last night instead of taking you to Grosvenor Square that you would be unable to control your inner cravings and seduce me after casting me off so brutally.'

'For which I apologise—although it would appear that in no way did you object to being seduced. You could have walked away, but you chose not to. Where Dhanu is concerned, I thank you for everything you have done for him. He became very attached to you in Berkshire and has missed you not being there. In future I shall make sure he is kept safe, so you need not concern yourself.'

'Not concern myself?' Her face became suffused with fury. 'How can you say that to *me*? Of course it concerns me. Had I not been present on the two pre-

vious occasions—the first when he almost fell foul of those two assassins—he would be dead now.'

William looked at the proud beauty who was glaring at him like an enraged angel of retribution and realised that she was on the brink of tears. His conscience smote him. 'I know he would,' he said softly.

Desperate to get away from him before she broke down and made a complete fool of herself, without another word she turned and opened the door, waiting for him to pass through.

In deep reflection William stood perfectly still, unable to believe the tempestuous, brave young woman who had stood up to him so proudly. Her stormy eyes were shining with unshed tears. He felt a consuming, unquenchable need to see her again soon when her ire had died down, to put things right between them. His attraction to her was disquieting. He was unable to put her from his mind. The sweet fragrance of her perfume lingered everywhere, drifting through his senses, and the throbbing hunger began anew.

He walked slowly to the door, where he turned and looked back at her.

'Would it make things easier for you if I were to tell you that I am in love with you?'

She was thrown completely off guard and everything in Rosa's world halted. Her shock and surprise were genuine. Dumbstruck, she stared at him. The declaration hung in the air between them as the blood pounded in her ears with all the force of a summer storm.

'Oh!' was all she could think of to say. He couldn't possibly mean it. Could he? 'Are you really?'

'Absolutely,' he assured her, in such a matter-of-fact voice that she could be forgiven for doubting it.

'I—I am shocked. I—don't know what to say.'

'You don't?' He laughed softly. 'You surprise me. I've never known you to be lost for words.'

'But when— How?' She gave him a sceptical look. 'You—you are not joking?'

'No, Rosa, I am not joking. I do love you—quite desperately, in fact. When I thought I'd lost you it was a terrible feeling. I love you. I love you with my whole life.'

She looked at him hard, trying to read what was in his eyes. His words and his expression filled her with such confusion that she was forced to look away.

With a little smile playing on his lips, he turned from her and strode across the hall.

'Where are you going?' she asked, taking a hesitant step forward.

'Home.'

'Home? But—you can't say something like that and then just leave.'

'I can and I will. Think about it, about what I said. I told you, you are as stubborn as a mule, so stop kicking. I know you feel the same as I do—I felt it when I held you in my arms, so don't spend too much time on analysis and dissection. Follow your heart, Rosa, and not your head. I know my declaration has taken you by surprise and I am willing to wait for what I want from you—which has nothing to do with your wealth. I always get what I want in the end.'

To find herself tongue-tied had never been part of Rosa's character. William's unexpected declaration had changed everything. It had toppled her precarious assurance and with it all the judgements she had made of this man who said he loved her. With a small gasp she covered her mouth with the back of her hand and looked away, but not before she had caught the smile on his face and observed him raise an amused eyebrow at her confused image.

She stared at the closed door for a long time after he had gone. Had he been serious? What on earth made him think that he loved her? Such a declaration she had never imagined she would hear from him and she was unsure how to respond. Nothing had prepared her for this and she was as afraid of her own feelings as much as his. With him there would be no reserve on her part, no subterfuge for the sake of self-preservation.

What was she to do? Everything lacked reality. How should she deal with this? Her mind returned to the period between his kiss at Ashurst Park and him coming to tell her that he would not marry her. How happy she had been then, having discovered feelings for him and could live in the hope of her feelings being returned. Those days and all her hopes had fallen to ashes. Suspicion had taken place of hopes and dreams, suspicion that came in the form of Lady Caroline Willoughby.

But if he was in love with her, Rosa, she must have been completely mistaken about that?

Rosa's aunt and uncle returned home shortly after midday. Mrs Loxley was quick to inform Rosa's aunt about Lord Ashurst's visit and was surprised when her employer appeared to be extremely pleased by his night-time visit instead of being shocked. Clara immediately sought out her niece, who seemed somewhat preoccupied. She carefully considered the strained smile Rosa had pasted on her delicately structured face. As much as she made the pretence, her niece couldn't hide the effect that Lord Ashurst's visit had had on her.

'Tell me what happened last night, Rosa. Under what circumstances did you feel compelled to invite him to stay here?'

Rosa was still reeling from William's incredible confession, trying to analyse it, afraid to hope and unable not to. Drawing a long breath, she began telling her aunt some of what had transpired—about Dhanu and the two men, how one had escaped and the other was arrested, and how Lord Ashurst had come to be drugged—but she did not tell her what had transpired between them after that.

'What made you bring him here? Why not go on to Grosvenor Square?'

'He—he didn't want anyone to see him in that state—and your house was much closer.'

'And yet you managed to get him up the stairs.'

Rosa lowered her gaze lest her aunt saw the truth in her eyes. She must not know that anything improper had occurred. 'Yes. He—he passed out almost immediately. Archie fetched Dr Walsh to examine him. He was convinced he'd been administered a narcotic and that he would sleep it off.'

'And this morning? How did he seem?'

'If he was still suffering the effects of the drug, then he gave no indication of it. So much has happened that I could never have believed would happen.' Her aunt was silent and attentive as she told her about William's declaration of love. 'I've asked myself what it can possibly mean. He seems to have had a complete change of heart and it's left me so confused I don't know what to think.'

'It's quite incredible, I agree. Did he propose marriage?'

'I don't think he would have told me he loved me if that was not what he intended.'

'I think you are right, but I remember how angry you were when he called off the wedding.'

'Of course I was. But since he left me earlier, I've had cause to scrutinise and analyse my feelings. One thing that has become clear to me is that my initial outrage was due to wounded pride and humiliation rather than injured virtue. Does that make sense to you?'

Clara returned her smile with understanding and settled herself more comfortably in her chair. She suspected Rosa hadn't told her everything, that there were some things she preferred to keep to herself. 'So where does Lady Willoughby fit into the picture?'

'I no longer think she does. I might have been mistaken where she is concerned.'

'What will your answer be if Lord Ashurst proposes marriage? Will you be prepared to give him a second chance?'

Rosa sighed deeply. 'In truth, Aunt Clara, I don't know.'

'Then what are your feelings with regard to him?'

Relenting, Rosa sighed deeply and confided some of the thoughts that were beginning to trouble her. 'In the beginning he saw me as little more than a means of paying his debts and financially securing his future. Now there is no longer money involved—truly— I have no idea how I feel. But what I do know is that there is something between us that seems to draw us together. He fills me with such confusion that I do not know what to think. He has a habit of encroaching on my thoughts when I least expect it.'

As the days slowly slipped by, much to Rosa's surprise and impatience and apprehension there was no word from William. A gold-embossed card arrived from Lady Willoughby. It was an invitation to Mr and Mrs Swinburn and their niece Rosa Ingram to attend a ball at Willoughby House, Lady Willoughby's mansion in Piccadilly.

Since coming to London Rosa had frequently attended parties at the houses of her aunt's friends, but this was her first ball. She was apprehensive and voiced her reluctance to attend to her aunt.

'William is bound to be there. Not having seen or heard from him since he left the house that morning, I am reluctant to come face-to-face with him at such a public occasion.'

'Of course you can. Besides, my instinct tells me Lord Ashurst might have had something to do with us being invited. To be invited to such an important occasion is an honour and a privilege and a true mark of distinction, for Lady Willoughby is only ever seen in the choicest circles and her friendship with prominent members of royalty means that her invitations are not to be refused. You must attend.'

Taking her courage in both hands, Rosa gave in, but she was uneasy.

It was at a soirée Rosa was attending with her aunt when she next saw Lady Willoughby. Rosa was about to rise from the sofa where she had been taking a quiet moment when Lady Willoughby put out a bejewelled hand and stopped her, her shrewd eyes assessing her from a tranquil face.

'Please don't get up, my dear,' she said, perching herself next to her. 'I saw you arrive with your aunt and I've been waiting for the opportunity to speak to you all evening. I'm so pleased you are to attend the ball I am giving before returning to Berkshire. William will be there, which should please you.'

Rosa stared at her. 'I—I beg your pardon?'

Lady Willoughby laughed her deep warm laugh and patted Rosa's hand. 'Forgive me, my dear. I do tend to be frightfully outspoken—too outspoken, my husband was always telling me, but that is my way. I know William quite well—from the days when he came from India to stay at Ashurst Park. He is always appreciative of a beautiful woman. The way he looks at you with particular interest tells me he has singled you out. In fact, you are the first woman he has shown a serious interest in since that unfortunate affair in India. You know about that?'

'Yes—he did tell me.'

'You will be good for him. You are just what he needs.'

'I—I'm sorry, Lady Willoughby, but...'

Lady Willoughby must have followed the thread of thoughts on her face, for she smiled knowingly. 'If it is any consolation to you, I know that William is very much attracted by you. I also know the two of you were to marry before you left for London.'

'He—he told you?'

'Oh, no, not William. The vicar of Ashurst—who was to perform the ceremony. I will not ask you what

happened—that is your affair—but when I saw you together in Hyde Park I could see there was something
between the two of you still.' Tilting her head to one
side, she said, 'You are in love with him, aren't you,
my dear?'

Rosa stared at her mutely, and Lady Willoughby
could read, by the sudden colour that sprang to her
cheeks and the confusion in her eyes, that she had hit
upon the truth.

'You can rely on me not to let what you say go beyond these four walls, if that is what's worrying you.'

Yes, Rosa thought, she could trust Lady Willoughby.
She liked her and felt comfortable with her, as though
she had known her all her life. It wasn't difficult to see
why William valued her friendship.

'I do love him, Lady Willoughby.'

'I thought as much—although I don't think he is
an easy man to love. Unlike many men of William's
background, he is a private man and stays away from
frivolous intrigues, even though several ladies have
made their availability known to him. When Charles
died so tragically, William was quite beside himself
with grief. It will take him a long time to get over what
happened and to adjust to his new life. Charles was a
highly likable young man, although somewhat wayward. He was the life and soul at any event, but he had
a weakness for gambling and lost a considerable sum
of his inheritance at the tables.'

'Why are you telling me this, Lady Willoughby?'
Rosa asked, her face impassive.

'Because you are different and I like you. Raised
in the Caribbean you do not altogether understand the
way of things here or society as we do. In that you and

William are alike—and I suspect he is in love with you. William is my dear friend as well as my neighbour, and I do so want him to be happy with the right woman—especially after what happened to Charles. He needs a woman by his side to share the burden of restoring Ashurst Park to what it was. My instinct and my judgement—which is hardly ever wrong—tells me that you are that woman, Miss Ingram.'

Realising that she had misunderstood William's relationship with Lady Willoughby, Rosa smiled. 'Thank you for saying that.' She lowered her eyes, a faint flush mantling her cheeks. 'And now I feel that I must beg your forgiveness. You see—I—I thought that you... that you and William were...'

'What?' What Rosa thought dawned on Lady Willoughby, which she clearly thought was hilarious. When she stopped laughing she sat back and took a deep, fortifying breath. 'Oh, my dear, how wrong you were—and quite naïve,' she said, not unkindly. 'I am far too old for William—although with one husband and a string of lovers behind me, I am easily tempted by a handsome face. At this present time my passions are directed to Lord Frampton—who is much older than me but he has a marvellous sense of humour, shares my passion for horses and is dangling his fortune before me like a carrot to a donkey.'

Rosa found herself laughing. 'You are quite incorrigible, Lady Willoughby.'

'I agree with you,' she said, getting to her feet. 'I have a dreadful habit of stepping forward instead of back. I have been incapable of learning by experience to conduct my life in less turbulent waters. Goodbye, my dear, and I am so looking forward to seeing both you and William at my ball.'

Rosa watched her cross the room to join a group of ladies, strangely touched by her concern for her well-being. Her words had dispelled any notions she had that she and William's relationship was anything other than platonic.

The night of the ball finally arrived. Rosa spent a great deal of time over her appearance, having sat for what seemed to be hours before the dressing-table mirror as Dilys swept her hair up into intricate, tantalising curls and teasing soft tendrils over her ears. Her gown was a dream of pale lemon chiffon, with a low bodice displaying more of her swelling breasts than she thought was proper, but her aunt didn't appear to think so. With a twinkle in her eyes she smiled with undisguised approval as Rosa fastened a diamond necklace around her throat and drop diamonds danced in her lobes, diamonds that had once belonged to Rosa's mother.

Fingering them lovingly, Rosa smiled at her reflection. 'Do you not think the diamonds are a little extravagant, Aunt Clara? Young, unmarried ladies don't usually wear diamonds.'

'No, Rosa.' Clara's eyes were sparkling with admiration as she looked at her niece. Her beauty was something to behold. 'You must wear them. After all, what is the point of having beautiful things if they are to be kept hidden away? A necklace of such beauty should be seen and appreciated and tonight is such a grand occasion, don't you agree? Now come along. Michael is impatient to see you in your finery. He will be so proud to escort such a beautiful woman on his arm. You look breathtaking. Why, look at you—daring, elegant and special, and so lovely. Any man, even one in his dotage, who sees you tonight, looking as you do, will surely find his heart going into its final palpitations.'

Laughing lightly, Rosa stood up and kissed her aunt tenderly on the cheek. 'Two beautiful ladies, Aunt Clara,' she said, looking fondly at her aunt attired in a gown of saffron silk and gold lace.

The preparations complete, they went downstairs to join Michael. He watched his two favourite ladies descend the staircase and the vision of loveliness he beheld made his heart swell with pride. When they were summoned to the coach Dilys carefully folded Rosa's velvet cloak about her shoulders. Despite her apprehension at seeing William—for she was certain he would be there—she was excited and light-hearted. It promised to be a glittering occasion.

The celebrated parties and balls given by Lady Willoughby when she was in town were typical of the London social scene, helping to draw some of the gentry from their country estates. Tonight's ball was to be a lavish and grand affair, with the cream of London society invited. The mansion was ablaze with lights and the roads around it crowded with vehicles. Footmen in powdered wigs and crimson and gold livery, bearing torches, met the guests and escorted them up the front steps to the house. Enormous bouquets of sweet-scented flowers in tall stands were placed around the hall.

From his vantage point on the gallery overlooking the hall, William lounged against a pillar and watched

Rosa arrive with her aunt and uncle. He smiled to himself, a mischievous, calculating smile, a smile those who knew him would be wary of. She was a cool vision of poised womanhood and undeniably the most lovely young woman he had seen.

As if sensing his eyes upon her, pushing back her hood Rosa looked up and saw him. His gaze slid slowly over her face. He inclined his head towards her, feeling an instant response to her beauty, her femininity, seeing how the light from the many candles lit up her hair like a silken sheath as she passed gracefully inside.

Caught in the spell of those compelling blue eyes, Rosa could not look away from him. He had given her two weeks to consider his declaration of love. Now she was faced with him she was overcome with relief and a strange light-heartedness, her fears and uncertainties vanishing like the morning mist. She paused a moment before following her aunt and uncle to where Lady Willoughby stood in the centre of the hall greeting her guests, continuing to look up at him. Holding her eyes with his own, a strange smile playing on his lips, he didn't move an inch.

He was attired in an exquisitely tailored claret jacket and pristine white cravat, the whiteness emphasising his dark, lean features. The meeting was more difficult than Rosa had anticipated. So much time had elapsed since she had last seen him—the events of that meeting, of their loving and how he had left her after telling her he loved her, still vividly clear in her mind.

Dragging her eyes away from his, after handing her cloak to a servant she proceeded to join her aunt and uncle to be received by Lady Willoughby, but she could not stem the wave of happiness that swept over her, making her forget the doubts that had assailed her during their time apart, driving out the anxieties. She yielded to the sudden temptation to let herself enjoy the evening, which already held the promise of enchantment.

Full of vibrancy and a striking presence, Lady Willoughby was full of smiles as she received them. 'Good evening, Mr Swinburn—Mrs Swinburn,' she said in her deep, throaty voice, her eyes beaming a welcome to Rosa. 'And Miss Ingram. How nice of you to honour us with your company. I am so delighted you were able to attend.'

'Thank you for inviting us, Lady Willoughby,' Uncle Michael said, inclining his head as he took his hostess's outstretched gloved hand.

They climbed the wide staircase to the grand ballroom, with its highly polished parquet floor, Venetian mirrors and crystal chandeliers. Between the long French windows opening on to a balcony were huge urns on pedestals, bursting with a profusion of flowers. Elegant gilt chairs were placed at intervals along the walls. Footmen passed among the guests with salvers of champagne. Inside the supper room tables were laden with an amazing feast—a riot of plenty to be eaten off Sèvres plates and wine to be drunk from Venetian glasses. The whole was an elaborate display, exquisitely beautiful, for this ball being given by Lady Caroline Willoughby.

Rosa was dazzled by the fashionable company, recognising several faces from her drives through the park and visits to private drawing rooms with Aunt Clara. She felt a sudden shyness on joining these distinguished, sophisticated members of society—this gay, rakish and exclusive set who graced the echelons of London society. Looking like a vision from heaven, she entered the ballroom on her uncle's arm and almost immediately drew the attention of most of those present.

Michael gently squeezed her hand in the crook of his arm, sensing her hesitance. 'Don't be nervous, my dear. Within no time at all your dance card will be full. But make sure you save a dance for me. I do declare this is going to be the most enjoyable evening I've had in a long time.'

He was proved right. Within minutes Rosa's dance card was almost full, although she was disappointed that there was no sign of William. Laughter and frivolity surrounded her and she found herself responding to it automatically. It was during her second dance, her partner a flamboyant young lord with an impudent grin, when she next saw William standing on the edge of the ballroom. She could feel his presence with every fibre of her being and an increasing comforting warmth suffused her. A strange sensation of security, of knowing he was close at hand, pleased her.

On his way to the ballroom William had been accosted by some friends and acquaintances, one after another eager, male and female, demanding his attention, which had prevented him from seeking Rosa out. He had watched her take to the floor with her partner and his heart wrenched when he looked on her unforgettable face, so poised, so lovely that he ached to hold her. Her whole presence seemed to blaze across the ballroom at him, eliminating all else.

Clara had watched him from the moment he had

entered the ballroom. Countless young women vied for his attention all the time. Lord Ashurst, she noted, treated them with amused tolerance, for his attention was on only one female.

'Lord Ashurst is here, Rosa,' she murmured to her niece when she concluded her dance. 'He looks at you a great deal.'

Rosa glanced in his direction. She saw his head above the crowd and instinctively knew he was looking for her. When his eyes locked on to hers and he smiled, a lazy cocksure smile, she felt her heart turn over exactly as it always did when he looked at her. She saw the glow in his half-shuttered eyes kindle slowly into flame and deep within her she felt the answering stirrings of longing, a longing to feel the tormenting sweetness of his embrace and the stormy passion of his kiss.

She watched the tall, daunting, devastatingly handsome man head in her direction with a feeling of anticipation, not in the least surprised when the throng parted before him like the Red Sea before Moses.

After politely greeting her aunt and uncle, he settled his attention on Rosa. 'As you do not appear to be taken for this dance, I wonder if I might—'

'Oh—but my next dance is with Uncle Michael.'

'I don't think he will mind if I steal you away,' he said, looking to her uncle for permission.

Michael laughed. 'You have my full permission, Lord Ashurst. You will make my niece a far better partner than I.' He looked at his wife, holding out his hand. 'Clara—shall we?'

Rosa watched as the two of them swept onto the floor. At the same time William slipped a hand beneath her arm to whisk her into the dance as the orchestra struck up a waltz.

'Come. I would have this dance with you before you are swept away by yet another overzealous swain.'

On the dance floor Rosa abandoned her waist to his encircling arm. It was as steady and firm as a rock. He held her close to his firm body, closer than was proper, she thought, but she could not have objected if she wanted to. Feeling as if she were in a dream, she placed her gloved hand in his and looked up at him as he whirled her round with a relaxed grace. He was a superb dancer. As he spun her into the dance she seemed to soar with the melody. It was as if they were one being, their movements perfectly in tune.

They danced in silence for a few moments, a silence in which William noted the strange lights dancing in her shining hair and her slender shoulders gleaming with a soft, creamy lustre. 'You look ravishing,' he murmured. 'And this is pleasant, is it not, Rosa?'

Feeling his arm tighten about her, Rosa looked into his eyes. 'Do you usually snatch your partners away from their chaperons in that way?'

He raised one well-defined eyebrow, looking down at her. A faint half-smile played on his lips as if he knew exactly what was going on in her mind. 'Only when I think they might need rescuing.'

'And what made you think I might needed rescuing?'

'Come now, Rosa. Admit you would rather be dancing with me than your uncle. Besides, I could not resist the opportunity to dance with you—the most beautiful woman in the room.' His hooded eyes captured hers. 'So, have I given you enough time to consider what I confessed to you on our last meeting?' he asked, twirling her round.

'Yes—although I'm disappointed that you left it so long to see me,' she admitted, feeling the music possessing her as her body moved to the melody, melting into him.

'Can you not now agree that if we are to get to know each other on more intimate terms,' he went on, lowering his head so that his mouth was very close to her ear, 'it should allow us privileges above the usual stilted decorum of strangers.'

'But you and I are not strangers, are we?'

'Have you missed me?' he asked.

Gazing up at him, she was happy to see his eyes were serious and devoid of his usual arrogance. His question and the anticipation of her answer was warmly evocative when he spoke and she felt as if she were dissolving inside when those soft, mellow tones caressed her senses. She wanted to tell him that she had missed him more than she would have believed possible, that she had missed his presence, his quiet strength, his lazy smile and the way he was looking at her now.

'Yes,' she admitted softly, feeling his warm breath fan her cheek, which was almost her undoing. 'After saying what you did, when you left me I was so confused I didn't know what to think. Before I left Berkshire, when you came to tell me you were not going to marry me after all, I was too hasty to have you gone. I'm sorry. I was hurt and upset, but I realise now I should have given you the opportunity to explain in more detail why you had changed your mind.'

'I should have made the opportunity. I should have

told you. I should have made you listen. I want to explain everything to you—when the music ends I will.'

'Thank you. I would like that.'

'You are not still angry with me?'

'Why? Should I be? I know I said things—we both said things...'

'Forget them. It was a misunderstanding. A silly, pointless misunderstanding. Everyone says things they don't mean in the heat of the moment—and as I recall,' he murmured, a spark of laughter in his eyes, 'the temperature was definitely heated on one particular occasion that I strive to recall all the pleasurable details.'

Rosa flushed and her heart began to throb in deep, aching beats. The reminder of that night she had lain in his arms, his touch, had been branded on her memory with a clarity that set her body aflame. She raised her eyes to his, seeing them darken and his expression gentle. 'How could I possibly forget.'

William's lips curved in a soft, satisfied smile and tenderness washed through him at the sincere honesty of her reply. 'As an experienced man of the world I never would have believed that I would fall victim to a beautiful, innocent young woman who has the power to amuse, enchant, bewitch and infuriate me as no other woman has done before.'

The tenderness in William's eyes warmed Rosa's heart.

'You dance divinely, by the way.'

'So my two partners have told me.'

'Saucy minx,' he murmured, smiling.

'And you dance very well, too.'

'Praise indeed,' he quipped, sweeping her into another dizzying whirl.

Content to let the music carry them along, they fell silent. Rosa gazed up at William's achingly handsome face and into his bold, hypnotic eyes, lost in her own thoughts, before she realised that his gaze had dropped to her lips and his arm tightened around her waist, drawing her against the hard rack of his chest.

'Don't look at me like that unless you want me to kiss you, Rosa,' he murmured huskily, his eyes dark with passion.

Rosa's cheeks burned. The reminder of his kiss, his touch, had been branded on her memory with a clarity that set her body aflame. She raised her eyes to his, seeing them darken and his expression gentle.

'You, my love, are blushing.'

'Any female would blush when you say the things you do and look at them like that. Please stop it, William. People will notice.'

'Then let us go somewhere more private.'

Before Rosa knew what was happening, William had deftly danced her through one of the French windows on to the balcony, drawing her away from the light and standing close beside her near the balustrade. Warning bells began ringing inside her head, telling her of the impropriety of being on the balcony alone with him, but she felt far too light-hearted and happy to object and refused to listen to them.

Chapter Ten

Appreciating the feel of the cool air on her face, Rosa breathed deeply, aware that William was watching her.

'H-how is Dhanu?' she asked, breaking the silence that had fallen between them. 'Has he got over what happened to him?'

'Yes—which is surprising.' His expression became grave. 'Unfortunately the constables had to let Kapoor go.'

'What? But—but why? I don't understand.'

'They had nothing on which to hold him. There's not a scrap of evidence against him. He had done nothing to justify arrest. Kapoor said he and his friend were walking in the street on that night when they encountered you and Dhanu. He told them that when the barrels toppled over they went to offer their assistance, but their actions were misconstrued. Fearful of being arrested, his friend—always of a nervous disposition—ran from the scene. Apparently he hasn't been seen since—although as a foreigner becoming lost in the murky underworld of St Giles, anything could have befallen him.'

'I see. And—and now what? Do you think he will return to India?'

'Not for one moment—not until his assignment has been accomplished.'

'Don't you know where he is?'

'No. He'll surface at some time, I suppose, and when he does I'll be ready for him.' William moved closer to Rosa, looking down into her dark eyes. 'I am well aware that my behaviour of late must seem somewhat bizarre to you—coming to London and declaring my undying love for you. Since I cannot think of any excuses off the top of my head, I realise that nothing will do but the truth.'

'I would appreciate that. Please don't laugh at me… but—well, when Lady Willoughby called on you at Ashurst Park saying she had a proposition to put to you, I—I thought…'

'What? What did you think, Rosa?'

'That knowing you were in dire straits—she might have come to offer you the money to retain Ashurst Park?'

William's eyes twinkled with humour. 'I think what you would really like to know is did she ask me to marry her in return?'

'Well—yes. That is what I thought had happened,' she said, having decided not to divulge her own conversation she had had with Lady Willoughby. It had been a private conversation with an acquaintance, an acquaintance she was looking forward to becoming a friend if she returned to live in Berkshire.

'Caroline Willoughby and I are friends, Rosa—good friends. Nothing more than that. She did offer to buy the estate that day, but I refused her offer. I have told you how I obtained the money.'

'Yes, the gentleman who also came to inform you that your friend—Tipu, had died. The news must have come as a terrible shock and must be painful for you.'

'Yes—more so when the messenger informed me that he had been poisoned by the Rajah's wife.' He shook his head slowly as fond memories of his friend entered his mind. 'Poor Tipu. He did not deserve to die like that. His letter to me, written in the final moments of his life, was an emotive one. With not long to live and knowing of my struggle to save Ashurst Park, he bequeathed to me an astounding sum of money. Ahmet, the messenger, was Tipu's most trusted servant. He is also here on behalf of the Rajah of Rajinda—Dhanu's father.'

Moving closer to her, he stood, looking down into her expressionless face. 'So you see, Rosa, I find I can now court you honourably, as you should be courted— on my terms, knowing that my feelings for you are not influenced by any mercenary motives.'

He pulled back slightly and took her face between his hands, staring passionately into her eyes. 'Forget about Caroline Willoughby. Yes, she did offer to buy the estate, but I sold her a small parcel of land adjoining her own. Nothing more than that. You were the woman I wanted to marry. The more I saw you the more I wanted you. I'm not referring to your beauty,' he added softly. 'I've known many beautiful women, but not one of them was like you. You have given me a sense of belonging which, after India, I thought I would never feel again.'

She quivered at the intensity of his passionate gaze. 'You told me you love me. Is it true?'

He nodded. 'I do. Very much, as it happens. When you came to see me at Ashurst Park I felt there was a connection between us. And every time we've been together since, my certainty has grown stronger. I'm not one to wear my heart on my sleeve, but I've never experienced anything like what I feel for you.' He sighed, brushing his hair from his brow with his hand. 'In the beginning I tried telling myself ours was a practical match, for the sake of saving Ashurst Park. But that did not take into account my feelings. I wanted to court you as a lover. Your father's money got in the way of that.' He held her eyes with his. 'Does that make sense to you?'

Rosa looked at him silently, seeing in his eyes the naked strength of emotion that had unsettled her so deeply when he had held her in his embrace and kissed her. Gone was the awful feeling of loss, of lost opportunities. She did not glance away, or try to get away to quiet her own inner tumult.

'Yes—yes it does. But I also believe your feelings for Lydia Mannering didn't help.'

William swallowed audibly. 'That I cannot deny.' Taking hold of her shoulders he drew her close, needing to feel the nearness of her, the warmth of her. 'But things have changed since then—much has happened. My remembrance of her has become diminished by the passage of time and meeting you. Only now am I able to see myself in a whole new different light. Now I have you. In degrees of love, I have to admit that my feelings for you transcend anything I have felt before.

It seems impossible and yet I know it is true, for here I am, totally enamoured with you.'

Releasing her he looked down into her upturned face. 'As my wife, I promise you that you will never want for anything. As for your wealth—put it to some good. I am sure that between you, you and your Aunt Clara with all her charities will work something out.' His gaze caressed her face. 'And you, Rosa? How do you feel about me?'

Her hand was captured and she found his eyes looking straight into hers. She was trembling. He tightened his grip on her fingers and almost pleaded, 'Say it, Rosa. Say you love me. Admit it.'

'Yes,' she whispered, 'I—I do love you.'

He smiled. 'I knew it. It wasn't so hard an admission to make after all.'

'No, it wasn't difficult because it is true. I love you. I believe I always will.'

'I want you to share my life. Let me explain how it's been for me, how leaving India affected me to the point where I did not think I would survive it. I want you to understand.'

They stood gazing at each other for a long moment, in a silent communication more eloquent than words.

'Tell me,' Rosa said at length.

'I have a strong affection for India. India was my life, my work. It went way beyond the Company. I could think of no other way of living. Even after my parents died I still had India and my work. Yes, I was a soldier and I have known days when I struggled in battle to stay alive. I was as much a native as you were on Antigua. You, more than anyone, should understand how I feel. I felt it was my home. Like my father before me I loved India with a single-mindedness and passion. People have died, Rosa—Tipu, my dearest friend died—and I felt a deep sadness and regret that I was unable to help him. I felt the same when I learned of Charles's death. I wasn't there for him, either. Now I feel as if I have a second chance, and I intend to make Ashurst Park what it once was. For me, things changed all the time—some good, some not so good—but India was always there. It is in my blood. In my soul. It will always remain in my mind and never leave me.'

Rosa was moved by the intensity of his words, his manner. She looked at him in a new light, seeing a side to him she had never known existed. Why, she thought, he is grieving. Why hadn't she seen that? He'd never spoken of the sacrifice he'd had to make when he'd had to leave India for ever. Despite the noise of the laughter and music drifting through the French windows, the night wrapped itself around them. For a long moment they stood together in silence at the balustrade, then Rosa said, 'I do understand.'

'I have told you this because I want you with me at Ashurst Park as my wife. I confess that at present I am finding all that has happened difficult to deal with. It is important that you know how I feel. Now your wealth is no longer an issue I can tell you that I have chosen you not only because I love you and that you are a lovely and desirable woman any man would be proud to have as his wife, but because I see in you all the qualities I want in the woman who will be my wife and companion.'

'Aren't you being a little presumptuous, my lord?' she exclaimed, a smile quirking her lips.

His eyes danced with mischief and he grinned. 'Where you are concerned, my dear Rosa, I have to be.'

'As yet I have not said I will marry you.'

'No. But I hope you will,' he said quietly.

'Then, yes, since you ask so nicely.'

'Thank you. There is so much about you that I love. There is a fascinating quality about you. I see your goodness and honesty and sincerity. You are realistic and generous and temperamental—all admirable qualities— and I believe you were destined to be a countess. We are well matched, equal.' His gaze settled on her mouth and he watched as her tongue passed over her full bottom lip in the most seductive manner that made him acutely aware that his body was stirring to life with alarming intensity. 'Shall I go on?'

'There is no need,' she said softly.

'Then before your aunt comes looking for you, I think it's time you kissed me. We haven't much time left and I don't want to waste a minute of it.'

Happy to do as he asked, Rosa leaned forward and placed her lips against his. Her eyes darkened with a love she wasn't trying to conceal from him any more. 'What do I have to do to please you?'

He smiled down at her. 'I am open to suggestions. Show me.'

William's lips were warm and then hot—a combination that was astonishingly delicious. Rosa's own mouth opened beneath his willingly. Nothing in her imagination or her memory had prepared her for the intensity of his embrace, or the eagerness of her own response. It was as though it had never happened to her before, had never felt his arms about her, had never felt the touch of his kiss or his naked body pressed to hers. Neither wanted to let the other go.

When they finally drew apart he cupped her face in his hand and looked deep into her eyes.

'Is this what you want, Rosa—to be my wife? I want you to be sure—without doubt.'

'Yes, William. Without doubt I am very sure.'

'We will discuss the matter of our future later, but now...' Lowering his head, he captured her lips once more.

The only thing that marred the days before the wedding was the fact that Kamal Kapoor was still lurking on the streets of London somewhere. Knowing this and taking no chances, William made sure that Dhanu was watched at all times. Ahmet, determined that the Rajah would see his eldest son returned to his rightful place, was at his side all the time. He was impatient to return to India as soon as it could be arranged. William was in agreement and, despite the threat Kamal Kapoor still posed, he reserved comfortable quarters for Dhanu, Mishka and Ahmet on board a Company vessel that was to leave London just days after his marriage to Rosa. Previous to sailing, he would have the passenger and crew lists checked to make quite sure Kapoor was not on the vessel.

'Try not to worry so much, William,' Rosa said gently, knowing how concerned he was about the young boy, trying to maintain an air of calm. 'With everyone watching Dhanu, nothing will happen. Hopefully he will be halfway to India before Kapoor realises he is no long in England.'

'I hope you are right. Kapoor is a dangerous individual. There's no telling what he will do.' He sighed, taking her in his arms. 'When we have seen Ahmet and Dhanu on the ship back to India, we'll go directly to Berkshire. Does that appeal to you?'

'Absolutely. I cannot understand why anyone would want to be in London all the time, surrounded as we are in Berkshire by the delights and pleasure of the countryside.'

'I agree, but as young as you are, there will be times when you will hanker for the gay life of the London social scene—for the theatre and the balls where you can enjoy yourself. It will be an exciting diversion from the quietude of Ashurst Park where there are few distractions.'

Rosa looked at him with amused amazement, her lips quirking at the corners as she tried to suppress a smile. 'I am able to enjoy myself perfectly well in the country.'

William gazed down into her eyes, unable to imagine a future without her by his side. She was smiling up at him, a smile that brightened the room and warmed his heart, and the closeness and sweet scent of her heated his blood. He was impatient for the wedding to take place, when he would make her his wife.

Rosa became the Countess of Ashurst. The wedding was a quiet affair, hardly the kind befitting an earl, but this was how they wanted it to be. Nevertheless, it was a day of great celebration.

Aunt Clara and Uncle Michael were delighted at the way things had turned out, but Aunt Clara wanted to make quite sure that marriage to the Earl of Ashurst was what Rosa wanted.

'Will marriage to Lord Ashurst please you, Rosa? Are you quite certain that this is what you want?'

Ever since William had declared his love and asked her to be his wife, Rosa had gone through a great deal of deliberation and heart searching, before deciding that, for better or worse, she would become William's wife. She could hardly believe how deep her feelings were running, and the joy coursing through her melted the very core of her heart. She loved William and that perfect certainty filled her heart and stilled any anxiety she might otherwise have had. The feeling was so strong there was no room for anything else.

Smiling, she hugged her aunt. 'Yes, Aunt Clara, it pleases me very well. I love him—I think I have always loved him.' Her whisper was soft and happy.

'Then that is all I ask. I shall be glad to see you properly wed,' she murmured, dabbing at her eyes. 'My dear sister, your mother, would have been so happy for you—and your grandmother, also. I know you are still in mourning, but she would not have wanted you to wait. She would have told you to grasp the moment.'

And so it was that Rosa, holding a small posy of roses at her waist, her hand resting on her uncle's arm, walked down the aisle of the candlelit church to marry William Barrington, the Earl of Ashurst. When she saw him, the few invited guests faded into the shadows beside him. Attired in an olive-green coat, dove-grey trousers hugging his long legs, overwhelming in stature, his dark hair smoothly brushed and gleaming, his presence was like a positive force.

William sensed her entrance and his glance swept the church until, drawn by her beauty, his eyes met hers, wide and direct. The vision of almost ethereal loveliness he beheld, her face serene, snatched his breath away. Something like terror moved through his heart. Dear Lord, he prayed, help me protect and cherish her all the days of my life.

He stepped out and took his place in front of the priest, waiting for her in watchful silence. There was a cool impertinence on his face when he looked at her, his eyes bold and with a twinkle of appraisal in their depths. His lips curved in a crooked smile.

Rosa caught her breath and for a brief moment experienced the same pleasurable feminine sensation she felt when he looked at her with his enigmatic gaze. Scarcely aware of her actions, she moved to stand beside him as he inclined his head to her.

Taking her hand, his long fingers closing firmly over hers, when she raised her eyes to his, he saw in their depths a gentle yielding that almost sent him to his knees. He smiled and she responded to that smile and, in that moment of complete accord, their marriage felt right.

Later, the celebrations over and the guests having left for their respective homes, William and Rosa were alone at last. The room was hushed and dimly lit around them. William met Rosa's gaze beneath the long curving sweep of her lashes and admired the flush on the creamy skin of her cheeks, the slim, straight nose and the delicately formed lips, which seemed to beckon the touch of his own. He lifted his hand, his fingers gentle on her jaw, sliding his parted mouth along the smooth satin flesh on her slender neck. He pulled back and saw the yielding softness in her eyes and somewhere deep inside him he felt the stirrings of an emotion that made him reach out and draw her into his arms. She melted against him. The hot, sweet scent of her was intoxicating.

'Happy?'

'Ecstatic.' She ached with the happiness she felt.

'Your cheeks are pink. You look radiant.'

'Because of you.'

'I love you, Lady Ashurst, and now we are alone I will prove to you the ardour you have stirred in me.'

With his eyes holding hers like a magnet, with infinite care he unpinned her hair. When the last pin was out she gave her head a gentle shake and her hair tumbled down her back in a living, shining mass. William marvelled at its luxuriant, thick texture and colour, running it through his fingers, pausing now and then to kiss her lips, her cheek, her neck.

Rosa's eyes drifted closed and her breath came out in a sigh as she kissed him softly and felt his lips answer, moving on hers. Drawing back, she looked at him, seeing how his eyes were beginning to smoulder.

'Let's go to bed,' William murmured, his long fingers beginning to unfasten the buttons down the front of her dress.

'Shall I ring for Dilys to come and undress me?'

'Since I gave your maid permission to retire and there is no other lady's maid on hand, allow me to oblige. Besides, I prefer to do the undressing myself. I would like to see what I missed on the night when my brain was fogged with the drug Kapoor fed me.'

The sight of Rosa's naked body—a miracle of ripe curves and glowing flesh, every shade of pale gold in the wavering blur of the flickering light—made William's heart slam against his ribs. Her legs were long and perfect, her breasts high and proud. Every nerve William possessed stilled as slowly his gaze traced the gentle swell of her thighs, over her taut stomach and minuscule waist.

Rosa's throat dried. His gaze focused upon her body and the ardour in his eyes was like a flame to her senses. She was unable to free her rational mind from the overwhelming tide of desire that claimed her, fuelled by a whirlpool of emotions.

'When you've looked your fill, William, kindly remember you are supposed to be a gentleman and take off your clothes, too—unless you intend to make love to me with them on.'

Nimble-fingered and driven by a sense of racing urgency, Rosa began fumbling with the fastenings at his throat. Desire a physical torment, he disposed of his clothes and, drawing her close, held her tight against him.

'You take my breath away,' he whispered.

Winding her arms about his neck, she placed feather-light kisses on the solid wall of his chest and his sinewed shoulders. William's heart constricted with an emotion so intense, so profound, that it made him ache. His hands glided restlessly, possessively, over her—her breasts, the small nipples quivering against his palms—sliding his hands down her back and over the gentle swell of her buttocks. Her breath was sweet against his throat. She was warm, womanly, long and slender, curving against his body, doing what she could to get even closer. William's male body rejoiced in it.

To Rosa, the moment was one of poignant discovery as her fingers slid through the short, dark matting of hair on his chest. His jaw was set, his mouth firm yet sensual, his eyes hard and dark with passion—and she could not believe he was hers—her husband.

When he pulled her down onto the bed their restraint broke. As he held her tight against him, his kisses consumed her in the violent storm of his passion. His mouth moved to circle her breasts, kissing each in turn—his lips then travelled down to her stomach, caressing, teasing, until Rosa moaned with pleasure and soared with every long sweep of his hands on her flesh.

She was operating wholly on instinct since her wits had flown. Her neck craned back and her fingers laced through his thick hair as she abandoned herself to his lips, his hands, intimate and provocative, exploring the secrets of her body like a knowledgeable lover, savouring the exquisite tension, initiating new delights. Pleasure burned through her, expanding, mounting, until her body shuddered with the force of her passion. So lost was she in the desire he was so skilfully building inside her that she scarcely noticed when he shifted position and eased her body beneath his own. The warmth of him pressed fully against her as she wrapped her arms about him, opening up to him, her kisses driving him on, inciting his passion until he could no longer control the force that had claimed him and she gasped as the bold, fiery brand intruded into her delicate softness, penetrating deep within her. No holding back, she strained towards him with trembling need, each instinctive, demanding thrust pushing her closer to the edge and bringing exquisite pleasure.

William revelled in her eagerness, in her unfettered sensuality, a sensuality that spoke to his own as she responded to his passion, his desire. No moment had ever felt like this. He was filled with a sense of rightness, as if to possess her had been his goal ever since she had sought him out at Ashurst Park. They strained together, no longer two separate entities, but one being, swept away, hurtling and twisting, onwards and upwards in a frenzied wildness, striving to reach the same goal.

Afterwards, when their passion had finally exploded in a burst of extravagant pleasure, in languid exhaustion and bone-deep satisfaction, they lay close together, limbs entangled, facing each other, breathless from exertion, bodies aglow, limbs weighted with contentment, clinging to the fading euphoria. William listened to her contented sigh and watched her open her eyes. Smiling, she nestled closer. William placed a kiss on her forehead.

'You are exquisite, my love. How do you feel?'

'Wonderful,' she whispered, firm in the belief that her husband was a man of extraordinary skill and prowess. He had taken her not just sexually, but with a deeper, infinitely more alluring need—something profound. 'I have no doubt in my mind that you are the same man who made love to me before.'

Shuffling onto her stomach and raising herself up on her elbows, her hair falling over his chest, she gave him a slumberous smile. 'What we did was very special to me.' She placed a soft kiss on his lips. 'Thank you.'

Rolling her onto her back, he swept the hair from her smooth cheek, his eyes warm and serious and very tender. 'It was my pleasure, Countess.'

The words were so painfully exquisite that Rosa thought she would die of it. 'I have to ask myself is this the man who once thought love had no place in his life, letting me believe that you had no love to give. What happened to change your mind, William?'

'You, Rosa—and Dhanu. I have come to love that boy as if he were my own. Can you ever forgive me for what I did to you—when I broke off our wedding?'

'There is nothing to forgive, William. I know why you did that. Until we met again in London I had not realised the full extent of how your leaving India, your cousin's death followed so soon by your friend Tipu had damaged you emotionally. Now I fully understand. But things change, people change—you have changed. In fact I think you are rather wonderful and one day I will give you a son.'

'Suddenly that no longer seems important. I have come to realise that as much as I want a son, I want you more, so feel free to fill the nursery at Ashurst Park with as many daughters as you wish.'

Nothing touched Rosa more than this, which was all the proof of his love that she needed. Nestling closer to him, Rosa closed her eyes, letting the warmth deepen inside her, driving out everything else. 'Then what are we waiting for?' she breathed. 'I don't want this to stop—ever.'

Touching her cheek with his fingertips, and then wrapping his long fingers around her chin, he tilted her head back, his eyes smiling into hers. 'Anything to oblige.'

Again his mouth covered hers, and so the night went on.

The East India Dock was a scene of great variety and activity. The Company was rich and powerful and well organised, owning the largest ships that used the port of London. The smell of coffee beans, tar, timber and hemp, permeated the air. The vessel in the fleet that was to return Dhanu to India was boarding.

Dhanu was eager to return to India and yet he was upset because he was leaving William and Rosa. All the way to the docks he tried to be brave and not cry, but when he saw the huge Company vessel that was to take him home, his face was alight with excitement. For William and Rosa it was a time of sadness. Dhanu had come to mean a great deal to them both, yet as much as they hated the prospect of parting from him, they were hopeful for his future with his father.

They were wrapped warmly in winter clothes, for the weather was extremely cold with a thin layer of ice on outer reaches of the still water in the dock. William was uneasy as he made arrangements for the baggage to be taken on board.

'I'll go on board and make sure everything is in order.' William's unease had transmitted itself to Rosa and she wanted to make sure the quarters he had reserved were adequate for their journey to Bombay.

All of them went on board. Mishka and Dhanu settled happily into the cabins allotted to them and, after saying farewell, William and Rosa left the ship, pausing when they stood on the dock to take a last look at the mighty vessel.

William observed the sadness of Rosa's expression. 'What are you thinking?' he asked, tucking her hand into the crook of his arm.

She shrugged. 'I was just thinking of Dhanu going back to India. It's right that he should go back to his father but I can't help wondering what the future holds for him—heir to a rajah. It seems such a heavy burden for such young shoulders.'

William nodded. 'My regret is that Tipu will not be there to watch over him, to guide him through the years. But the Rajah loves his son and I know Dhanu will make him proud.'

The man standing on the dock as silent as a shadow watched William Barrington leave the ship. His features became ugly, contorted with anger and a wild hatred. If what Barrington had told him was true and his sister had been banished, then nothing remained of the prestige that had marked his existence at the court of the Rajah of Rajinda.

Raw emotion and immense disappointment that he had failed in his mission to rid his sister of Dhanu had robbed him of any kind of reason, any kind of judgement. He blamed William Barrington for having made it impossible for him to get at the boy and he wanted to make him suffer with his bare hands, until he was too helpless to ask for mercy. His eyes narrowed and gleamed with a murderous light. This time he would not drug him, which had been his only means of punishing him when they had met at the children's institute, he was going to kill him.

His eyes were intent on William.

Sensing he was being watched, William turned his head and scanned the crowd of people milling around him. Kapoor was standing openly on the edge of the dock, making no attempt to hide himself. He bore no resemblance to the man who had once enjoyed his elevated status as the Rani's much-favoured brother, lavishly dressed in colourful silken robes and glittering with exquisite jewels. Now he was dirty and unkempt—his time spent in London had not been kind to him. William felt tension coiling in the air around him. The shock of seeing Kapoor had worn off and he appraised the situation. Kapoor's eyes were wild and darker than blood, but the ferocious rage and hatred contorting his face told William that he was very much alive.

'Damn you, Kapoor. I might have known you'd be waiting.'

William moved slowly, his eyes fixed firmly on him. Kapoor confronted him, then, with a roar of rage, flung himself at William. The two men scuffled, becoming a twisting, writhing mass. Condemned by his struggle for power in a faraway court, Kapoor must have known in his heart that it was too late for him. Finding himself released from his adversary's grip, he stepped back. For a moment he looked at William, his eyes red from exhaustion and tortured by a sense of failure.

With her heart in her mouth, Rosa watched in horror as the scene began to unfold before her eyes. She watched William reach for him, but Kapoor slipped out of his grasp and fell backwards. Teetering, he took a step back, but finding only air, losing his balance, he fell over the edge of the dock. The ice cracked beneath his weight and he disappeared into the dark watery depths beneath.

With her heart beating heavily, running to the edge of the dock she stopped and looked down. Kapoor had disappeared. There was nothing but a black hole in the thin layer of ice.

'The ice! He's gone through the ice! What can we do?'

They waited a moment, hoping Kapoor would surface, but there was no sign of him. What had happened had drawn a large crowd. Acting swiftly, William thrust Rosa away from him. After removing his jacket, grim-faced, he moved to the edge of the dock. Aware of what he intended, Rosa stepped forward, horror written all over her face.

'William—no. You cannot go into the water. It's freezing. Kapoor may be dead by now.'

'She is right.' Having accompanied them off the ship, Ahmet stepped forward, concerned by William's decision to go into the icy water. 'It will be impossible to withstand the cold beneath the ice for long.'

'I have to. I have to do this. I have to see if I can find him. Until I see for myself if he is alive or dead, this will never be over.' Tying a rope around his waist, he handed it to a stevedore. 'Haul me out if I'm down there too long.' His face was closed when he looked at Rosa for a moment, then he turned and plunged into the water. A gasp went up from those gathered around and people struggled with one another to see what was happening in the water.

With silent horror, Rosa fixed her eyes on the spot where William had disappeared, unaware that she was holding her breath while she willed him to reappear. Ahmet came up beside her and took her hand in a firm grip in an attempt to allay her fears.

'He'll be all right. He'll come out. Wait and see.'

Rosa couldn't bear the waiting. William was in great danger. He had been under the water a long time. Why didn't he come back up? And then the sight of his dark head surfacing revived her spirits.

Shaking his head and gulping in air, he disappeared

once more. The longer he remained under the water the more Rosa felt as if she were dying. Her soul, her very life, was concentrated in her eyes, fixed on the place where he had gone under. A boat had pulled up alongside and then, miraculously, William surfaced, his hand clasping Kapoor's coat. Immediately they were both hauled into the boat and rowed to the edge of the dock. It was plain that Kapoor was dead. Having hit his head on something sharp when he had fallen, Kapoor had a deep gash that marred his forehead. William climbed up, his body shivering with cold. Their driver appeared with a travelling rug and draped it about him. Gratefully he wrapped it around his body.

'Best get you home, sir, before a chill sets in.'

William looked at Rosa. Her face was drawn and ashen. He went to her, water dripping from his wet hair.

'I'm all right, Rosa. Don't worry.'

'What will happen to Kapoor?' she asked, looking at the Indian's lifeless body being lifted out of the boat.

'The constables will take him away. There will be questions asked, which I will deal with. Come, let's see Ahmet back onto the ship. There's nothing else we can do and I must get out of these wet clothes.' He turned to Ahmet. 'Now you can return Dhanu to his father without the threat Kapoor posed hanging over you. He would have known that you would be leaving some time and must have been watching the dock for some time.'

'Yes—and now it is over. Thank you, Lord Ashurst, for what you have done and for the kind hospitality you have shown me. The Rajah owes you a great debt.'

'The Rajah has already given me a great deal, Ahmet. I am in *his* debt.'

With nothing else to be said, Ahmet bowed his head and, turning from them, boarded the ship.

One week after Dhanu had departed for India and after Rosa and William had spent an enjoyable evening at the theatre with Aunt Clara and Uncle Michael, later, sated and content, in the huge four-poster bed, William drew Rosa towards him.

'Ever since we returned from the theatre you have been preoccupied, my love. I know you have something on your mind. Would you like to tell me about it?'

Sighing, Rosa rolled onto her stomach, resting her arms on his chest and looking down at his face. 'I've been doing some thinking.'

'Oh? What about?'

'My wealth. Since you don't want it—'

'And I no longer need it.'

'Quite. Well, you know how I want to put it to good use—to use for the good of others. I would like to know more about the work of abolitionists of the slave trade. I know there are numerous committees working hard. There are tracts and petitions to organise and it all costs money. I would like to make a considerable contribution. Tell me what you think?'

'I commend your actions, Rosa. Since coming to London and taking my seat at Westminster, I have listened to and spoken to leading activists and given them my full support. I intend to do my best to campaign for abolition. The work has been ongoing for decades—gathering pace all the time, and it will not stop until there is emancipation of all slaves.'

'It will be a great day when it comes—I hope in my lifetime. There is also something else I would like to do. It's something I've given careful consideration to for some time now and I hope you will approve.'

Liking the feel of his wife's naked body pressed to his own, settling himself into a more comfortable position William wrapped an arm about her slender waist. 'Pray continue. I am all ears.'

'I would like to have a large fund made available to Aunt Clara so she can open an orphanage for all the children in her care. The institutes are by no means adequate, although they are better than nothing at all, but I know it is her dream to one day open an orphanage and even a school where the children can be educated and properly taken care of. Along with her associates she works hard to raise funds, but it is never enough.' She fell silent, looking at her husband, waiting for his reaction. When he was not forthcoming, she prompted, 'Well, tell me what you think—and please understand that this is important to me.'

'I can see it is—and I am not surprised, knowing how much you enjoy working with your aunt. I have no objections. The money is yours to do with as you please and I cannot think of a more useful or deserving cause. I will help in any way I can—and,' he murmured, his slumberous gaze becoming fixated on her lips, 'you might also find ways to coax some of my own newfound wealth out of me. I'm open to persuasion.'

Rosa laughed, lightly placing a kiss on his lips. 'I'm sure you are, but please behave and keep your lascivious thoughts to yourself and be serious for a moment. Before we leave for Berkshire I would like you to accompany me to my lawyer to set things in motion. Perhaps he will oversee the proper distribution of the funds. Aunt Clara has been so good me and I know she will be so happy to see her dream achieve fruition.'

Laughing softly, William rolled her onto her back. 'I, too, would be happy to see my wishes achieve fruition,' he said, cupping her face in his hands and proceeding to plant tantalising kisses on her cheeks, her lips, 'if I can just stop you talking for long enough.'

'But you will come with me—to see the lawyer,' Rosa murmured, almost losing the will to think clearly as his fiery tongue began to play havoc with her ear.

'Anything you ask, my love,' he murmured, claiming her lips at last.

Approaching Ashurst Park for the first time as the Countess of Ashurst, Rosa could not believe her good fortune. Today it was blanketed in snow, the sky an unbroken blue above, whereas in summer it would be surrounded by a riot of flowers, the lawns mown, and beyond the surrounding trees, well-tilled fields stretched time out of mind into the distance.

When she had first set eyes on the house with its eye-catching façade, she had fallen in love with it and had dreamed of one day entering as its mistress. And then she had found a way when she knew Lord Ashurst was in need of a rich wife. When he had agreed to her terms she had thought all her hopes were about to come true—his rejection had been a bitter blow.

But now, she thought, her eyes straying from the approaching house to the man by her side, how things had changed. And how very lucky she was. As he surveyed his ancestral home his eyes held a sadness as he reflected on the past. His sadness transmitted itself to Rosa and she took his hand.

'What is it, William? Why the sadness?'

'When I arrived from India and entered the house, knowing what had befallen my cousin—his death— I felt that the house had lost its soul. It was full of ghosts—of old sins—of grief. Remembering the happy times when I came here as a youth—the house was always filled with laughter—I wondered if it was possible for those times to come again. Could I bring it back?'

'Oh, William, I am sure you can. We will do it together. It will be a long climb back, but it will come. The children we have in the future will bring happiness— and never forget that we have each other.'

He looked down at her, loving her. Already he could hear the children's laughter coming to him over the snow from the house. He glanced ahead and felt the tension ease. His face relaxed and he smiled.

* * * * *